LORD EDGINGTO

BOOK 14

DEATH AT SILENT POOL

A 1920s MYSTERY

BENEDICT BROWN

COPYRIGHT

For my father, Kevin,
I hope you would have liked this book an awful lot.

The Beginning of the End

READER'S NOTE

Welcome back to another Lord Edgington mystery. I try to keep the series interesting by approaching each book in a new way and, in this one, I wanted to challenge myself to create something quite different.

I recently finished the final Izzy Palmer novel, which was probably the oddest book I'll ever write, and my next project will be my jolly and light-hearted annual Christmas book. So, with this one, I wanted to inject a change of pace. There are elements of thriller mixed into the classic mystery plot, and it is a little more serious than some of my books. It may well be Lord Edgington's most challenging case yet, too. However, it still has the usual mix of humour and intrigue along with a pack of truly treacherous suspects.

You'll find a character list, historical information and a glossary of unusual words at the back of the book.

I hope you love it!

CHAPTER ONE

Grandfather had been sitting in his favourite armchair, mutely staring into space for what felt like hours.

"You don't think he's gone back to his old ways, do you?" our footman Halfpenny asked in his typical, worried tone.

"No, of course he hasn't." My grandfather's right-hand man Todd normally knew the lay of the land, and I had to hope he was right.

"It's the darnedest thing," I explained. "We were sitting here discussing a recent case, and he seemed to fade before my eyes."

"So he hasn't moved since?" Todd asked in the manner of a doctor, checking his facts.

Studying the mute Marquess of Edgington, I considered my answer. "His expression has certainly changed. For a while he was smiling rather inanely." I chose this word to knock my thin-skinned grandfather from his stupor. I thought he might lurch upright with a scowl to say, *Christopher, I do nothing inanely. Everything I do is perfectly ane.* Though I've no idea whether *ane* is a real word.

As my rudeness had no effect on him, I continued my explanation. "A few minutes later, his pupils grew wider, as if he were deeply afraid of something. Then soon after that, he began to look puzzled and has remained in that state ever since."

The three of us were standing in a line in front of the eccentric detective, but Todd now moved to one side to get a different view of his master. "Which case were you discussing?"

"It wasn't one of our own. The last thing he mentioned was the matter of the missing rubies in Belgravia."

Our head of household was usually the picture of discretion, but he couldn't resist showing his excitement over the Vorontsova case. He actually rubbed his hands together. "The one with the suspicious Russian émigré, the disappearing necklace and the heartbroken Duchess?"

"Yes, Todd, but don't get too excited." It really has come to something when it falls to me to encourage restraint. "I don't believe that Grandfather is any closer to locating the loot than the police are."

Halfpenny looked just as puzzled as his seemingly comatose employer. "What or who or why is the Vorontsova case?"

"You haven't read about it in the papers?" I betrayed a touch of amazement.

The ever-proud footman puffed up his chest. "I don't read the papers. I believe that it is better to be happy than knowledgeable."

I felt certain that my grandfather – had he been with us in anything but body – would have railed against such an ostrich-like attitude. However, after a moment's thought, I began to doubt myself. Isn't it possible that an existence oblivious to the evils (and even the wonders) of the world is superior to a well-informed person's life of worry? I had never expected our slightly creaky footman to spark such a deeply philosophical reflection.

Rather than concern himself with this dilemma, Todd was quick to explain the circumstances of the crime. "Countess Marina Vorontsova is a White Russian émigré with connections to the royal family, or at least that's what she says. She's thrown herself on the mercy of a series of wealthy aristocrats of whom she claims to be a distant relation. They were only too happy to entertain the flamboyant young woman at first, but when it became apparent that she didn't have a mountain of Muscovite treasures to pay her way, noses turned up, and several doors were slammed in her face."

"How do the rubies come into it?" For a man who claimed to take no interest in current affairs, Halfpenny was most intrigued.

"They belonged to the Duchess of Hartlepool." Todd knew just as much about the salacious affair as I did. "She heeded a request to admit Countess Vorontsova to her home. The countess showed up in her finery, with a grand bejewelled tiara on her head, and was shown into the Duchess's private quarters."

I admit that I was eager to contribute and took over the next part of the story. "No one knows what was said during the meeting, but the British Duchess was called away on other business, and so the countess finished her tea and was shown from the room by the butler. When the lady of the house returned, she noticed that someone had rifled through the drawers in the neighbouring boudoir and her priceless ruby necklace had been stolen."

"Gosh. How exciting," the footman responded.

I let Todd take over once more. "That's not even the most interesting part. The alarm was raised before the Russian countess could leave the house. A servant stopped her, the police were called, and the suspected thief was searched."

"Well? What did they find?"

"Nothing." He pulled proudly on the bottom of his waistcoat. "Countess Vorontsova had nothing of value about her person but for the tiara, her Russian passport and a purse with a few shillings."

I couldn't hold it in any longer. "Don't forget the red powder!"

Todd bowed appreciatively. "Of course, Master Christopher." We made a fine double act, and Halfpenny's anticipation only grew. "In the room where the rubies had previously been stored, the police discovered a fine red powder. They couldn't identify its provenance but, judging by the traces of the substance that were found nearby, it appeared to have been ground up using a small glass paperweight as a makeshift pestle."

With this summary completed, my grandfather's sitting room fell quiet. The only sound was the soft inhaling and exhaling of our golden retriever Delilah, who was asleep at her master's feet.

"What a conundrum that is." Halfpenny licked one finger to run it along the parting in his thinning hair.

"Wait, look!" Todd drew our attention back to my grandfather. "Lord Edgington's expression has changed."

I half hoped that the story might have pulled him back to us, but he was just as unresponsive as before.

"I think he looks rather peaceful," Halfpenny concluded with a smile. "Perhaps he's thinking of the time when his own children scampered about the halls of this grand old house, and our dear Mistress Katharine had a kind word for everyone she met."

Just as the dear fellow's nostalgia was in full flow, my grandfather sat bolt upright in his chair and the footman nearly had a heart attack.

"I've got it!" the famous detective said with a clap of his hands.

"What have you got?" If I wasn't on hand to ask such simple yet essential questions, our investigations would surely grind to a halt.

"The Vorontsova case – I know how it was done!"

"Congratulations, M'lord," Todd politely replied, but a faint glimmer in his eye said, *Are you going to tell us?*

Grandfather was up on his feet and strode across the room with his fists raised in celebration. "It's so obvious when you think about it."

"Of course it is," I said, and the glimmer in my own eye at that moment probably said, *Now hurry up and tell us what you know!*

"Was the red powder the police found important, sir?" Halfpenny dared ask when it became increasingly clear that Grandfather would not divulge any of the details until we'd shown that we were suitably amazed.

"In a way, yes, and in another way, no, not at all." He closed his eyes as he stood in front of the window that looked over the great lawn.

I was sorely tempted to shout, *Do stop prevaricating and get to the point!* As I am a well-bred young gent and would never be so rude, I settled for an overacted yawn and a glum look at my nails.

To explain this behaviour, I should probably tell you how we had spent our summer. We certainly hadn't set sail for adventures on the continent as my grandfather had been promising for... I can't recall how long. Far from it, we'd taken a town house in Soho and spent two whole months investigating the minor intrigues of several notable public figures, none of which I had managed to solve. I was beginning to think that the promise I'd shown as a detective had already petered out.

He countered my display of ennui with a challenge of his own. "Very well, Christopher. Before I explain what really happened, would you care to hazard a guess?"

Having recently reached the grand old age of twenty, I was almost a grown man, but this didn't stop me sparring with my mentor at every given opportunity. "A guess, Grandfather? Do you really think that an apprentice to the matchless Lord Edgington would ever rely on anything so unreliable and insubstantial as a guess?" I didn't wait for him to answer but ploughed on with the first thing that popped into my head. "My *hypothesis*, Grandfather – that is to say, the conclusion I have come to after many hours of quiet consideration – is that the clothes the countess was wearing are key to solving the case."

I bowed confidently and, when I straightened up once more, the three of them were looking at me as if I'd said something really very stupid indeed.

"Her clothes?" Todd echoed in a questioning tone.

"That's right." I put my hand to my breast pocket in a Napoleon-esque manner. I wasn't about to admit that I didn't know what had happened to the rubies. I was having far too much fun. "Or more importantly, the tiara which she wore upon her head."

Grandfather said nothing, but he had the air of a man who was very much looking forward to revealing the evidence of his genius.

"The way I see it," I continued, as I copied his confident stride towards the window, "this fake Russian – who is as much a Romanov as I am a Rockefeller – this impostor visited her supposed relation one quiet Wednesday afternoon wearing a tiara of all things. It was no doubt studded with gems of all colours, and I suspect that the red stones were made of paste or melamine or something of that type. When the countess was left alone, she exchanged the fake gems for the real ones. The red powder she left behind was from the counterfeit stones, which she had crushed with whatever heavy object happened to be at hand."

I was surprised to see that two of the three men were now looking at me as if I'd said something really very clever indeed.

Grandfather put one finger to his cheek as he regarded me. "You know, Christopher…" He even bit his lip for a moment, and I prepared myself for the worst. "You know that your 'hypothesis' is almost exactly the same as my own."

I laughed like a sheep. Not that sheep laugh of course, but I'm sure you know what I mean. "You're talking rot, man." I had to swallow then; his assertion had knocked me aback. "I can't be right. I made up that silly story on the spot because I couldn't imagine how the rubies had gone missing. Now stop playing and tell us how it really happened."

Our expectant servants' eyes flicked between the pair of us as Grandfather began.

"Assuming that Countess Vorontsova is the culprit, and that she can make solid objects vanish into thin air, then the only solution I can find is that she wore the tiara knowing of the Duchess's rubies. She went there to steal them and, as you said, swapped the imitations for the genuine articles before destroying the evidence."

The resultant silence was interrupted by the slow handclap of our footman. "Bravo, M'lord! And you, Master Christopher. Bravo!"

Grandfather came to put his arm around my shoulder and joined in with the praise. "You've done an excellent job, my boy. I am truly proud of you."

I kept expecting him to tell me he was joking or find a flaw in my analysis, but his expression was so sincere and so kind that I could tell that he meant what he was saying. I can't describe how bad I then felt for ragging him (every day for the last two months).

Todd stepped forward to shake my hand. "We must telephone the police and the newspapers at once to tell them of your great feat of deduction."

"And you managed it in half the time of his lordship!" Our head footman finally stopped his applause, but only because he had gone to fetch the phone, which was standing on a small trolley in the corner of the room. "Really! Who takes tea on a Wednesday afternoon in a tiara?"

"Who indeed?" Grandfather cut into their jovial chatter, and the moment that I'd foolishly allowed myself to believe was not coming had surely arrived.

"I beg your pardon?" My throat was quite dry.

"Who would go about the place in a tiara?"

I didn't answer as Halfpenny froze where he stood, and Todd's hand came to a rest on the handset.

"Yes, there is only one person I can think of who wears the same tiara wherever she goes." Grandfather returned to his favourite contemplative spot beside the window and our newly alert dog, Delilah, sat next to him to observe our reaction to her master's reversal. "A woman by the name of Countess Marina Vorontsova, who comes from an ancient and noble Russian family. A woman who clings to the only vestiges of her former wealth and power that she retains. The very same woman who carries her passport with her despite the fact that, were it a forgery, it would be a simple matter to prove."

"So you're saying she really is Russian, and she didn't crush the gems with a paperweight?" My voice was so quiet that these words must barely have reached his ears.

"Let's not get ahead of ourselves. Shall we?" He clicked his fingers twice, which Halfpenny apparently understood as a sign that he required tea. He hurried from the room and would reappear a short time later with a pot and two cups. In the meantime, Grandfather continued to correct my guess that I had disguised as a hypothesis. "Countess Vorontsova is known for her flamboyant sense of dress, as every newspaper article concerning the theft has gone to great pains to remind us. Therefore, were someone wishing to incriminate her, they could rely on her to

14

wear her ruby-studded tiara to visit the Duchess that day."

"But why would anyone want to perpetrate such evil against a near penniless émigré?" I asked, aware that I'd changed my tone since describing the woman as an impostor mere moments earlier.

"You tell me, Christopher." He took a few steps closer. "What do we know of this would-be burglar?"

I racked my brains as, in all honesty, I knew very little that I hadn't just described. "There was her flamboyant dress and…"

"Yes?"

"And her apparently genuine Russian heritage. And… And she was almost out of money and went begging for assistance from a number of potential benefactors."

"Well done. That is the very detail that most interests us."

"Is it?" I replied, as Halfpenny wasn't there to be surprised by everything he heard.

"Can you tell me what connected the people she visited?"

I tried to recall the list of names from the newspaper articles I had read. "There was the Duchess of course… and the wife of a bishop who publicly snubbed her in a theatre. I remember a baroness, a minor earl, and I believe she'd even made a petition to the husband of the King's cousin. I don't see how any of this can explain the countess's motives though."

In the end, Grandfather answered his own question. "You said it yourself when you explained your excellent theory. The people she visited were the countess's relations. Each had some connection to Mother Russia."

"I'm afraid I don't see the relevance," Todd kindly said so that I could continue staring into space and, I can only assume, dribbling.

It was at this moment that the tea arrived. Halfpenny presumably set about pouring, stirring, adding milk and the like, though to be quite honest, I paid no attention. All I can say is that, approximately two minutes after I heard the door swing open, a teacup magically appeared in Grandfather's hand.

"It seems reasonable to conclude that, if the Duchess of Hartlepool agreed to see Countess Vorontsova in her private apartments, she believed the link to her family to be genuine. If that were the case, and we are finally open to the possibility that the countess was not there to steal gems, then we must question whether her host intentionally tried to incriminate her."

He was hardly generous with the evidence he'd provided, but he had given me just enough to connect up the scraps. "The Duchess knew what the countess would wear on her head and plotted to make it look as though the Russian noble had stolen from her."

"Precisely!" He increased his pace to get through the rest of the story. "I first considered whether it all came down to a longstanding rivalry between the Vorontsovs and another well-established Russian family to whom the Duchess of Hartlepool can trace her ancestry."

"That would make a lot of sense," Todd agreed. "That's the kind of thing that happens in the Russian novels I've read."

Grandfather hadn't finished and waited patiently for his turn to speak again. "However, if she were trying to cast a shadow over a rival, there was no need to go about it in such a complicated way. If anything, the trick with the fake rubies suggested that the countess was to blame but simultaneously made it almost impossible for the police to charge her."

My brain was racing to find a solution to the case before us, but I was destined to fail once more.

Lord Edgington failed to suppress a self-satisfied smile. "It took me some time, but I finally noticed one key fact." He paused to make us wonder what this might be. "The supposed crime occurred in the first week of August."

No one said a word.

"The first week of August is famous for…" He gave us another chance, and just as I was about to say, *School holidays,* he provided the correct answer. "Glorious Goodwood, gentlemen. One of the most important horse racing events of the season traditionally begins at the end of July and continues for several days. And to whom, may I remind you, is the Duchess of Hartlepool married?"

It was rather an obvious answer, but I hadn't said anything for some time, so I thought I should give it a go. "The Duke of Hartlepool?"

He would have clapped his hands together again, but he was holding his cup and saucer. "The Duke of Hartlepool indeed. A man whose stable of horses fared poorly at this year's meetings and, I must imagine, lost no small amount of money in backing them." He had played his trump card and took a well-deserved sip of tea as if to say, *Now that is how you solve a taxing case.*

"That's fascinating," the man who'd previously claimed to have no interest in current affairs remarked. "So the Duchess made it look as though she had been robbed in order to claim insurance money on a set of jewels which have probably been pawned on the sly to pay off her husband's debts. You truly are a wonder, your lordship."

"Thank you." Grandfather rewarded himself with another sip and a brief *ahhh* of satisfaction.

"I will telephone Chief Inspector Darrington forthwith to tell him of your discovery, sir." His retainer had already picked up the handset.

"That is very good of you, Todd. Of course, Christopher helped solve the most difficult element of the case. I really only read between the lines from there. It is the foremost rule of any good detective to question what at first seems apparent and then—"

"...To question it once more," I said to complete one of his many such maxims.

"You are correct yet again." He was in a particularly good mood that morning, but there was something still on my mind.

"If I may put one small question to you, Grandfather."

"Of course, my boy, of course. How may I be of service?"

"I was just wondering whether you're any closer to solving the disappearance of Patience Hindmarsh at Silent Pool."

He set down his cup of tea on the table beside him with a brief clatter, and his smile vanished. "Ah, yes... Silent Pool..." He opened his mouth to say more, but nothing would come.

CHAPTER TWO

Forgive me, if you will, if I now jump back in time a short while. I'm normally a linear storyteller – A to B without a stop in between, and that sort of thing – but I feel that I would be remiss not to tell you of our brief visit to Silent Pool before we met the Hindmarsh family themselves.

Some weeks earlier than the scene I have just described, an old friend of my grandfather's called us out to that beauty spot in the heart of Surrey to examine a violent scene. You will remember, of course, that we had been staying in the capital for some time by this point. A trip to the countryside was not on our agenda for the month, but I can't say I truly minded. As much as I loved the shine and swagger of London, and its great green parks were only a stroll away from our house, I missed Surrey's rolling hills and verdant vistas.

I believe my grandfather felt much the same way. "It's the smell that informs one's senses that you've left the city behind," he proclaimed as we stepped from his favourite Aston Martin Cloverleaf.

I was tempted to tell him this was surely down to the horses that made use of the bridle path in front of us, but I don't think he would have looked too kindly on the observation.

"Something in the air tells you, *This is where we are most free. This is where man should truly be.*" He took another lungful of clean country air, and I'm fairly certain he caught that *odeur de cheval.* He grimaced and quickly changed the subject. "Chief Inspector Darrington told me to meet him here at eleven on the dot, and he is never late."

He raised his watch from the outer pocket of his waistcoat, and I caught sight of the second hand, ticking towards the hour. The hour was reached, and Grandfather's look of expectation turned to one of bewilderment.

"It appears that he is late," I dared point out.

"Impossible!" He looked up at the sun then, as though he wished to argue with the passing of time. "I've known the man for decades. Darrington can't possibly be—"

It was at this very moment – one minute and seventeen seconds past eleven, to be precise – that a black Austin 7 drove off the road behind us and came to a stop a few feet away.

"I'm terribly sorry that I'm late, Lord Edgington," Darrington announced as he stepped from the vehicle, his white hair somewhat less kempt than usual, and with what appeared to be feathers speckling his uniform. "A cart carrying a great number of chickens overturned near Cobham. The road was blocked. I normally allow extra time for delays, but I had not expected to have to chase a gang of errant poultry around a duck pond."

I couldn't help but smile at this small victory. Grandfather may have solved any number of minor crimes that had affected his high-society chums over the course of the summer, but he'd been wrong when it came to the chief inspector's punctuality. And yes, now that I say it, I'm aware just how petty that sounds.

"It's over this way." Darrington pointed to a narrow path over a remarkably crooked stile. His resolute manner was more flustered than normal, and I came to doubt that it was merely the chickens that had brought about this change in him.

We followed in silence, and the steady rhythm of his boots on the dry path beneath our feet was like the bass drum keeping time on an ominous piece of music. I can't say why I felt such dread at that moment; I knew nothing of the circumstances that had called us to that woodland setting. I knew only that our companion wished to consult my grandfather on a puzzling case.

Perhaps my mentor experienced that same sense of apprehension, as he remained quiet until we reached the lake. Thanks to its name, I'd assumed there was a body of water nearby, but I had never before visited the area, though it was only a short drive from Grandfather's estate.

"It's quite lovely," he said as we stopped to enjoy the view. The sun was not yet at its apex, and it cut through the trees to overlay an intricate pattern of sparkling light on the surface of the water. A family of ducks was crossing the small lake, and an ever-expanding triangle of ripples accompanied them on their journey. The water itself was of a colour I had never previously seen. It was vibrant green in places, turquoise in others, and so clear that I could almost see to the bottom. On the far side, a grey heron stood looking unconcerned by our presence, and here and there, yellow leaves floated like small boats. It was the very spot for a picnic, but I knew we were not there for anything so jolly.

"I suppose it is," Darrington responded a little gruffly. "I can't say I noticed." He cast his eyes across the water at an old stone building on the far side. It must have been built as a mill a century or so earlier, as the remnants of a water wheel were still visible. "This way, gentlemen."

He continued on the path that skirted the edge of the water. "The press don't know anything about the disappearance, and I'd like to keep it that way for the time being. You can be sure that it will cause quite the scandal considering the family's high standing. The woman's husband, Abraham Hindmarsh, has a reputation for being a formidable character."

I turned to my grandfather and, not for the first time, felt as if I knew what he was thinking. He was turning over the scant facts that we now possessed in order to construct a simple narrative in his head. He was flicking through relevant news stories in which the Hindmarsh family had featured in order to form a profile of their dealings. And yet this did nothing to limit his shock when we reached the badly damaged Bentley.

"My goodness, what a sight." He stopped dead in his tracks to take in a very different view from the one we'd previously admired.

I could only think that the scene had been left as it had been found by the police. The doors were open on both sides of the luxurious vehicle, and I immediately noticed splashes of red on the cream leather interior. It was only when I circled the scene that I realised it had crashed into a box tree by the water's edge.

Darrington cleared his throat and gave us a brief precis of what he knew. "There is blood on the seats and doors but none on the steering wheel or dashboard. As a result, some far cleverer officers than I am believe that the crash itself is unlikely to have caused whatever injury its driver suffered."

Grandfather didn't disagree, or at least, not verbally. He gave no hint of his first impressions as he knelt down beside the open door to look inside. "You mentioned a disappearance?"

"That's right." Darrington walked to the other side of the car to peer through it. "Patience Hindmarsh hasn't been seen for three days. Her youngest son found the vehicle on Thursday afternoon. Josiah says he went out looking for his mother when no one had seen her for some hours. The house is just a short walk from here. It sits on the feeder lake to this one."

Grandfather looked along the path that went deeper into the woods. I felt that there were a hundred questions which we would have to answer, but he was not yet ready to ask them.

Glancing down at the grass beneath my feet, I spoke for the two of us. "It doesn't appear as if cars drive this way regularly; how would the son have known where to look for her?"

Something in Darrington's manner suggested that he'd asked the same question of his subordinates. "Josiah claims that he came here as his mother once took him to this spot on a walk."

"Did you find his fingerprints in the car?"

I received a curt nod in reply.

My initial thought was that the son had hurt his mother in some way – perhaps even killed her – then claimed to find the abandoned car to explain the presence of any evidence that would link him to the crime. Thinking beyond this, I might conclude that this was too obvious a solution, but when did the obvious become less likely than the improbable?

Darrington had more to say. "Josiah's fingerprints were discovered on several surfaces, including the wheel and dashboard. However, we also found traces of his father and four siblings. Since it was the largest car in the family's possession, the Bentley was used when they went out together en masse."

"Which sounds as though we have reached a dead end." There was a finality to Grandfather's words, almost as if he could see no point in continuing the investigation.

"Might there not perhaps be another route to the truth?" the chief inspector asked, most diplomatically.

His former colleague could only reply with a question of his own. "Did Josiah say whether he went inside the car?"

"He says he climbed in through the front passenger door and looked under the seats in case he could uncover any clues. When he found nothing, he retreated to the house in case someone had received word from his mother."

Now that the expert investigator had begun, there was no stopping him. "I assume that the missing woman's husband is the same Abraham Hindmarsh who is the Member of Parliament for Guildford?"

"Quite right." Darrington was something of a mystery to me.

Though I had met him on several of our cases, he was the definition of a closed book and rarely talked about anything but his work. The one thing I knew about him with absolute certainty was that he'd spent time in the army. Everything he did was precise and careful, as though he'd been taught to take the measure of his every movement to an eighth of an inch.

He placed his boots together, much like a soldier giving a salute. "Hindmarsh is a capable man with a truly uncompromising nature. Nothing he has told us made me think it any less likely that he was behind his wife's disappearance."

Grandfather stood up and, without taking his eyes off the car, walked slowly away. "I'll reserve judgement until I've had the chance to interview him."

"I'm afraid that won't be possible."

"Why? Has he no tongue? Or has he left on an arctic voyage?"

Darrington pursed his lips before responding. "He refuses to have anything more to do with the investigation. He claims he has told us all he can and will not allow my officers onto his land until we discover something new. I specifically suggested that he at least speak to you, but he refused point blank, and his butler saw me from the property."

Grandfather's expression only became more serious, but he did not reply. I expected him to demand to see the missing woman's husband or at least list the reasons why this was an unsatisfactory outcome. On the contrary, he merely stared at the damaged vehicle and said nothing.

It was around then that I found the courage to look inside the car. There was a lot more blood than I'd been expecting, and I soon pulled my head back out again. I'm normally not squeamish at such moments, but there were great long splashes of rusty red across the seats and in the footwells. It looked very much as though the missing woman had been slashed with a knife, and it was hard not to think the worst.

A story of my own formed in my head, and I decided to voice it aloud. "Perhaps someone tried to take Patience Hindmarsh against her will. She fought with the driver and the car crashed into the tree. Rather than risk her escaping, the assailant produced a knife and attacked her."

Grandfather nodded gravely. "The whole affair leaves a nasty taste in one's mouth."

Darrington took a few steps closer to address us both. "That wouldn't explain what happened to the body, though. You'll have to follow me."

He turned to lead us on the final part of the tour, and the three of us walked on around the lake. The path soon became more overgrown as we approached the old mill building. Our guide stopped from time to time to point out dry red specks on the undergrowth.

"It's lucky that there's been so little rain this summer or we would have lost much of the evidence. It has been three days now since she disappeared. Abraham Hindmarsh prevented his children from contacting us until he was certain their mother had really gone, so we're fortunate to find anything at all."

Grandfather gave me a pointed look, and I knew just what it meant. Perhaps Mr Hindmarsh wished to avoid wasting the police's precious time, or perhaps he was hoping there would be nothing to find by the time they were called.

On we walked through that quiet wood. The only sound was the snapping of twigs beneath our feet and the rustling of the leaves overhead. I had the ridiculous thought that murder shouldn't be allowed to happen in such an idyllic spot – that the natural world should be protected from man's barbarities – but I knew better than to say anything so naïve to my wise companions.

"There's a lot more blood inside the mill house," Darrington told us. "The building belongs to the family, though the lake is public property. Patience Hindmarsh's predecessors were farmers in these parts before making their fortune in industry." He pointed deeper into the woods. "I have one last thing to show you."

I could only think he'd followed the grim trail several times already, as he easily found his way. The traces of blood to which he now pointed were lower down than before, and I noticed a clear path through the undergrowth.

"The specialists we've had down here say that the broken branches and flattened leaves suggest that a body was dragged through here. If it was Mrs Hindmarsh, we think the killer was looking for a place to dump her."

As he finished this statement, we came out beside a shallow pit, where long-dead inhabitants of the area had extracted chalk. It would have been a miserable final resting place, so at least poor Patience was spared that injustice.

"Why would he have changed his mind?" I had to ask. "I can understand him removing the body from the car if he didn't want anyone to know that she was dead, but why go to the trouble of dragging her here only to rethink the plan?"

"Fear of discovery," Darrington replied, and a further explanation was provided by the sound of a car speeding past not so very far away. "There's a road just beyond that thicket. The killer must have realised that this wasn't so isolated a spot as he had imagined and made other arrangements. There's a deer path that leads all the way to the road. Either he had an accomplice, or he went to fetch his own car and came back for his victim."

"It doesn't sound as though much thought went into this rushed and violent crime." Grandfather viewed the case dispassionately, but I was incapable of any such thing.

I turned back towards Silent Pool, even though it was no longer visible through the dense underwood. "It's a horrible way to die, no matter where her body is."

CHAPTER THREE

Grandfather wrote to the Member of Parliament for Guildford, requesting the chance to discuss his wife's disappearance. The reply was much as Chief Inspector Darrington had predicted. Abraham Hindmarsh would not allow us to visit his house or speak to his children. We were barred from investigating the case, and there was nothing we could do about it.

By the end of the week, the story was released to the press, and there was even a sizable reward offered in exchange for information on the missing woman's whereabouts. With the tale of the stolen rubies and the Russian émigré losing its initial lustre, they were hungry for a new story to distract from the typical gloomy news of industrial stagnation, record national debt and an overvalued pound.

Politician's Wife Vanishes, the Times reported, under a photograph of Patience Hindmarsh looking noticeably lost and nervous. *Police Pursue Criminal Connection in Hindmarsh Case,* the London Chronicle announced within days, though the story that went with this claim offered little new information. *Silent Pool Dredged: No Sign of Body* was the news the following morning. *Patience Hindmarsh: Chance of Survival Slim,* the Comet attested, quoting a source close to the investigation.

It was interesting to see that the papers were willing to point fingers at her overbearing husband, indirectly at least. The stern visage of the honourable Mr Hindmarsh was everywhere in London, peering out at me from newspaper stands in Piccadilly Circus and billboards on the Strand. No one wrote the words, *Abraham is the likely killer,* but I read more than one account of his quick temper, dour attitude and sharp tongue. He'd made a name for himself working under the Foreign Secretary, Lord Darnley, but I had to assume that his name was not always whispered in the most positive of tones.

Grandfather quickly became preoccupied with the case. He read every word that was printed, rang Scotland Yard daily to receive updates and consulted friends and former colleagues in the very highest places in order to share information and present his theories. None of it did any good and, before long, the summer ended, and we returned to his estate at Cranley Hall.

"The problem is that we are so far removed from the investigation that it is nigh on impossible for me to grasp the motivation of any suspects," he told me a day or two after we had settled back into our old routine.

We were sitting in two grand armchairs on either side of a large bay window. Delilah was snoring happily at her master's feet, and the house was quite serene that shiny September morn.

That did not mean for one moment that I would let him get away with hyperbole. "Didn't you once tell me that there is no such thing as an impossible case, and the only limitation is the detective at its helm?"

He looked across at me with an expression that said, *I may well have uttered such words, but I'd rather not acknowledge them.*

"Of course, it is tempting to believe that the woman's husband is to blame," he told me instead.

"Undoubtedly."

"By all accounts he is a surly brute even by the standards of the House of Commons, but without knowing how he treats his family, there is no way—" He stopped himself then, presumably remembering another of his aphorisms that he was on the point of contradicting. "Or rather, it is extremely difficult to say what kind of man he is."

I had complained of such quandaries any number of times, only to be told not to feel sorry for myself. All the same, I decided to be nice. "I sympathise, Grandfather. I honestly do. In all the time we have been working together, we have never once had to conduct an investigation from such a distance."

He clicked his fingers twice at this moment, though I couldn't begin to imagine why. When no response came, he looked about the room, realised we were alone, and stood to ring the bell for our head footman.

"The one good thing that has come of this whole sorry affair is that it has presented a much-needed distraction from our other unsolved case. Even if we never find an explanation for Patience Hindmarsh's disappearance, I can say with some confidence that the theft of the Duchess of Hartlepool's rubies will—"

He fell silent at this moment and his eyes glazed over in a way that I had never seen before.

"Grandfather?" I asked, but there was no reply. "Grandfather, are you quite all right?"

I waved one hand before his face in the hope that this might stir him, but he merely blinked and continued to stare at me like a waif peering through the window of Fortnum & Mason's chocolate department.

"You rang, M'lord?" Halfpenny sang as he entered the room a short while later.

He cheerfully sailed across to us, and something about his arrival must have sparked a reaction in the detective. Grandfather's smile disappeared, and a look of wonder occupied his features.

"What's the matter with him?" the footman asked in something of a whimper.

"I can't begin to imagine. He was chattering away just a few minutes ago, and now this."

We stood watching this strange sight and might well have continued indefinitely had Todd not appeared.

On seeing us there, he came to inspect his master for himself. "How unusual."

"He's been like this for some time," I explained.

"You don't think he's gone back to his old ways, do you?" our footman asked in his typical, worried tone.

"No, of course he hasn't." My grandfather's right-hand man—

Wait, I've already told that part of the story. I've talked in great detail about my grandfather's revelation with regards to the Vorontsova case, and my own minor success in making sense of the disappearing rubies. What I haven't explained is what happened next.

"I was just wondering whether you're any closer to solving the disappearance of Patience Hindmarsh at Silent Pool," I mused, only for my grandfather to put down his cup of tea and his smile to vanish. "Ah, yes… Silent Pool…" He opened his mouth to say more, but nothing would come.

For a moment, I was worried he'd fallen into that inexplicable trance again, but then the phone that Todd was still holding began to ring and the Chief Inspector's voice broke through the silence.

"Hello, Todd? Is that you?"

"It is, indeed, sir," our trusty retainer replied. "How may I be of assistance?"

"There's something of an emergency. You must tell the former superintendent that we need his help directly at Silent Pool."

"Has there been another murder?" I was quick to ask, and Todd repeated the question down the line.

The chief inspector's response became muffled and slightly metallic as it passed through the wires. "Not yet, there hasn't. However, judging by the interactions I've witnessed between the various parties here, it may only be a matter of time. The one good thing that has come of this morning's misadventure is that Abraham Hindmarsh is now resigned to our presence on his property. He's willing to let you investigate."

Grandfather was already on his feet and spoke with the confidence of a man who expected his every word to be heard and heeded. "We will be there forthwith, Darrington. I am already on my way."

We left Todd to conclude the conversation and took the stairs down from Grandfather's suite of rooms. As we reached the western corridor of Cranley Hall, I had a question for my mentor.

"How many of your various members of staff do you expect to accompany us on this particular case? Do you imagine that the man who weeds the paving stones in the garden will come in handy? Or will you restrict yourself to your usual core group of cook, footman and factotum?"

He did not stop or even change his expression to any great extent. He communicated his emotions solely with a sideways glance, but this was plenty to tell me that he was unimpressed.

"The house is a mere eight miles from here. I have no reason to think that we will have to stay the night, and it would be presumptuous to enlist the help of my servants. A chauffeur will suffice."

I thought back over our past cases to the times when his insistence on bringing a large number of paid helpers had seemed quite unreasonable. Before I could point out any contradiction in his logic, he let out a bird-high whistle and called to our canine companion.

"Do keep up, Delilah," he shouted along the corridor. "Our presence is required at the scene of a possible crime."

Much like me, she could summon no response, though this did raise a new question.

"You're bringing your dog?" This was me speaking, not Delilah. "Isn't that just as presumptuous as bringing an entourage of servants to wait upon you?"

"No, of course it isn't." He was shooting along the corridor at such a pace that even this challenge couldn't slow him down. "It's simply good practice. Any gentleman detective worth his salt has a hound at his side and a novice assistant to round off the trio. She is just as essential to my process as you are."

I tried not to take this as an insult and failed. I waited for my hairy equal and we ran after our master and out of the house. A grand estate, a dubious politician and the no doubt despicable Hindmarsh clan awaited us.

CHAPTER FOUR

The enormous manor house which had been built overlooking the larger of the two lakes at Silent Pool was remarkably modern. Most of the stately homes I'd visited with my grandfather were either from centuries past or built to look as though that were the case. Lodine – as a sign informed me the house had been christened, but I would soon discover no one actually called it – couldn't have been more different.

The first thing that stood out about the L-shaped building was its asymmetry. One side had three peaked gables, the other none. At one end of the grey slate edifice was a rounded tower that looked as if it had been transplanted from a Spanish castle or a primitive oast house. At the other end was a plain wall hewed from local stone. Though all of this was in keeping with the architecture of the Arts and Crafts movement of the Victorian era, I had the definite feeling, as we stepped from Grandfather's black pre-war Napier limousine, that the house had been constructed this century.

It was located close to the edge of the lake, so there were no formal gardens in front of the property as you would normally expect from a country house. Instead, the grounds spread out into the woods behind the building, and a stone terrace bridged the gap between the front door and the water. The overall effect was dramatic, and yet it was quite appropriate for its wild surroundings.

"It's good of you to come so quickly," Darrington said with an air of hesitation. He was only standing a few yards from the house but looked at the front porch as though it were a man trap. "Mr Hindmarsh has been informed of your visit. He's very particular about who enters his property."

Grandfather was immediately curious, and I was reminded once more that the missing woman's husband would be considered the likely culprit until a more promising possibility presented itself. "What did he make of the news of our arrival?"

Delilah had exited the car last and sat beside the chief inspector, awaiting his response.

"It's hard to say." Darrington had always seemed a thoughtful, careful sort of man, but there was an added reticence to everything he did that day. It was as if he felt the need to consider the sensitivities of the case before choosing each word. "He's been on edge ever since I first spoke to him. However, the possibility that one of our witnesses is afraid of your oracular talents surely can't prove that he was involved in the crime."

"You're quite right." Grandfather turned away for a moment, and it was clear he only half believed this.

The scene was very much like the one we had inspected some weeks earlier, though grey clouds had blocked out the warming sun we'd previously enjoyed, and a few wisps of fog hung over the lake. Such is the way of things in Britain in the autumn. Our allotment of sunshine had apparently been used up for the year, and I felt it likely that we would have to wait until the spring to see that celestial spectacle again.

"Perhaps we should seize the moment and enter the house," I suggested when my two more experienced associates stood there looking as ominous as the sky overhead.

Darrington huffed his agreement, Delilah wagged her tail, and Grandfather's moustaches wiggled a fraction. We moved towards the house, where a uniformed constable was waiting to open the door for us. I had to think myself lucky that I'd never had such a boring job. It goes without saying that there are any number of advantages to being born with a silver spoon in one's mouth, but I couldn't think of anything more tedious than standing on guard outside a house. It certainly wasn't going anywhere.

The rubber-cheeked officer was over the moon to perform this small duty for us. "Good morning, gentlemen. Welcome one, welcome all," he said a little informally, and Grandfather studied him as though he represented a rare species of porcupine.

The entrance hall, which we now… entered, was a spectacular sight. Two curving staircases swept down to us from the first floor and, on either side, a gigantic modern mural covered the walls. To tell the truth, I'd never seen art quite like it. Painted in beige and white monochrome, there was a modern city skyline seemingly emerging from the clouds on one side and an oddly geometrical depiction of Silent Pool on the other. It was both heavily detailed and yet stark. Underneath, a white, tiled floor shone in the light that came through three porthole windows above the door, and I hadn't the faintest idea what I thought of anything I saw there.

Before I could decide, I noticed a young woman dressed all in black. She reminded me of a novice nun and, in keeping with this impression, she turned away demurely from us as we crossed the hall. She was carrying long runs of fabric in contrasting shades over each arm and disappeared through a shadowy doorway.

"She's an impoverished relative by the name of Charlotte Elliott," Darrington explained once we'd followed a corridor off the hall towards the back of the house. "She has no real connection to the case, from what I can tell, but my men have interviewed her."

This gave me a number of points to scribble down in the notebook in my head. The first was, *She's definitely the killer!*

The rooms we passed were bright, airy affairs, but they were connected by dark passages that felt as if they'd been added as an afterthought. I nearly walked into my grandfather, and I couldn't see Delilah, though she was only a few feet in front of us. It's hard to say how she knew which route the chief inspector intended to take, but I could hear the swish of her tail and her soft panting as she successfully led the way to the tower I'd spotted from outside.

The deeper we went into the house, the more of its inhabitants we saw. It was not only footmen and maids who caught my attention, but five well-dressed people in their twenties, lounging in lounges and reading in reading rooms. They were all of a piece in the style of their expensively tailored clothes, but their colouring and features were on a scale from dark to pale. Despite this, I was willing to bet that they were the siblings of whom the chief inspector had spoken.

When we reached the gloomy parlour in front of the tower, Darrington paused before knocking on the thick black door.

"You may enter if you must," a voice inside said by way of a welcome. "The door is unlocked." The deep, irritable tone in which the man spoke gave the sense that he had no interest in whatever would happen next.

"Thank you, Mr Hindmarsh, sir." Darrington seemed excessively cautious, and I got the feeling that he'd already endured several difficult conversations with the man and wasn't looking forward to this further meeting.

"Come in, gentlemen." Abraham Hindmarsh said without turning around. "I won't keep you long." He stood with his back to us as he placed a tray of some sort into a glass-topped display cupboard.

"Moths," he said, apropos of seemingly nothing. For a moment, it sounded as if he were insulting us, but then he spun around to explain. "I collect them and mount them. It's a minor distraction from my duties, but one which requires no small amount of patience and dexterity."

He was a huge man, built very much like the tower in which we now stood, and it was hard to imagine his thick workman's fingers lending themselves to such an intricate hobby. It was also hard to imagine, based on this strange welcome at least, why he had called us to the house.

"I'm honoured to meet you," my grandfather began when no one else broke the stalemate. "I'm acquainted with the Foreign Secretary, and I've only heard him say good things about you."

A suggestion of a smile shaped Hindmarsh's thin lips. "That is very kind of Lord Darnley and equally generous of you to say so. I have learnt much from his tutelage since he made me Parliamentary Under-Secretary of State for Foreign Affairs." He clearly took some pride in this wordy title.

I know that promising assistants to famous detectives are supposed to excel when it comes to analysing suspects and grasping the subtext of a conversation, but I was at a loss as to why no one had mentioned the matter we'd gone there to discuss. Even with these opening salvos dispatched, the two men stood watching one another like boxers waiting to see who would get things started. Admittedly, I'm also no expert on pugilism, and I might well have mixed my metaphors there.

"Mr Hindmarsh called me this morning to attest to a disturbing development here at Silent Pool," Darrington announced when, I could only imagine, he'd grown tired of whatever was happening.

"Oh, really?" Grandfather turned these two words into a question. It was not a grammatically correct question, of course, but he had always been a *do-as-I-say* sort of person rather than the alternative.

"That's correct." Hindmarsh shook off the daze that had come over him and searched for a more complete answer.

While I waited, I glanced at the rows of glass cases which went around the edge of the circular room. I was puzzled to discover that

36

almost every moth on show was of a similar size and species. This was not the collection of some great naturalist who wished to contrast various specimens. It was the display of a man who was making do with what was at hand.

"I imagine that you have read about the events that recently unfolded here." He did not turn these words into a question but ploughed on with what he wanted to say. "Well, this morning, someone tried to murder me."

"That's terrible. How did it happen?" Grandfather pretended to be shocked. I cannot say why he would feign any such thing, but I'm certain that's what he did. He was never particularly convincing at times like this, though perhaps he wanted Hindmarsh to know that he was being insincere.

Hindmarsh took longer than necessary to answer this simple question. He walked over to the desk that was directly in front of the door and pointed to the high-backed chair that stood behind it. "I was sitting here working and rose to consult a book when a bullet whistled through the room."

All eyes turned to the chair, and I could make out a small hole three quarters of the way up it.

Grandfather's reply was just as cautious as Hindmarsh's short summary of the attack. "Did you pursue your assailant?"

A pause. A shift of the eyes. "It didn't even occur to me. I dropped to the floor and hid." Hindmarsh had a roughness to his manner, and yet he spoke so carefully that, were I a cynic, I would have said he was lying. "I relied on the fact that, if a man is such a coward that he would shoot me through a door, he was not about to confront me face to face. I heard the sound of footsteps retreating, and my heart rate had almost returned to its usual level when my son Ezekiel burst into the room to check that I wasn't hurt."

Grandfather hadn't gone to inspect the door or the chair. He stood right where he was and asked another question that wasn't a question. "Your son had heard the gunshot?"

"That's right. He was in a room along the corridor and came immediately."

Lord Edgington's eyes possessed a certain glow when he was on a scent. "And yet he didn't cross paths with whoever fired the shot?"

"That's exactly…" Hindmarsh began before correcting himself. "Or rather, I can only imagine that's what happened."

He received a brisk nod in response before Grandfather motioned for me to inspect the door. I did as instructed – when do I not? – and sure enough, there was a small hole just above head height.

I was surprised that I hadn't seen it when Darrington knocked to gain entrance. The two-storey tower was brightly lit, and I would have expected the light to shine through the hole out to the corridor. I opened the door to see why this had not been the case and realised that the would-be assassin had pointed the gun at a downward angle in the hope of hitting his mark. While the bullet hole lent some small gleam to the outer chamber, it was not the bright bolt of sunlight cutting into an Egyptian tomb that I'd read about in so many adventure stories.

I stepped out of the room and closed the door to spy through it on tiptoes. Although the hole was perfectly aligned with the chair, this did not explain why the attempted murderer would have chosen such an unreliable method if he'd really wanted to kill the man.

When I returned to Hindmarsh's office, Grandfather was sitting quite comfortably in one of the two armchairs in front of the desk. He was still engaged in his piece of theatre and now rested his right ankle on his left knee in a shockingly informal manner.

"I will summarise what I understand so far." He was definitely playing up to the image of the eccentric detective. "Someone from your household – we must assume the assailant was known to you in order to access this part of the house – someone from your household came here with a gun and, without knowing exactly where you were in the room, placed it against the door and pulled the trigger. Is that right?"

"I believe it is." Hindmarsh had grown even more circumspect. He presumably found the sight of the revered Lord Edgington (who was flanked by a chief inspector of the Metropolitan Police and a boy who had fortuitously guessed the motives behind a few simple murders) somewhat intimidating.

"Then perhaps you can explain why I have identified not one but two bullet holes when you only heard a single shot."

The game had been building up to this. Hindmarsh spun around to look at the evidence that only my grandfather had spotted. I imagine that he'd seen it as soon as we entered the room, such was the deftness of his six or seven senses.

His victim took two steps closer and froze with a look of horror on his face. "I can't imagine…" It seemed that words would desert him entirely, but then he found some more. "I suppose the blighter must have shot twice…" He knew this sounded wrong and was once more forced into a correction. "Or perhaps he had a trial run when I wasn't here."

"Yes, of course," my wily grandfather replied in a perfectly trusting tone of voice. He'd caught the man out, but he wasn't ready to reveal what he knew just yet. "Yes, that must be it."

CHAPTER FIVE

In ideal circumstances, my grandfather would have broken from the interview to inform me of his conclusions at this point. I would have asked him what he really thought about the second bullet that had buried itself in the wall just a few inches from the chair. Subsequently, he would have insisted that I already knew what it meant, forcing me to make a wild guess which, at least once in a hundred tries, might turn out to be accurate.

As none of this was possible, I decided to raise a point of my own.

"You were unwilling to allow us to visit until now," I told Hindmarsh. "Your wife has been missing for the best part of a month and—"

"It's only been twenty-two days."

I continued in the same insistent manner as before. "Your wife has been missing for twenty-two days, and yet it is only now that your life appears to be in danger that you allow the finest detective in Britain to take on the case."

He opened his mouth to answer, but I believe he changed his mind. "Who are you, sir?"

"My name is Christopher Prentiss." I moved around the table to look at him a little more closely. It seemed that something of Grandfather's theatricality had seeped into me. My response was prickly and direct. "I am Lord Edgington's assistant, and we've come here to uncover what really happened to your wife."

Far from revealing that I'd intimidated him, Abraham smiled ever so smugly. "Oh, the little grandson. I thought you were still at school."

"I was still at school until I finished school." In my head, this had sounded really very pithy. "And now I'm not at school and—"

Thankfully, he interrupted before I could say the word school again. It was much harder to play the steely interrogator than I'd hoped.

"Well, Christopher Prentiss, you and your grandfather are both welcome here. You may not believe me, but I want nothing more than Patience's safe return."

I looked at the chief inspector and his former colleague, but they were evidently happy to let me take charge. The only problem was that I didn't know what to say next. I wandered around the room and stopped in front of the door, by which time my thoughts were a little more organised.

"Do you accept that you are a suspect in her disappearance?"

There was no hesitation now. He responded in a heartbeat. "I would think far less of the detectives leading the case if you didn't consider my involvement. A husband of a missing woman must inevitably be at the top of any list of suspects." It is much easier to be tough on witnesses who disagree with me, but this man kept telling me I was right. The blackguard! "Just because I am a highly respected Member Of Parliament, that shouldn't change the procedure you follow."

The longer he spoke, the more dramatic his voice became, which was a common feature of the politicians I'd met. There was something oddly hypnotic about his delivery. Much as the lilting tones of an operatic tenor can send me to sleep, I would have liked nothing more than to pull up a chair and drift away.

"I believe that you and Patience had a volatile home life." I was basing this assertion on the picture that my grandfather had painted of the man over the last few weeks.

Hindmarsh pursed his lips, and I knew I'd finally scratched his well-polished surface. "I loved my wife."

Past tense, I thought, but it could hardly be used as proof of his guilt, and so I kept on at him. "You loved her, but your life here was not an easy one."

"It's not that at all. You need only speak to my sons, Ezekiel or Josiah, or even my younger daughter, to know that we share a happy home."

I could not fail to notice just how selective he had been when providing these references. There was evidently something he wanted to hide, but it was hard to know how to get from where we were now to the truth.

Luckily, I wasn't alone. Grandfather picked his moment and seized the conversation once more. "Lord Darnley may say good things about you, but he is not the only acquaintance we have in common. I have heard it said on a number of occasions that you control your family as if you are a general and they are your troops. Few of them have laid eyes on Patience for the best part of a decade, and the rumour is that you did not allow her to leave the house. So forgive me for reading between the lines, but perhaps your perception of a happy existence is distinct from theirs."

It was hard to know to what extent Hindmarsh's reactions were genuine. Much of the time, he seemed supremely confident, but flashes of fear shone through.

"I love my wife and children and want only what's best for them." That superior tone had returned. "I am a modern man, but that does not mean I would allow any of them to be corrupted by the world in which we live. All five of our children still reside here at Silent Pool, and Patience has done a wonderful job raising them... despite her troubles."

The way he pronounced these last three words put an idea in my head.

"Did she drink?" I don't know how I reached this conclusion, but as soon as I said it, I felt that I was right.

Grandfather's eyes suddenly widened and, when no response was forthcoming, he hurried the man. "Didn't you hear the question, Mr Hindmarsh? My grandson asked whether your wife was a heavy drinker."

Hindmarsh gazed down at the desk in front of him and wouldn't look back up for some time. "Yes, she was... or is. In the last year, things became more strained between us, and she turned to alcohol. I really have no idea why she would have left the house when she did. I don't know whether she's alive or dead, and I can't tell you who would want to hurt her."

"Do you deny that you kept her as an effective prisoner in this house?"

In a split second, a look of rage came over the brawny man's face and his response burst from him. "A woman's place is in the home. I did nothing more than make Patience abide by her marital vows, and I do not regret my actions in any way."

In the silence that followed, a shock of anger fizzed within me. I cannot say that Hindmarsh's view was a rare one – such outdated beliefs are still far too common in unenlightened societies such as our own – but it was anathema to me.

If Grandfather felt the same, he hid it well. "I assume that I was

43

correct in my assertion that other members of the family hold a different perspective on the harmony you described. Presumably some of your children took exception to their mother being locked up at home. Which is why today, a short time after her disappearance, one of them came here to punish you for what they believe you've done."

It was the silent member of our party to whom Hindmarsh now turned. No, wait, not Delilah, who was calmly watching the interaction from under one of the cases of dull brown moths. The politician sent his pleading look in Chief Inspector Darrington's direction.

"This is ridiculous," Hindmarsh said with little conviction. "My children and I may not agree on everything, but I can't imagine for one moment that one of them would wish to harm me."

Even the deferential chief inspector (and Delilah, for that matter) looked dubious at this moment. "We understand your position, sir. But is there someone in particular with whom you cross swords?"

"Swords?" Hindmarsh showed another hint of panic. Could he really not perceive any danger from within the family, or was this a ruse? "I've had crossed words with each of them, but we muddle through. I refuse to believe that a member of my own family could be responsible for this or Patience's disappearance."

Before he could say another word, a cry carried along the corridor and a great commotion sounded from somewhere in the house. Grandfather was the first to react, but Delilah shot past him through the door I'd left open. This time, she knew exactly where she was going and followed the screams and shouted insults all the way to the front of the property. I chased after them to the largest salon we'd seen. It was decorated in a starkly modern style, with a thick blue carpet and angular furniture that looked as though it had been fashioned on a distant planet.

There was no time to think too much about the décor as, against the wall opposite us, one of the Hindmarsh brothers was holding his sister by the throat.

"Take it back, you witch!" the young man cried. "How dare you tell such lies about our father!"

44

CHAPTER SIX

The first thing that puzzled me was why the three siblings who were not involved in this confrontation did nothing to intervene. Had I been in their shoes, I would have at least tried to talk the man out of his attack, but instead they cheered the quarrelling pair, much like gamblers at a cock fight – another form of combat about which I know very little.

"Choke the life from her, Ezekiel!" a small, rather hunched figure shouted, though he was soon drowned out by the third and final brother.

"Elisheba, kick him until he lets go."

There was one woman who hadn't said anything, but she watched her sister being strangled with just as much interest as her brothers did. I would have guessed that she had an old-fashioned Biblical name like her siblings, but I was yet to learn anything else about her.

"You'll do no such thing." Grandfather spoke with impressive authority, and I knew the aggressor would loosen his grip. "Release the poor woman this instant or I'll do something that you'll be lucky to live to regret."

He grasped his amethyst-topped cane in both hands, as if he were about to break it in two. I knew what that elegant silver tube concealed, and so it was a good thing that Ezekiel let his sister drop to the floor with a resigned huff.

"I wouldn't have killed her." His belligerent manner very much reminded me of his father's.

Elisheba, the woman who had slid down the wall and was now clutching her sore neck, was looking at her brother with a glint of excitement in her eyes. This was not the reaction I had expected, but then nothing I'd seen in that house was how I'd imagined it would be.

Her lip was bleeding and there was a glowing red welt on her cheek where I had to conclude her brother had slapped her. Despite all this, she looked as though she'd happily go for another round with him and said just as much.

"Ezekiel, you coward. Come back here and tell me how you really feel!" When her demand was met with silence, she licked her bleeding lip and continued. "You're just like Father. When you can't bend a woman to your will, it terrifies you."

"I'm scared of nothing and no one." Her wide-necked brother stamped his foot, as though he were about to launch himself forward. It was an empty threat and simply caused his sister to laugh.

"Stop this." Abraham's voice travelled ahead of him so that all eyes were already on the doorway by the time he ambled into the room. "Do you think you'll achieve anything in life by fighting one another?"

I was surprised to discover that even the previously outspoken Elisheba would not answer back to her father. Her gaze fell to the floor, and she and her siblings froze where they stood, like sculptures in a landscape garden.

"She started it, Father." Ezekiel was at least twenty-five, but he sounded like a child at that moment. His large hazel eyes looked around for help, just as a little boy will search out his parents after falling over. "She was saying the most horrible things about you. It only makes sense that she's the one who shot through your door."

"I don't want to hear that," Hindmarsh responded. "I don't want any of you suggesting that a member of our family is responsible for the violence that has been perpetrated here. Do you understand?" When required, he could be stentorian in his delivery, and the words rattled the rafters of the hall-like salon.

For their part, the five grown-up children fell quiet. The factions in their ranks were already quite clear, but they couldn't meet one another's gaze, and they certainly couldn't look at their father. We would learn nothing more about them until he had gone.

Grandfather must have known this, as he turned to our host and spoke more warmly than at any time that morning. "Mr Hindmarsh, I truly appreciate your time and assistance. There is clearly quite some work ahead of us, and I will need your children's help to get to the bottom of this terrible business. I don't wish to bother you any more than I already have."

Mr Hindmarsh looked uncertain how to proceed. It was evident, to me at least, that he did not want Grandfather to dig too deeply into his family's affairs, and yet the esteemed detective had spoken so reasonably and politely that it was hard to disagree.

"Of course, Lord Edgington," he eventually replied with a mechanical bow of the head. "If there is anything that any of us can do to aid your investigation, you need only ask."

He didn't immediately leave but glanced around at his offspring. I believe the look he gave them said, *Don't do anything that will make matters worse.* He bowed before exiting the room, and his lolloping gait reminded me of one of his sons. There was something unusually pronounced about the curve of their backs, and I wondered whether he and the boy who had supported Ezekiel in the fight suffered from the same congenital condition.

Once he had gone, it was Grandfather's turn to admonish them. "Your father is right in what he said. You mustn't turn against your siblings. They are the only ones you will ever have."

It is hard to say whether his audience gave this message any credence. They had separated into their two groups, with the adherents of Abraham Hindmarsh leaning against the mantelpiece on one side of the room and the defenders of their mother's memory arranged on a sofa on the other.

Though they gave no sign of having heard, my grandfather continued on the same theme. "My brother died when I was around your age, and not a week goes by without my wishing he had lived longer. Whenever I'm reminded of his generosity and sense of humour, it stings my heart as if I'd just heard the news of his demise."

There were even more dramatic repercussions to his brother's death, and I didn't blame him for not going into them.

The rather muscular, masculine-looking girl who had watched the fight so impassively would be the first to respond. "Those are pretty words, Lord Edgington. But we would have to possess an ounce of kindness in the first place for the same to hold true in this house. Our father brought us up to regard such things as weaknesses. As he loves to remind us, a hard heart cannot suffer."

Grandfather took a moment to smooth his black silk cravat. "Are you so callous and pebble-hearted that you feel no sorrow for your mother's disappearance?"

Ezekiel and his short-statured brother both mumbled words of agreement, but the others were less sure.

"Mother was different," the girl who had been the victim of Ezekiel's throttling replied. "You know it's true, Hosanna."

Her dark-haired sister looked unwilling to support her, but eventually consented. "Mother was far kinder than Father ever could be. She tried her best to make us more human. It wasn't her fault that Father controlled and repressed her."

"Do you want me to strangle you next?" came Ezekiel's response. He was the tallest of the five and looked to be the most dangerous. He was broad too, with large, Neanderthal fists much like his father's. Three of his siblings were dressed in formal attire – one brother wore a black suit, and the girls were in long dresses. Ezekiel, though, must have removed his jacket and rolled up his shirtsleeves when the fight began, as his thick arms were on display.

Hosanna showed no sign of being intimidated but looked at her brother with the same impassive gaze as she'd viewed the confrontation. I found this more frightening than Ezekiel's threats, but then I am someone who shows my emotions at all times through the ever-changing expression on my face. I'm like a sentimental thermometer in that respect.

Grandfather looked from one sibling to the next, and I knew that he was memorising features to distinguish them. Hosanna had a square jaw and dark hair. Ezekiel was the bruiser I've already described. The brother I took to be Josiah was, for want of a nicer word, the runt of the litter. Elisheba was strikingly pretty, with pouting lips and golden hair that outshone her siblings'. And the third brother, whose name we still hadn't learnt was... Well, he was rather moon-faced and dim looking and was the only one of them in a checked beige sports jacket. He had taken his sister's side in the argument, though, which suggested he was a nicer sort than either of his brothers.

This is what I noticed about them, but there's a good chance that Grandfather had learnt a lot more. Either way, he stood there for a moment before pointing his finger at the girl who had nearly been strangled. "You—"

"My name is Elisheba," she replied.

"I know your name." For the length of this sentence, Lord Edgington's manner was not so different from their autocratic father's. Perhaps he realised this, as he immediately softened his tone. "Miss Hindmarsh, I would appreciate it if you could come with me."

CHAPTER SEVEN

"Perhaps you should start by telling us what made your brother so angry."

Grandfather stood in front of a large family portrait that hung over the mantelpiece in a stately room off the one we'd just left. The décor was more traditional here, with heavy wooden furniture and a Welsh dresser displaying a large collection of Dresden porcelain. As for the portrait, it had evidently been painted some time ago, as the five offspring were still children. It looked as though Ezekiel and Elisheba were the oldest. The slight and kyphotic Josiah was the youngest, and square-jawed Hosanna and the other brother (whose name I still didn't know) were in the middle somewhere.

"I would think it was obvious." Elisheba struck a defiant attitude from the start. "I told him outright that I believed Father was responsible for Mother's disappearance. If you knew what our dear daddy is really like, and how life was here before that day, you would understand entirely. My brother Ezekiel, however, will not hear a word against him. He would rather strangle me to death than hear the slightest criticism of his hero."

The manic glint that I had noticed in Elisheba's eyes when we'd first found her was now extinguished. That hunger for violence and perhaps even self-destruction had been replaced by a pensive look.

"Then it falls to you to tell us why you believe your father is responsible for whatever happened here three weeks ago." Grandfather watched our suspect as she moved to an armchair before the window. She was framed by a brief burst of golden sunlight which only made her vividly bright hair shine more intensely.

"Father is a bad man. There is no other way to say it. He has raised us to be wolves, rather than decent human beings, and it really is no surprise that this family is disintegrating before our eyes."

Elisheba raised her chin a fraction and looked straight ahead. Normally, when one of our suspects is as beautiful as she, I am instantly convinced of her innocence and go to great lengths to explain away any potential evidence against her. The young lady and her siblings were a frightening mix of furious and self-assured, and I can't say I felt any such compulsion this time.

As the only official there, Chief Inspector Darrington sat in the chair opposite her and issued a request. "Can you be more specific, Elisheba? If more lives are at risk, time really is of the essence." Something about the way he pronounced her name made me think that they already knew one another.

"Father was never interested in our education, but he did enjoy probing and baiting us to see who would react. From an early age, he teased and taunted and told us that we were weak. He dangled his approval over our heads as a prize that we could gain should we live up to his expectations."

"So you're saying that he raised you to compete with one another?" Grandfather crossed his arms and looked a little impatient. Her statement was bold but vague, and it was hard to get any real sense of what she was trying to tell us. "My dear, you will have to be more explicit."

"I'm sorry." She picked at a loose thread on the arm of her chair. "You will have to ask him, but I do not believe his goal was to watch us fight; he simply wanted the four weakest specimens to die away so that a great victor could emerge in his image. He was trying to create one implacable super-man who would one day serve as his replacement. Ezekiel has always been the likely contender."

I was convinced that something had been left unsaid in all of this but, presumably realising that Elisheba was unwilling to utter it, Grandfather changed the subject.

"Then tell us about your mother. It seems that few people outside of this house know a great deal about her. Can you tell us why?"

She broke off the thread on her chair with one fierce tug, and then her words came more freely. "Mother was a good person, but Father spent his time trying to mould her into the woman he wanted in a wife. It was easier to shape us, as we had no knowledge of a world without him, but Mother resisted and was punished."

This time, no request for clarification was needed as she soon explained herself. "He built this house to be her prison. That's why it's so isolated. When they were first married, she was too outspoken and liberated for his liking and so, fifteen years ago, he brought us to the countryside to keep her away from his precious friends and powerful acquaintances. He never allows anyone to visit. Even friends and family are kept away. The only exceptions are our staff and his dead sister's daughter who lives here with us. To be quite honest, my dear cousin is little more than a servant to him, so it was no great sacrifice to give her a small room in return."

"That is Charlotte Elliott," Darrington explained. "The young woman we saw on the way to Mr Hindmarsh's office."

Grandfather presumably made a mental note of this and pushed the witness for more. "But what of last month? What happened between your mother and father before she disappeared?"

She had become more skittish, and her gaze jumped about the room as she prepared her response. "She hadn't seemed herself for months. Normally, I would have expected her to confide in my brother Lemuel or me, but she said that there was nothing wrong. I kept asking all the same, but she refused to tell me. And then, on the morning that she disappeared, she had a terrible row with our father. I could hear their shouting from the other side of the house. I believe he even threw a plate at her."

"Did you hear what caused the argument?" I asked, almost instinctively.

She turned to look at me and seemed surprised that I had spoken. "I did not. In fact, I'm afraid to say that I stayed where I was in my studio. Father's voice thundered through the beams of the house like a call down a telephone line, but I couldn't make out what was said. All I know for certain was that he was incensed. It's easy to tell his mood from the way he speaks, and I'd rarely heard him so angry."

"Was there any suggestion that he was having an affair?" Grandfather was never normally so direct, and I noticed a flicker of hesitation in Elisheba before she replied.

"It's possible. My mother had told me many times that there was no love left in the marriage, and I've often questioned whether Father has a mistress or two in the city. She had definitely been more unhappy over the past year."

"We heard that she began to drink," I mentioned, as I thought I should make the most of my lucky discovery.

Elisheba nodded. "Yes, but I cannot tell you whether she was sad and so turned to alcohol or it was the other way around."

"What about money?" Darrington put to her. "Might that have caused the schism between them?"

She said very little without first pausing to think. "My father adores the stuff and was rarely generous with what he had. Mother had very little use for it, though her inheritance paid for this house and everything it contains."

"Was the fortune she inherited still in your mother's name?" A hint of excitement glimmered in the chief inspector's eyes as he struck upon a possible motive for Abraham to have killed his wife.

Elisheba looked out at the sparkling lake through the window. "On paper, yes, but my father is very good at getting what he wants, and my mother had long since given up standing in his way. What I can tell you is that her father didn't trust his future son-in-law. He made sure that the bulk of the family estate would remain in Mother's name after they were married. As a result, it will pass to us, their children, in time."

"So your father couldn't have divorced her without losing a large part of his wealth?" Grandfather was quick to conclude.

"That's correct." Elisheba said no more than this. It was enough to plant any number of thoughts in our heads, though this in itself made me question her motives. "Mother was definitely the wealthy one. I don't know how much Father has in his own name."

"What about this morning?" I asked, as we'd mainly concentrated on her mother's disappearance and ignored the attack on Abraham Hindmarsh. "Can you explain who would have shot a gun into your father's office?"

Distress rippled across her features once more. Her emotions changed back and forth like a weathervane. "Everyone assumes that I tried to kill him, but any one of us could have gone to the cabinet where he keeps his weapons and picked out a rifle or what have you." She paused, perhaps realising that this was far from proof. "Father thinks that he has fought to protect this family, but all he's ever done is harm us. So I wish I'd had the courage to end his life years ago, for my mother's sake at the very least, but I've never been able to stand up to him. Ever since I was a child, I find myself practically immobile whenever he speaks to me."

She sounded as sincere as any witness we'd interviewed and, while it was true that I'd been fooled in the past, I didn't think that would turn out to be the case this time. As she relaxed a little into her seat, I could sense the suffering she'd endured at the hands of a callous, domineering father. Everything she'd told us could be verified by talking to other members of the household, and though she clearly didn't get along with all of them, her account of life at Silent Pool fitted with what we'd already seen there.

My grandfather cleared his throat to ask an important question. "You've only spoken about your mother in the past tense. Are you so sure she is dead?"

She sat straight back up again, and her gaze became oddly focused and intense. "I have no doubt whatsoever. How else could you explain the sudden disappearance and the blood all over her car? The police believe that her body was dragged from the scene. If Father isn't to blame, then why would he forbid us from talking to the police until today?"

"And if he isn't the killer—" I began, and she soon cut me off.

"If he isn't the killer, then one of his acolytes must be. Either Ezekiel decided to help him out of whatever hole he'd dug, or little Josiah was trying to curry favour as he always does. They're a despicable bunch who are all the more dangerous for believing otherwise."

The spite had returned to her voice, and she had to bite her tongue to stop from saying anything worse. For the first time that morning, it was my grandfather who needed time to reflect on the story we'd heard. He leaned against the wall in, for him at least, an almost slovenly fashion.

"That is certainly a sad story. However, I must ask what other factors could have brought about the current situation. It is apparent that there is a split between those of your siblings who take your mother's side and your two brothers who, as you so aptly put it, are considered your father's acolytes. Might the rivalry between you explain what happened to Patience?"

She shook her head forcefully, and that sour expression remained. "I can't imagine how it would. Ezekiel and Josiah idolise the dishonourable fraudster for the constituency of Guildford, but they had no specific issue with our mother. She always tried to be kind to them, no matter how she was feeling." She touched the red mark on her cheek then and seemed more sure of herself. "No, it all comes back to him. I'm certain."

"And what of the others?" I asked. "What of Hosanna and…" I searched my brain for the name of the fifth sibling that she had mentioned a minute or two earlier.

"Lemuel."

"Yes, Lemuel. Are you sure that things were so harmonious between them and your mother that an innocuous argument couldn't have led to violence?"

She barely let me get the words out before correcting me. "You don't know my mother, Mr Prentiss. She was a truly good person and would have done anything for us." She swept the hair from one side of her face, and I realised once more how beautiful she was and just how frightened she made me. "The only person with whom she quarrelled was our father. I don't know how many times I can tell you the same thing, but there is no doubt in my mind that, whether he delivered the blow that killed her or not, he was to blame for her death."

I considered asking another question but, in the stillness that followed Elisheba's final, resolute statement, a shot rang out.

CHAPTER EIGHT

Everything was happening too quickly. We hadn't had time to explore the house yet, let alone meet the staff, rifle through the missing woman's papers, interview enough of the suspects to have a feel for the case or let Delilah into the gardens to do what she had to do at that time of day. A shot rang out, and I thought it highly unlikely that the killer would have missed this time.

For a moment, I had to wonder whether Elisheba was expecting this very thing, as she reached the door even before my grandfather. Our dog was hot on her heels, and this time she had the scent of gunpowder to follow. I trundled along despondently at the back of the group. It's all very well being the grandson of Britain's greatest living detective – according to the London Chronicle, at least – but murder is a sordid affair and there is nothing pleasant about finding a body.

We passed the siblings' nervous-looking cousin as we sought out the source of the bang. I don't know what happened in the ten or so seconds between our dog entering the room and my arrival, but it hadn't made Abraham Hindmarsh any less dead.

Even though she'd spent the last twenty minutes telling us just how much she disliked her father, Elisheba was still shocked to see his immense bulk laid out on the white carpet of yet another expensively decorated "lounge". I use that word in particular as there was nothing so stuffy or old-fashioned about it to mistake the place for a salon or a parlour. It was a lounge for certain.

The only splash of colour came from the sprays of blood that had shot from the dead man's chest and back as the bullet cut through him. Every surface had been as blank as a freshly purchased notebook before that moment. But what colour his blood had lent the place! A spray of red had made it onto the previously spotless white wall behind. Another decorated the carpet in front of him, as if a house painter had come through the place with his equipment moments earlier.

Delilah knew to stand back from the body, but she released a sympathetic whimper which, by most accounts, the dead politician did not deserve. In keeping with what she'd previously told us, Elisheba was motionless in his presence, even as her siblings and the constable from the front door arrived.

"Father!" Ezekiel yelled on seeing the man laid on his back with his arms splayed out to one side and that bright stain on his breast.

The eldest son ran towards the body, but Grandfather raised one hand to stop him and so he crouched down where he was instead. The dead man's eyes were still open, and I looked into them in case some fragment of an image had remained there to tell us who was responsible for his death. I'm aware that this isn't possible, but it was a traumatic moment, and I wasn't thinking logically.

The one thing we could say with any certainty was that Elisheba had not pulled the trigger. Of course, her siblings weren't to know that.

"She did this!" Ezekiel said, pointing to his sister. "Admit it. You blamed him for what happened to Mother, and you took your revenge."

The accused still couldn't make a sound. She fell to her knees just as her brother had, and so my grandfather responded on her behalf. "Elisheba was with us when your father was murdered. I cannot speak to her wider involvement, but she was not the person who ultimately killed him."

"Perhaps he did it to himself out of guilt!" Lemuel, the brother who had stayed quiet through our first encounter, tried desperately to find an explanation. "Is there a gun nearby? Could he have dropped it when he fell?"

Grandfather had already examined the scene and knew the answer. "Not unless it has fallen behind a sofa or beneath one of the chairs. And besides, in all my years as a detective, I have never known a man to shoot himself through the heart. It is an unnatural position for the hand to take and potentially a slower, bloodier death than a bullet to the head."

Despite this, the hunched figure of Josiah dropped to the floor to look for a weapon. Only a few seconds passed before he rose once more and gave a brief, dispassionate shake of the head. Considering that we'd been told how greatly he admired his father, he was oddly unemotional throughout.

The only one of the dead man's children who did not contribute to the undertaking was Hosanna. She stood in the doorway and watched her siblings as though she were nothing more than a paid observer. We'd learnt little about her from Elisheba, and I was curious as to what role she fulfilled in the family. She did not appear to be one of her father's favourites, but I'd seen nothing to suggest that she was aligned with Elisheba and Lemuel.

What a family! Fallings out, warring factions, a missing mother, and now the controlling patriarch had been murdered. I doubt I've ever met such a horrible lot.

"I'll need you all to tell me where you were in the moments before you came here," the Chief Inspector announced when no one had said anything for some time.

"I was getting a cup of tea." The constable spoke in a shamed voice, before realising that the question wasn't directed at him and quietly shuffling from the room.

I was interested to note that, despite the strength of emotion on display when we'd seen them fighting, none of the man's children cried at his death. Even Ezekiel, who was still kneeling a few feet from his father, would shed no tears.

Hosanna was the first of them to answer Grandfather's question. "I was in my studio. I… paint." She found the second sentence more difficult to utter than the first. It was apparently easier to describe her whereabouts at the time of her father's murder than admit to her artistic endeavours.

"I was reading in the room opposite Hosanna's," Ezekiel added.

With each person who answered, our focus would shift, and it was now Josiah's turn.

"I was playing the piano next door."

Only Lemuel remained, and I could already tell how nervous he was to go last. He opened and closed his mouth like a trout in a net, then held a hand to his throat as if it was terribly dry. "I was there too. We each have a room for our pastimes."

"Yes, but you didn't come out immediately when I called your name," Josiah reminded him, and the youngest brother's eyes narrowed to show just how suspicious he was.

"Because I'd fallen asleep, and it took me a few moments to rouse myself."

"You'd fallen asleep before lunch?" Ezekiel shot to his feet, apparently just as angry as he'd been the first time we'd seen him. Like his brother's, there was something too practised and overdramatic about this response. "I've never known you to nap at this time of day."

Hosanna stepped in to prevent another fight, and I felt more confident that she occupied the middle ground between the rival pairs. "There's no need to take that tone, Zeke. Lemuel came out of his room shortly after. It'll do you no good to scare him into confessing to something he didn't do."

With confrontation avoided, silence came over them like a veil dropped from on high. I've often noticed this phenomenon shortly after a body has been discovered. Loved ones (or otherwise) of the deceased suddenly fall quiet to take stock of the new world in which they have found themselves. I don't believe it is merely to pay respect to the dead, but to make sense of what has happened. It is a silence that the victim might previously have filled – an absence that is instantly noticeable.

My grandfather can be a sympathetic soul when it's required and stood respectfully to one side as Hindmarsh's offspring each experienced the moment in their own ways. The only interruption was the arrival of their cousin. Charlotte Elliott looked more out of place each time we saw her. As she spotted her uncle's corpse, she emitted a strangled moan, and Elisheba ran to comfort her.

Perhaps it was in response to Charlotte's genuine sadness, to which none of them had come close, but the siblings delivered a sudden rush of evidence to rule out their involvement in the crime.

"I feel I should remind everyone that I've never been much of a shot," Josiah informed us in a hushed voice.

Hosanna responded in a similarly defensive tone. "None of us is except Ezekiel. Father was the marksman. He was desperate for us to learn to hunt and fish. That was one of the many ways in which we let him down."

"I heard something shortly before the gun was fired," Lemuel decided to add. "I thought I was imagining it at first, as it was ever so soft, but I believe that someone had placed his ear against the door to listen to what was happening in my room."

The expression on Ezekiel's broad face changed, and I could tell that this news had sparked a significant memory. "That's right. I heard the very same thing. I thought it must be you, Charlotte," he said, looking across at his downtrodden relative.

"I've been nowhere near your studies." Her voice was higher than her cousins', and there was a note of submission which I felt must come from living in her reduced state. Though the chief inspector had told us that she was an unlikely suspect, I was eager to find out whether that was true.

"I didn't say I was in my study," Ezekiel snapped. "How did you know where I was?"

I was expecting the previously fierce Elisheba to savage him for this comment, but she still had an oddly far-off look in her eyes, and it fell to Hosanna once more. "Really, Zeke? Can't you leave such pickiness to the detectives?" She ran one hand through her long straight hair. "It's obvious that we'd be in our studies. We spend most of the morning there. Now stop trying to solve the case and let Lord Edgington and the police do their jobs."

She fell heavily into an armchair and stared at the floor, apparently no longer interested in what would happen next.

"Thank you, Miss Hindmarsh." Grandfather paused over the penultimate word, and I wondered what had occurred to him. "Can you tell me what you heard before the shot was fired?"

She turned from the floor to peer up at the ceiling. "It was much as my brothers said. A few minutes before Daddy was shot, I heard someone in the corridor. I really didn't think anything of it other than that it was an odd time for the maid to be there."

He nodded at his former colleague, and Darrington left the room to discover where the maid was at the time of the killing.

"And you, Josiah?" he asked the remaining brother. "Did you hear anything?"

"No. No, I didn't." He said this most belligerently, as though hoping for an argument. "But as I was playing the piano at the time, it's hardly surprising that I failed to notice a slight noise at the door."

I turned to the most reasonable person there just as Hosanna asked the next question. "You were playing Bach, weren't you?" Hosanna asked her brother in order to confirm the story.

"That's right. It was 'The Goldberg Variations'."

The idea entered my mind that the piece of music Josiah had been playing might lead us to the killer, but it seemed unlikely.

"So no one here was involved in your father's murder?" Grandfather put to them. "We know he didn't do it himself, that the disappearance and possible death of your mother gives you all a good reason to slay him, and yet you would have me believe that wasn't the case."

"As a matter of fact—" Josiah began in response to this sarcastic claim, but before he could say anything more, his older brother had kicked him in the back of the leg to make him stop talking.

Lemuel went to stand beside Elisheba, and, for a moment, the room was split along familiar lines. On one side, Ezekiel and Josiah glanced at one another, apparently unable to say anything more, and standing in the middle was Hosanna, who looked just as reserved as ever. It was hard to imagine how she had remained neutral for so long.

I've come across enough splintered families to know that the relationship between parents and child is rarely simple. My own father has spent most of my childhood at his job instead of at home with his family, and my grandfather's parents were so distant that it's a wonder he didn't turn into a homicidal maniac himself.

Perhaps that's the strangest part of it. For all the bad parents who raise bad children, there are always exceptions. There are uncut diamonds who emerge from the roughest of backgrounds, and saints who've been treated so badly that the real miracle is the fortitude they showed to survive. It would have been foolish to assume that every last one of the Hindmarsh siblings had the capacity to kill, but it was our job to work out which of them was the murderer.

Ezekiel turned to look at the girl he had almost strangled less than an hour before, and I could see that he truly despised her. He didn't have to say anything; it was there in his eyes. He blamed Elisheba for what had happened, even if she was the only person who definitely couldn't have done it.

CHAPTER NINE

"I don't like it," I told my grandfather once we'd sent the suspects back to their studies.

"A man has been shot through the heart. How were you hoping to feel?" he replied in the same ironic tone of voice that he'd used to address our suspects.

"I don't mean that I was hoping to extract any level of satisfaction from the terrible event. I mean that we're facing a real puzzle."

"Well, Christopher, our cases are rarely simple." He cast his gaze through the window to the terrace at the front of the house. The other wing of the L-shaped building was visible, and his eyes lingered there for a few moments.

I needed to slow things down and express myself more clearly, so that's exactly what I tried to do. "Grandfather, you really aren't listening. Things are different here. So much has happened in a short space of time. Everything points to Patience being dead. Elisheba was almost throttled by her own brother and Abraham is… Well, he's there on his back on the carpet, and no amount of scrubbing will remove the stains."

"You're right," he said before focusing on entirely the wrong thing. "Of course, whoever thought that a white carpet was a good idea must have had the doolally tap! I really don't understand modern trends in interior design."

I raised my voice to put my message across more clearly. "Really, Grandfather. Must you be so flippant? What scares me most is that you don't appear to have the faintest clue what has been going on in this family. I think you're as lost as I am, and that is far more terrifying than the dead body that we haven't even taken the time to examine."

He crossed his arms and looked amused for all of three seconds before the spirit went out of him. He allowed his body to become looser – his hands fell to his sides and his shoulders slumped. "I don't know how to tell you this, Christopher, but you're quite right."

I resisted jumping in the air with joy. It wasn't the moment – though I can't deny I planned to remind him of these words at some point in the future.

"I can't understand what any of this means yet," he continued.

"But I don't treat any case lightly. I may have become desensitised to the death of a man whom even his greatest admirers would struggle to defend, but I will seek out his killer with all my usual dedication."

I didn't reply immediately. Instead, I wandered over to look at the dead politician on the floor of his extremely modern lounge. We knew when he'd been killed, so there was no great hurry to inspect the corpse on that account. We knew how he'd been killed, too, unless there was something we'd missed. The only thing we couldn't say for certain was who had killed him… and why… and why now… and any other essential fact that might lead us to the culprit.

"I felt it was going to happen," I said as I inspected Hindmarsh's pale, lifeless visage. His eyes were still staring up into space, which made perfect sense as he was dead, and he'd looked that way ever since we'd arrived. "I don't just mean because of the bullet holes; something told me as soon as we got here that death would come calling before long."

Grandfather nodded, but he let me speak.

"I can't explain it, but there's something about this family that's all wrong. They barely have a good word to say about one another. I may not always get along with my relatives, and I haven't forgotten the fact that there have been some real terrors in our family, too, but this is different. It feels as if none of them can see any good in the world."

"I do know what you mean," he interrupted. "Abraham scarred his own children through his heartlessness. It does not sound as though it was one particular event, so much as year upon year of mistreatment and neglect. The best you can say about them is that Elisheba and perhaps Lemuel loved their mother."

"Elisheba also believes that Abraham was a murderer. What if one of her siblings discovered that to be true and punished him for it? The obvious choice would be Lemuel, who is terribly nervous about something, but it would be much easier for Ezekiel or Josiah to get away with the crime. They idolised their father; if they finally realised what a monster he was, perhaps they could have killed him, knowing that no one would suspect their involvement."

He smiled then and my words gave him a dose of pep. "No one except us, Christopher. We are here to question the unquestionable and probe the improbable."

A sash window on the other side of the room was open a fraction, and I felt a gust of wind caress my fringe. "It's all very well asking questions, but it's answers we need, and I don't know where to start this time."

I must apologise for being so melodramatic. I can't say I was at my most confident after failing to solve even the simplest cases that had come our way recently.

"Why don't we start with the holes in your argument?" He did not wait for a reply. "For one thing, you didn't mention Hosanna. She may seem calm compared to the rest of the family, but that is no reason to disregard the possibility that she could kill."

He raised an extra finger on one hand as he worked through each point. "And then there is the idea that our investigation will be more difficult because the suspects are somehow inhuman or immoral. I would say that was hugely preferable to previous cases in which everyone seemed so normal and innocent that it was near impossible to imagine who could have committed the crime."

I felt a little silly then and couldn't help smiling. "So what you're saying is that I should pull up my bootstraps, buck up my ideas, and stir my stumps."

"Well, not in so many words, but it won't do you any harm. The most important advice I can give you is to focus on the simple things." He took a few steps closer so that we were only a foot or so apart. "Our investigation has barely begun. We will start with Mr Hindmarsh, then move on to his wife before considering which of their children could be behind these violent acts."

When it least mattered, my grandfather could be dismissive and pernickety, arrogant and insensitive, but when I really needed it, he was capable of making our manic world seem sane again. With these few words, he had instilled a sense of purpose and positivity within me. I felt as though I could have marched to Mount Olympus to fight the Nemean Lion… Although, now that I think about it, the Nemean Lion probably lived in Nemea, wherever that might be.

"Christopher, are you ready?" Grandfather was standing at the door, and I realised that I had been daydreaming about the frightening, though slim, possibility of my turning into an ancient Greek hero.

"Ready and raring to go!" I lied as I considered exactly how one went about wrestling a lion without getting terribly bitten.

I took a great gulp of air and sallied from the room, only to be confronted by the staff of the house, who apparently had some questions for us.

"Lord Edgington," the butler muttered with downcast eyes. "I must say that I have great respect for you, sir, and I don't mean to show any impertinence by asking whether what we have heard is actually true."

Grandfather looked at me even as he stepped forward to answer. "If you are asking about your master, then I'm afraid I must confirm that he is dead."

A maid I'd previously spotted was absent, so Darrington was presumably still interviewing her.

"It's a tragedy," declared the woman whom, based on her oversized pinafore, I took to be the cook. "A real tragedy, sir. We can't begin to imagine why anyone would do such a thing."

This perspective was quite different from the one we'd had from the victim's eldest daughter, and the young scullery maid soon elaborated. "Poor Mr Hindmarsh was awful good to us, sir. He really was a fair and generous master."

"Especially come Christmas time," the rather rotund butler confirmed, and his jowls wobbled as he spoke. "There was always a hefty envelope for each of us on Christmas Eve. He even gave me a bottle of his favourite port wine on my birthday."

There was one person there who said nothing. Hindmarsh's niece, Charlotte, stood further along the corridor looking wan and withdrawn. She was one of those people who would be terribly pretty if she ever happened upon a reason to smile, but that did not appear to be her lot in life.

Darrington appeared from behind her and waved to get my grandfather's attention.

In return, Lord Edgington nodded and tried, in some small way, to address the servants' concerns. "I'm sure that Mr Hindmarsh was an exceptionally good employer. He would have been very happy to know what loyal and grateful staff he had. You can rest assured that I, the Metropolitan Police, and of course my capable grandson will leave no stone unturned in our pursuit of the truth."

Something rather unexpected happened at this moment. They all began to clap. His words had evidently had the desired effect, and the butler in particular looked most encouraged. I was a little taken aback by it all. My father has always said that only Americans and the easily amused applaud anywhere outside of a theatre, though I have long since learnt that Father is a notorious grump and his opinions on most things in life should be taken with a jar or two of salt.

"Will you be partaking of lunch, M'lord, Lord Edgington?" the overly obsequious major-domo continued.

"That would be lovely. Thank you…" He extended the word past its usual length in order to elicit the man's name.

"Blunstone, sir. And it will be an honour to serve you at table." With any concerns about the murder apparently forgotten, the man was happy to have someone new to attend to and roused his troops. "Chop-chop, everyone. We have a busy day ahead."

CHAPTER TEN

The Silent Pool staff dispersed about the house like mice looking for hiding places, and I would have stopped to talk to the lowly cousin, but Darrington waved us over once more.

"I've spoken to the housemaid, and she claims that she's been nowhere near the wing where the siblings have their studies since much earlier this morning. The constable on the door reports nothing suspicious either, though he was in the kitchen at the time of the killing." He stroked his chin then as if to draw the next comment from his mouth. "I can make no sense of this case. I hope you've done better than I have."

Grandfather looked uncomfortable, or perhaps bilious for a moment before confessing the truth. "We're in no position to identify the killer yet, but I do have a number of points I would like to explore. First of all, we must find—"

As he was speaking, there was a knock at the front door. We followed the corridor around and came back to the entrance hall, just in time to see Blunstone usher in two uniformed officers.

"Ah, this way, gentlemen." Darrington was about to lead them to the scene of the murder when he remembered we were still there. "You have the run of the house, Lord Edgington. I'll keep you informed of any discoveries we make as the experts search the scene for clues."

He and my grandfather had known one another long enough not to need to say anything more, and the chief inspector hurried off with his subordinates. To my surprise, Grandfather turned and led me outside. Delilah was quick to follow and quick to disappear off into the gardens.

"I thought we were going to probe deeper into the lives of the victims and their potential killers?" I said as he stood glaring at the exterior of the room where Hindmarsh had just been murdered.

He ignored my question and asked one of his own. "Tell me, Christopher, what do you notice from here?"

I stood some way from the house and wondered what miniscule detail he wished me to observe. "The weathervane above the tower is pointing west... ish."

"That's very interesting, but unless the bullet was blown off target by a sudden gust of wind, I doubt it will prove significant."

I tried again and looked a little further down. "A tile or two has become dislodged from the roof. I believe that there were gales recently and—" I'd realised by now that this was just as irrelevant as my previous comment and changed my tune. "I really cannot say what you want me to notice, Grandfather. I'm looking at the façade of one wing of a very impressive house built at great expense by a heartless man who was kind to his servants. The downstairs window is open. The room just above it has a rather nice balcony, though I haven't noticed any others around the house, and the flowers at ground level are clematis. Is that of any value?"

"You never can tell." He walked back towards the house. The constable who'd been guarding the door that morning wore an awkward smile as we passed. Presumably he realised that he was at fault for leaving his post in search of refreshment at the time of the killing. Or rather, I hope he did.

One of the advantages of Hindmarsh's murder – if one were to look for a bright side to such a nasty incident – was that we could now nose about in his office to our hearts' content. When we got there sans chaperone, Grandfather was immediately drawn to the desk, whereas I couldn't help looking at the cases of moths. As something of a bird watcher myself, I do appreciate the joy of observing and cataloguing animals in their natural habitats, but I find it difficult to imagine why anyone would wish to knock such miraculous beings on the head and pin them to a dull white board.

I had the definite feeling that Hindmarsh had extracted pleasure not just from the chance to study the creatures he had killed, but from his dominion over them. The question which immediately came to my mind was whether he had been doing the same thing with his family. He had prevented his wife from seeing anyone, and she barely left the house. As for his children, they were all old enough to have flown the coop by now, but none of them had done so. Had Abraham pinned them down in that beauty spot for life, or had they chosen to stay for some reason?

This reminded me of a comment that my mentor had made. "You stressed the word 'Miss' when you spoke to Hosanna," I reminded him.

Grandfather didn't look up at me but continued leafing through a pile of correspondence. "I wondered whether you would notice that.

What did you take from it?"

"Presumably, you had just realised how unusual it was for none of the five siblings to be married by their mid to late twenties. I believe it crossed your mind, as it has mine, that their father may have kept them here, just as he did his wife."

He nodded and clicked his fingers but, all the while, his eyes remained on the papers before him. "That's excellent, my boy. You are as whip smart as a fox who has forsaken the country for a nicely appointed flat in St James's. That is exactly what I was thinking."

I was hoping that he would reveal something more that I was yet to realise, but he was too busy for that. I moved on around the room, still confused by the paltry selection of moths Abraham Hindmarsh had obtained. I could only think that he went outside with a net one evening and made do with whatever happened to fly into it.

In fact, as the eminent detective alongside me rapidly rummaged through the private affairs of a murdered politician, I felt compelled to take out one of the trays to make sure that the moths were as boring as they looked. I half hoped that, under a different light, they would betray a pearly lustre that had not previously been visible. I even wondered whether they might possess a bioluminescence like certain fungi or sea creatures, which would make them glow in the dark. I was disappointed on both counts, and it was around then that Grandfather gave a frustrated groan.

"I was rather keen on the idea that everything that has happened came back to politics. I wondered whether a rival had paid a kidnapper to take Hindmarsh's wife so as to hold influence over him. It struck me that we might find some tantalising matter of state on which he was working or that he was secretly instrumental in the creation of the Kellogg-Briand pact, which was signed in Paris last month. But no, it seems that his main role in the government was helping to promote trade conferences abroad and boasting about the might of the British Empire. The man was Parliamentary Under-Secretary of State for Foreign Affairs, and yet from everything I see here, he was a glorified braggart."

"That's a real shame, Grandfather," I told him, as I struggled with the glass case I had pulled out. "But I don't suppose you could give me a hand putting this drawer back? It won't fit properly."

Still distracted by his own problems, and not in the mood to question why I was looking at the moths in the first place, he came to my aid. "Is it too much to ask for a little intrigue? Just for once, couldn't the explanation for a murder be a plot to hide the presence of international spies that had become embedded in the British government?"

I didn't like to tell him that such fanciful thinking was normally my job. He had seized the drawer of fifty or so dull brown moths and made more progress than I'd managed.

"It's all in the wrist, Christopher. You just have to…" He didn't finish the sentence as the drawer was still protruding some way from its casing. "Well, it really should be easier than that."

"I have an idea," I told him as I pulled it out again and looked inside the long wooden frame. "There's something blocking it at the back." I reached my hand inside and felt a small packet of papers deep within. I could barely touch them and had to roll my sleeve up before trying again. This done, I just about managed to flick them onto their front to pull them out.

"You're a little genius," Grandfather pronounced most inaccurately (on two scores). "There I was, looking in the obvious places while you thought carefully about where a man like Hindmarsh might hide something he didn't want us to find."

It was tempting to accept his praise, but I'm an irritatingly honest person at the worst of times. "You could say that was what I was doing, but a more precise description would be that I got distracted by some dead insects and stumbled across—" I paused then as I was uncertain what we'd found.

"Private letters penned in red ink!" He was certainly more cheerful than he'd been a few moments earlier. "I knew there had to be something. Hindmarsh stopped us from coming here until today because he knew we would suspect him of murdering his wife; there had to be a reason for him to think he was the likely suspect. Locking Patience up at home was part of it, but he is far from the first excessively controlling husband I've encountered. The rivalry he'd instilled in his children was another feather in his spectacularly ugly cap, but this may be even more important."

He seized the bundle, untied the presumably romantic red ribbon, handed me a letter and selected one for himself. We read in silence for a few moments, and it appeared that his missive was more interesting than mine, which mainly talked about a hat the writer had recently purchased.

"It turns out that, much as Elisheba concluded, her father was having an illicit liaison with…" He flipped over the page. "…his secretary who goes by the name of Nancy. He was carrying on with his own subordinate! Have you ever heard of such a cliché?"

"Regardless of whether they were backstabbing swine or star-crossed lovers, I don't see how their intimate communications are likely to lead us to the killer."

He didn't hear me at first, as he was too busy tittering to himself. "Yes, yes. You're quite right. I'll put them back where I found them immediately." This was a barefaced lie, and his eyes continued darting back and forth across the paper as he devoured poor Nancy's descriptions of her heartache (and shopping).

"Grandfather!"

"Come, come, Christopher. You're forgetting the Edith Thompson case of 1923. She was convicted of murdering her husband on the grounds of common purpose even though it was all her paramour's doing."

"A case which you have often said was a great injustice," I felt I should remind him.

"That may be, but what was the evidence that actually convicted her?"

We said the answer at the very same moment. "Her love letters."

"Fine," I eventually conceded. "But we don't have time to read them all. You should hand them over to a constable who can do the job for us."

"Oh, very well." He put the letter back into the envelope and perched on the desk to look pensive for a moment. "Abraham Hindmarsh really was a first-rate bounder. It's amazing it took so long for someone to murder him."

CHAPTER ELEVEN

As my grandfather was being his occasionally impossible self, and we didn't seem to be making headway on either of the crimes we were investigating, I decided to ask some questions of my own… to myself… in my head. I didn't hold out much hope for the process.

The first doubt that came to me was where the weapon that killed Hindmarsh had gone. The second— Actually, I'll just list them.

> **How did the killer run from the scene without anyone seeing him?**
>
> **What was the sound Lemuel and others heard outside the siblings' studies and studios?**
>
> **Did the fact that Josiah didn't hear said sound mean that he was actually the killer? Had he taken a short break from playing the piano to kill his father?**
>
> **Did it really make sense for Abraham Hindmarsh to invite us there if he thought we would suspect him of murdering Patience? Surely the fact someone was trying to kill him couldn't explain why he hadn't done a better job of hiding the incriminating letters.**

Oh! I think I might know that one after all.

I looked at the two bullet holes, and then the one in the door, and I suddenly knew what I felt my grandfather must have realised as soon as we arrived.

"The killer found Hindmarsh alone and shot him to death," I confidently announced, but this did not draw the reaction I had foreseen.

"I would say that was fairly obvious." Grandfather rose to leave the room.

"Yes, but the hole in the door suggested that he was too frightened of his victim to shoot him in person and failed in his first attempt."

He had a special smile for when I'd realised something clever. It was curiously slow to form but eventually stretched from cheek to cheek. "Keep going."

"I thought it was an odd way to kill someone, but now I understand what was happening. Hosanna told us that her father was the marksman in the family. He invited us here because he thought he'd divined a stratagem for deflecting suspicion onto someone else. By shooting through his own door, he wished to suggest that whoever had murdered his wife was now after him."

"Excellent!"

"That would explain the two holes. The first was a test when his children were out of the house – he missed the chair by some way and presumably realised that shooting through the door wouldn't work. He repeated the shot from within this room when there were people around to hear it. He was so confident that we would think him the victim that he didn't even remove the evidence of his affair. The arrogant so-and-so may well have been looking at the letters when we first came to speak to him."

I was hoping for one of the soft rounds of applause that he often gives when he's impressed by something. It never came.

"That's very good, and if true, it proves once more what cheek the man had." He shook his head and smiled. "Of course the question we should be considering is whether he went to these lengths because he really was responsible for his wife's death – be it a premeditated murder or an argument that got out of hand – or he was simply worried that we would blame him for it."

I joined him at the door, and we left together. "Either way, he was willing to incriminate his own children in the process," I pointed out. "By staging the supposed attempt on his life, he reinforced the idea that someone else in this house was willing to kill."

"That's the bounder we've come to know and love. Who would have thought that a politician could stoop to such levels?" He said this with a twinkle in his eye, and it was obvious that he was joking. "Come along, my boy. We have solved one minor mystery, and we must do our best to tackle some bigger ones."

We'd reached the entrance hall with its stark murals and the sweeping double staircase, and I noticed something through one of the porthole windows. "I think you should go ahead. I'll meet you there shortly."

"But you don't know where I'm going," he protested.

"Don't worry about me!" I didn't pause my retreat as he might have expected but kept walking out of the house. I passed the constable at the door and continued across the paved courtyard all the way to the edge of the water.

I wouldn't say anything for some time. I just stood beside the dead man's niece and waited for her to address me. Charlotte Elliott looked quite lost as she lingered there. She didn't turn to address me but stared across the glimmering lake as she spoke.

"When I was a child," she began, "I thought this place was paradise. My mother used to bring me here in the summer to spend time with my cousins, and I couldn't imagine a nicer place on earth."

"And what of its inhabitants?" I had to ask, as my grandfather had twisted my brain so that I must always focus on the tragic and suspicious. "Did you like them too?"

She tensed the muscles in her arms. "I love them, though I'm in no illusion as to how they view me." She paused then, and I thought I would have to help her along. "I'm the poor interloper – a mere charity case who has done nothing but sponge from their family since my mother died."

I had already realised just how rare it was to meet a witness who was so forthcoming with personal information. There were those who pretended everything was fine, even as the world was falling apart around them, those who lied, and others from whom it took my grandfather's powers of persuasion to extract the truth. Charlotte was clearly different.

"I know what it's like to be the odd one out in a family," I said, perhaps sounding a little hard done by. "I might be my brother's brother and my father's son, but I've never quite fitted in with them. I'm lucky to have a mother who knows how to unite us."

She pulled her arm across her body, as if trying to protect herself. "My mother was the only real family that I had. My father died when I was young and left us with nothing. Of course, I knew when I came to live here two years ago that Patience would rather I had never darkened her doorstep."

An interesting shift of perspective had occurred. Until now, even those in Abraham Hindmarsh's camp had painted the missing woman as a good person, but perhaps she wasn't so perfect after all.

Charlotte looked up at the vast expanse of sky above Silent Pool, and I took the chance to study her. She had skin as pale as a South Sea pearl, and hair so black and silky that it shone like polished obsidian. But her perpetually heartbroken expression seemed to overwhelm everything else about her. She was the kind of girl I might have devoted my time to making smile, had I not imagined that she was a savage killer, hellbent on claiming the Hindmarsh estate. Admittedly, she'd be far down the list when it came to inheritance, but such was the power of my grandfather's training that I was already doubting her innocence.

"You must have suffered a great deal," I said to win her over. "This morning especially."

She turned her head, and I felt she was judging me just as I had her. "It would be wrong to complain of my lot in life. Whatever happens next, I have been incredibly fortunate to spend so long here."

"Do you really think that the family would throw you out to fend for yourself?" I asked in a tone that showed I cared just a little too much.

"That's neither here nor there. The fact is that, for the rest of my days, the comfort of my existence will always be in the hands of someone else. If I had any money, I would train for a profession, but Mother was born with very little and died with just as much, and I am at the mercy of the Hindmarshes."

This was all very interesting, but I'd been trying to push the conversation towards the murder, and she'd skilfully diverted it in another direction. Did she know what she was doing, or was her mind on other things?

"Can you tell me more about your uncle? I believe your cousins made their minds up about him a long time ago, so it would be helpful to hear about him from someone more neutral."

She turned away from the lake and began to walk around the house to the elaborate gardens beyond. "I know that his children couldn't always see the good in him, but he really could be very generous. He despised my father and could barely tolerate my mother for her choice of husband, but he was always kind to me. One of my earliest memories is sitting on his knee as he bounced me up and down and sang 'Ride a Cock Horse to Banbury Cross'. My father had died a short time earlier, and it left a lasting impression on me."

I was struggling to make sense of the man who remained the first confirmed fatality at Silent Pool. Was he a heartless bully who kept his family trapped at home and raised them all to compete with one another? Or was he the soft-hearted father figure that his niece had just described? Perhaps he adapted his personality to what he felt was needed. He was admired by his staff, and his young (let's be honest, she was probably young) secretary evidently thought highly of him. But who was Abraham Hindmarsh really?

We had reached a row of long rectangular flower beds, and I could see Delilah rolling about in the distance. With the summer over, there was not much colour to be found, though I spotted a patch of blue flowering leadwort beside purple-leaved cabbages that brightened up the dull brown earth.

A discrepancy in Charlotte's account finally occurred to me. "When we spoke to Elisheba this morning, she told us that her father used you as little more than a servant. Why would she say such a thing if it weren't true?"

I saw her flinch again, and the muscles in her neck tightened. "I'm no servant. I have taken on certain duties in the house, and I've overseen the redecoration of a number of rooms, but no one took me for granted. Elisheba is a cherished companion, and I would never wish to say anything against her, but she's often claimed that her father treated me poorly when that simply wasn't true."

It was tempting to believe that she was hiding some dark truth, but perhaps her reticence came from a desire not to offend. For a woman in her precarious position, it was surely a good instinct to have, but one that I would have to persuade her to resist.

"I quite understand." I sounded just like my sly grandfather. "When speaking to your cousin earlier, I came to appreciate just what a capable and interesting individual she is."

"Yes, she's a charming person and the prettiest woman I know." She was quite rapturous in her praise. "As a child, I dreamed of having her golden hair instead of my dull brown locks." Even as she said this, her very much black (not brown) hair caught the light, and I wondered whether she could really think so poorly of herself.

"However, she is also stubborn and passionate," I continued. "We found her fighting with Ezekiel, and if the truth be known, she seemed quite excited by the conflict between them. It made me wonder whether someone in the family could be responsible for Abraham's murder."

She gasped at this as though she had never imagined anything so wicked. There was something almost too innocent about her, and I was certain she was hiding something. Maybe it was a trifling secret – the kind that so many of our suspects have, but it had certainly caught my attention.

"No one has been kinder to me than Elisheba." She paused then to impress this fact upon me. "She even calls me sister, sometimes, though I know I could never be so important to her. However, her rivalry with the others, and especially Ezekiel, is so intense that I believe it sometimes affects her view of the world."

I wouldn't let her get away with such evasion any longer. "Are you saying that her criticism of her father is unwarranted? I don't refer to your aunt's disappearance, but the way he treated his family before that. Did he not do all he could to rule them as a despot?"

"I really can't…" she began, but this was just a false start before she found an acceptable alternative. "Or rather, I don't believe that anything is so simple. It only makes sense that his children should take sides in the matter. Ezekiel and Josiah could see the goodness in their father. They believe that he acted as he did for their benefit, whereas Elisheba and Lemuel vocally disagreed and at times it would come to blows between them."

"Yes, but what do *you* think?"

She turned away then and moved faster along the path towards my dog, who had ducked down low as though ready to pounce. "I can't honestly say that I consider myself entitled to an opinion."

"Well now you are. You're a witness in an investigation, and I need to know how you see the matter."

I believe she was about to answer when a sudden, repeated sound travelled over from the bushes, and we both turned to see what new slice of the unexpected was coming our way.

CHAPTER TWELVE

Fine. I admit it. The sound that alarmed us was not the shriek of a dying man or the deafening bang of a pistol. It was a happy squeak as a small dog came barrelling into the light. He was little more than a puppy, and I could tell how happy Delilah was to have a companion. She barked to express this very thing.

"Oh, Samson!" Charlotte cooed as the tiny golden retriever rolled heels over head into the bigger dog.

"His name is Samson?" I could barely believe it.

"That's right. I've only had him a few weeks, but I'm quite in love."

As Samson and Delilah frolicked together, and Charlotte knelt to nuzzle her puppy, I added yet more questions to my list.

Is it possible for a person who owns such an adorable animal to be involved in a violent crime?

Is asking such a question just as bad as my previous propensity to believe that all women blessed with intoxicatingly beautiful eyes were inherently innocent?

What are the chances of Delilah's new friend having the same name as her biblical namesake's lover? And does this mean that my dear dog will somehow be responsible for the fluffy pup's eventual downfall?

I believe that I can answer this final pair of questions right now. One: Low, but not impossible. And two: no.

The cuddly tyke's emergence, and Delilah's joy as she nudged him with her nose as though she were his mother, had set me back to zero in my ever-so-soft interrogation. There really was no way to get to the heart of the matter with that whimsical creature licking our witness's face.

"How old is Delilah?" she asked, and I had to think.

"Well, she'd been around for a few years before I was born, and I've just turned twenty, so…" I did some adding up in my head. "No, that can't be right." I was almost as baffled by the canine mystery

79

I had just happened upon as Abraham Hindmarsh's murder. "Either this dog is immortal or…"

Apparently unable to make any sense of my babbly, Charlotte continued with the previous topic. "Everything has got worse since Patience went missing. The last three weeks have felt as though we were living inside an oven, waiting for the first of us to explode."

I had some questions about her understanding of household appliances, but I didn't interrupt.

"My uncle tried to pretend that everything was fine and that his wife would be back at any moment, but not a day went by without one of my cousins getting the needle. The scene you witnessed between Elisheba and Ezekiel was quite typical. What I can't tell you is whether it is connected to Abraham's death."

As she sat on the red flagstones to tickle Samson's tummy, and Delilah ran around us in happy circles, I tried to decipher what she really meant. She had avoided saying whether she thought one of her cousins could be to blame for either of the killings, but now suggested that the antagonism between them since their mother's disappearance could have led to their father's death.

"And if you had to choose one person as the likely culprit?" I tried again.

Her eyes flicked around the garden and back to me. "That's not fair," she complained, her voice rising. "How can you expect me to accuse a member of my own family of murder?"

This was another discrepancy. Just a few minutes earlier, she'd insisted that she'd never fitted in there. Now they were her family.

Of course, if someone had asked me to point the finger at one of my cousins, I… Well, as it happens, I've been in that very situation, and it wasn't as difficult as I might have imagined, but I could see that Charlotte would need more persuading.

"I'm not going to tell my grandfather to arrest whomever you suspect," I promised her. "But if there's something you know that could incriminate one of your cousins, you mustn't keep it to yourself."

Samson wriggled out of her hand to go chasing after Delilah, and, for a moment, Charlotte didn't move. "I don't want to cause anyone any trouble. I honestly don't know who killed Abraham or why he was murdered." It was clear that, despite all this, she was about to reveal her suspicions. "The only thing I can say is that there's something unusual about Josiah that I've never been able to define."

"Something not quite right?" I asked, as that was generally what forced people to identify loved ones as potential maniacs.

She nodded eagerly, as though this were the key piece of information that would help us make sense of the crimes. "He claims to idolise his father, and yet I'd never seen him look anything but sullen around him. In return, Abraham viewed Josiah as a promising failure. He admired Ezekiel, of course, but his poor youngest son was never able to impress him. And so I've wondered for some time whether…"

The look in her eyes was one of panic. I couldn't honestly say whether this was a sign of the shame she felt for making such an accusation, or because she realised that it might very well be true. "I can't help wondering whether Josiah killed his mother in order to win favour with Abraham and, when his father didn't approve, he shot him too."

Her head dropped, and she no longer had the courage to look at the gleeful animals who were threading in and out of the yew bushes. In the central square of the formal garden there was a circular fountain with a raised sculpture of Neptune (or possibly Poseidon, I can never tell the difference) gazing down at us scornfully with his pitchfork (or possibly trident, I can never tell the difference) raised to attack. Her eyes came to rest on the fearful figure, and it did nothing to lighten her mood.

"If you're right," I said when a short silence had passed, "then the responsibility falls on Josiah, not you. And if your supposition is wrong, then I promise that no harm will come of it."

I crouched down to squeeze her shoulder, but this only made her cry. I'd previously imagined her being more pretty with a smile on her face, and while that could still be true, she was simply exquisite in her sorrow. She was the kind of beauty to whom a Renaissance painter would have devoted a very sad painting; she would have made a perfect model for a melancholy study of the Virgin Mary.

"I'm sorry," I said, with little hope of reassuring her. "I really am sorry for everything that has happened to you. I doubt that much I can say will make it better, but I do promise that my grandfather and I will investigate the matter as discreetly as possible."

She wouldn't look up at me, but Samson tottered back over to us and burrowed his way onto her lap to offer some comfort.

Knowing that mere platitudes would do nothing to cheer her, I let her into my thinking on the case. "For my part, I've been wondering about your uncle since he was killed. The temptation is to assume that he murdered his wife before one of his children sought revenge, but as you've suggested, things might not be so simple."

I didn't expect a response, but she held her puppy tighter, and a few words emerged from beyond the screen of long black hair that hung loose at the side of her face. "In which respect?"

"Perhaps Patience isn't even dead. Couldn't it be that she finally made her escape?"

"How would that be possible?" There was a note of offence in her reply, but I continued, nonetheless.

"I don't know, but what if someone killed Abraham for an entirely different reason?"

She shook her head but said nothing.

"I think it's just as likely that he was having an affair with the wrong woman, and her murderous husband found out about them. Or perhaps Abraham made a fool of a rival politician in the House of Commons, and the fellow came here with a loaded gun. He could have snuffed out his candle in little more than an instant and escaped from the house. What I'm saying is that it wouldn't surprise me if the wretched man was blasted from the face of the earth for something he himself did."

My voice had grown steadily louder and more insistent as I spoke so that, once I'd listed these violent hypotheses, she looked quite scared. I saw myself through her eyes for a moment and remembered that this wasn't a normal topic to discuss with a nice young lady like Charlotte Elliott. This was the kind of conversation I could have with my grandfather and almost no one else.

"I'm so sorry," I said, and smoothed down the tie that, as it turned out, I wasn't wearing. I was dressed in a summer sweater and slacks. If she hadn't thought I was off my onion before, I can only imagine that had changed. "There's no need for you to worry about any of that. Leave everything to us."

I let out a carefree laugh in order to suggest that my eccentric behaviour was all part of the job. The way that she now stared at me told me that it hadn't worked. I opened my mouth to explain but was afraid that I would only make things worse.

"I should return to my duties." Getting to her feet with her little dog cradled in her arm, she mumbled a farewell and moved to leave.

"And I must get back to work." I bowed to her most formally while trying to make sense of what on earth had just happened.

CHAPTER THIRTEEN

Much as I'd expected, I found Grandfather looking for evidence on the whereabouts of Patience Hindmarsh. He was in a small room in the right-hand wing of the house, which I soon understood to be part of a row of similar spaces where she and each of her offspring pursued their various pastimes. They were arranged on either side of a short corridor and reminded me of the cells in which the inmates once lived in old-fashioned monasteries.

"What have you found?" I asked to be polite – though, in truth, I wished to talk about my own concerns with someone who wouldn't view me as a brain-sick madman.

"Very little whatsoever," he replied without looking up at me. He was back to one of the things he did so well: flicking through piles of books and papers in search of some titbit of evidence. "All I can tell you is that, based on her reading material, Patience appears to have been very knowledgeable about healthy living. She knitted, she sewed, and she read about the impact of improved dietary habits. There are books here on everything from vegetarianism to eating nothing but red meat. Have you had any more luck than that?"

The room had shelves on either side which displayed similar titles to the ones he had described. It was hardly the most appealing library I'd ever come across. There wasn't a single one of the great Victorian novelists represented. I would even have settled for a copy of Chaucer or some such, but this was not the place for someone with my tastes. In addition to her books, there was an easy chair, an immense potted plant with large rubbery leaves, a Singer sewing machine built into a small cast iron table and an ornamental spinning wheel in front of a pleasing arched window.

I pondered exactly which of my concerns I should share with him. "I spoke to Hindmarsh's niece. It turns out that she had a very different view of her uncle to that of his children. And Elisheba's claim that Charlotte is an unpaid servant appears to be untrue."

"Abraham Hindmarsh was a complicated man." Grandfather opened a book that, judging by the gold inlaid diagram on the cover, was all about the internal organs of the human body.

He held it upside down to see whether some significant note might tumble out. It did not. Instead, he ran his hand over the top shelf and found a framed photograph positioned face down. It was a picture of the Hindmarshes (Mr and Mrs) as they were in their youth. Patience had a large wave of hair pinned to the top of her head and wore a simple white dress with pearls. She had a nervous look on her face and stood with her back to her husband. For his part, Abraham was barely recognisable. He had not yet grown into his pigeon-like form and wore remarkably casual clothes. I would imagine that they were around the same age as their children now were.

The photograph – or was it a tintype? I really couldn't tell – was blackened around the edges, as though the darkness was creeping up on them. And yet they looked almost happy. It was hard to imagine that their distaste – perhaps even hatred – for one another would lead to tragedy.

"'The beginning of the end,'" my grandfather declared in a sombre tone.

"That's rather a dramatic interpretation," I rebuked him. "There's nothing to say how they were feeling at the time."

"It was not my interpretation, boy," he said with a tut. "Those very words are written in small letters under the photograph."

The septuagenarian's eyes – or at least his wits – were clearly better than my own.

"There you go then," I blustered. "More evidence that he was the villain that approximately half of his five children think he is."

I believe that he was about to criticise my mathematical proficiency, but he must have understood my thinking, as he put the photograph back where we'd found it and returned to his search.

I watched as he went about his work, his gloved fingers walking their way along the tops of the books, like a shopper browsing the shirts in Selfridges.

I returned us to the previous discussion. "Charlotte was reluctant to say anything unkind about her cousins and uncle, but I did manage to extract one particular suspicion from her."

"Oh, really?" He did not look up at me. "So she was no great admirer of her aunt then."

Not only had he changed the topic away from what I'd wanted

to discuss, he'd made it sound as though I had put Charlotte forward as a suspect in Patience Hindmarsh's disappearance. "She said that her aunt treated her as an outsider. But she didn't say outright that she disliked her."

Still rifling away to his heart's content, he thought up a whole new scenario. "I can see it now. The impoverished orphan driven to murder the cruel matriarch in order to keep her place in her uncle's home. It's an interesting prospect."

"No, Grandfather, you're not listening. Charlotte said that she believed Josiah to be the most bloodthirsty member of the family."

Though he was bent over a wooden chest, searching through a pile of what looked like personal correspondence, he had a very expressive back, and I could tell he found fault in what I'd said. "Did she use that actual word? Did she describe her cousin as bloodthirsty?"

I had to cast my mind back. "Well, no. She agreed that he was 'not right', but it's no great stretch of the imagination to understand what she really meant."

"I doubt that is enough to secure a conviction," he practically purred in reply, and his back became a little smugger than usual.

"Maybe not, but it fits with another thought I had. It's all too easy to believe that the two Hindmarsh children who butted heads with their father are the likely culprits. However, I think that we should watch Ezekiel and Josiah just as carefully as their siblings. Charlotte says that Josiah is driven by his failure. He has never lived up to his father's expectations and may have lashed out as a result."

There was no response. Even his back remained surprisingly impassive.

Once I'd grown tired of waiting for an answer that would never come, I changed the topic. "Why do you believe that something in this room could reveal what happened to Patience Hindmarsh? It's a large house, after all."

He glanced at me over his shoulder. "She shares a bedroom with her husband. We have seen nothing to suggest that she took any of her children into her confidence, and the other rooms we have seen would be too public to risk hiding any secrets there. Mark my words: this is the place."

I peered about the room in the hope that some snug little hidey-hole might reveal itself to me. It didn't, and so I turned to the door through which I'd entered. There was a small shelf just above it which held a number of cookery books. I took down a copy of Mrs Beeton's most famous work, but it looked as though it had never been opened. I believe you could find the same volume in my grandfather's library, and it would be in very much the same condition. I tried a few other titles without uncovering anything useful.

I was about to give up when Grandfather clapped his hands together in irritation. "We're getting nowhere. Perhaps this isn't the place after all. Perhaps she has a metal box in the cellar with her important papers inside, or maybe she dug a hole in the garden and buried them."

I couldn't bear to see him so downhearted and looked for a solution. "Have you looked at what's holding that pot off the floor?"

He turned to the immense terracotta receptacle and the plant with huge dark leaves sprouting from it but couldn't see what I saw.

"There are three evenly sized supports beneath the base," I told him. "One of them is hidden by the wall behind it. They are positioned in a manner by which the rear one could be removed and the other two would continue to hold the pot." I waved my hand in a rather superior manner as if to say, *Go ahead, my good man. I will wait while you prove me right.* I may even have smiled as I awaited the inevitable praise that would come my way.

"There's nothing there but a third flat brick."

"Oh." I can't say I wasn't disappointed. The supports were just the same thickness as a decent sized tome. It would have been a very good hiding place, had Patience decided to conceal an important book there.

"Philodendron," Grandfather muttered, having pushed the pot back against the wall. "That's the name of this plant. It originally comes from South America, but I saw one on display at the Empire exhibition in Wembley Park in 1924." I couldn't imagine what point he was making, but he'd crossed his arms most confidently. "Can you tell me what the word philodendron means in modern English, Christopher?"

"No, not—" I began, before realising that this wasn't true. "Well, philo means love, and I imagine the rest means bush or tree, seeing as there are other plant names which finish with the same suffix. Rhododendron for one."

He looked exceedingly pleased. "Precisely. Philodendron means *love of trees*, though it might be possible to mistranslate the word as *love tree*. I'm willing to bet that Patience made this mistake, as a love tree sounds very special indeed."

"Weren't you just criticising me for jumping to conclusions? What could possibly suggest that she valued it so highly?"

He frowned as he considered my point. "It's difficult to say. Perhaps it was the fact that she hid a small, though surely quite significant, bundle deep in its foliage where most people would never have looked for it."

He waved his hand in a rather superior manner as if to say, *Go ahead, my good man. I will wait while you prove me right.*

I reached into the centre of the plant and pulled out the previously described package. "Well, I never!" I couldn't understand how he had spotted it from several feet away.

Even before we'd removed the waxy brown paper that covered it, I hoped it would be a diary of some description. To my great excitement, he opened the book to show the large red letters on the first page. They read: *This is Why I Hate Him.*

"Now, Christopher," Grandfather said as he carried the slim journal over to the desk beside the spinning wheel, "what do you think about that?"

"I think you were lucky where I wasn't. I identified a good hiding place that you hadn't even considered, and *my* idea led to *our* discovery." I was tempted to point out that this was the second time I'd expertly located some evidence that morning, but his attitude suddenly changed, and his smile disappeared.

"You're quite right." He bit his lip as he examined the book's plain burgundy cover. "There is simply so much evidence to find wherever we go. A genuine glut of the stuff has presented itself, and it is difficult to know what deserves our attention."

He turned the page, and I was about to discover why Patience Hindmarsh had hated her husband when a scream carried along the corridor outside the room.

"He's dead," the shouter shouted. "My brother's been killed!"

CHAPTER FOURTEEN

I don't like it when people are murdered before we've had a chance to get to know them a little. I'd barely found the time to consider Lemuel's potential guilt, and now he was gone for good. There would be no illuminating interview in which Grandfather worked through a number of impressive techniques to extract our suspect's deepest secrets. To be quite honest, my only impression of the *middlest* Hindmarsh brother was that he seemed rather dim and perhaps easily led. It certainly didn't offer us much hope of finding his killer.

"Tell me again more slowly," Grandfather said in a clear, sympathetic voice as we spoke to Hosanna in the room a few doors down from Patience's sanctuary.

The siblings had called these spaces their studies, but it was hard to imagine that much study had gone on in Lemuel's. For one thing, there were no books of any kind – a cardinal sin by my reckoning, but I try not to judge people solely on their libraries these days. Instead, the walls were lined with cuttings from picture papers of healthy young men competing in cross-country races or training on running tracks in rain-swept parks. There was one particularly good photograph, taken from low down, of a group of clean-limbed fellows all negotiating a hurdle in a steeplechase. They were captured with the blur of motion and looked very much like a team of horses jumping a fence in the Grand National.

I admit that I was distracted by this singular collection of photographs even as I stood over Lemuel's body and his sister explained how she had found him there.

"I hadn't seen Lem since Father was killed, and so I came to look for him. It was unfathomably quiet out in the corridor, and I knew something was wrong even before I stepped inside." She once more broke off her description to comment on the fate of her poor brother. "This isn't fair. It simply isn't. Lemuel was the best of us, no matter what Father thought. I don't care whether he was good at school or destined to make a name for himself in politics – Lemuel was better than any of that. He had a kind heart, and I don't know how I can go on without—"

In a moment, her words dried up, but her eyes wouldn't shift from her dead brother, who looked oddly comfortable in a leather armchair beside the open window. It was a battered and misshapen piece of furniture that had obviously been used for decades. The arms were worn, and someone had stitched up the threadbare fabric in places to keep the stuffing from pouring out, but I had the sense that Lemuel had loved it. I could just imagine his parents demanding that he throw it out and the once cheery fellow paying them no heed. It was strange of me to focus on an old chair rather than examining the body, but I knew so little about the victim, I had to start somewhere.

Ezekiel and Elisheba appeared from their studies, which meant I could delay having to look into Lemuel's eyes for a moment or two longer. I must admit that I prefer it when people die with their eyelids firmly shut. I'd say about fifty per cent of murder victims are kind to the detective in that respect, but Lemuel was still gazing across the room as though wondering who might come in next. The manner in which he'd been killed was obvious, even from several feet away. Someone had tied something around his neck and pulled until he could no longer breathe. From the bright red line that the weapon had left behind, I had to conclude that a length of strong, fine wire had been used. Rope or string would have left a different pattern.

Despite his placid mien, Lemuel's face was discoloured and there were scratch marks where he'd tried and failed to prevent the inevitable. His fingers were bright red too, so it looked as though he had inserted them between his neck and the wire. If the truth be told, he was lucky not to have lost the tops of his fingers. Though this would have provided little comfort in his final moments.

"I'm sorry for what you have endured," Grandfather told the younger of the two sisters. "But have you seen anything that might help us identify the person who did this to him?"

All the emotion that had flowed from Hosanna was suddenly dammed. "No. No, I have not."

"Then perhaps you heard something?" I asked in the hope that this might break the deadlock.

Her gaze still gripped her brother's limp form as she shook her head. "Not a thing."

It didn't seem as though there was a great deal more she could tell us, and all I could do for the moment was stand and reflect upon the senselessness of the crime. I had not known Lemuel, but I could still feel sorrow for what had happened and the pain his death would bring those who loved him. It was already apparent on his sister's face.

Ezekiel had been standing in the doorway listening, but instead of sadness, he now showed his anger. "This has to stop. Whoever is doing this must realise that no good will come of it."

I found his performance excessively theatrical. He spoke as though the emotions he wished to convey were not his own, and it had taken me until now to realise why that was. Ezekiel was a copy of his father. He had been raised to be a politician and spoke in a forceful manner that left me questioning whether he believed a word he was saying.

"It can't have been Lemuel," Hosanna mumbled to herself, and I tried to understand what she meant. "This should never have happened."

Ezekiel put his hand on her shoulder. I expected her to turn to embrace him or perhaps push him away, but she didn't react at all, so her sister came forward to comfort her in his stead. Elisheba did not look nearly so moved by the sight of Lemuel's corpse as she had been by her father's. She stayed strong for Hosanna, who rested her head against her chest and unleashed great long cries. Elisheba's red dress turned a shade of purple as the tears soaked through the fabric and we waited for the last of the siblings to arrive.

I hadn't thought of it before, but there was loud music playing somewhere nearby. It had been going for some time and was certainly not coming from Josiah's piano. There were drums, a trumpet and a saxophone in the mix of sounds that carried down the corridor and, for a moment, it grew more raucous before the door slammed shut and we heard footsteps approaching.

"What's happened?" the final brother asked before entering. "What are you all—?"

Ezekiel turned and took a few steps closer to the door to cut him off. "It's Lem. He's the next of us to go." This time, he didn't even pretend to be upset. He spoke as though he were informing a teammate that one of their order had been dismissed in a cricket match.

It's a real shame, of course, I imagined him saying, *but the game isn't over yet and there is still hope of a win even if a good man had been lost.*

He punched Josiah on the arm, and I was transported back to my days at the Oakton Academy for Distinguished Young Gentlemen, where the most overtly effusive sign of affection it was acceptable to show a fellow pupil – if you didn't want to be called a big girl's knickers – was a slap around the back or a jovial fist to the ribs. I was so glad to have left that gloomy institution behind, but it seemed that whatever Victorian-style instruction the Hindmarsh brothers had received had travelled with them into adulthood.

"You know I don't often agree with Ezekiel," Elisheba declared to cut through the oppressive silence, "but he's right this time. If someone in this room is responsible, it must end now."

Hosanna had been the picture of stability for much of the day. She had barely flinched at the sight of her own father's corpse, but as we stood in our impromptu semi-circle around poor Lemuel, it was too much for her to bear; her anger poured out like molten lava.

"How can it just stop? You're naïve if you think that will happen." She glanced around at her siblings, her body shaking as the waves of emotion travelled through her. "Lemuel shouldn't be dead – not him. We all know that he was the only one of us who was worth a thing. Our parents were broken, and they made sure we were just like them, but Lemuel kept his innocence when we couldn't."

Elisheba tried to console her even as Hosanna slipped out of the loose embrace.

"I don't know why this is happening, but I know how it will end." In the midst of her fury, she fell quiet and turned back to the body. Moving on slow, quiet feet, she took five small steps across the room and, with two fingers outstretched on her right hand, she leaned forward to close her brother's eyes for the last time.

Something about this sent a shiver through me. It was an ancient gesture that put me in mind of the funeral rites from Greek plays – from 'Antigone' and 'Medea'. And I knew just then that Hosanna had been transformed by grief. She was no longer the steady centre of the family – the middle ground between two divided camps. Hosanna was mad with rage at the thought that the one good man amongst them was dead.

"It must stop," Grandfather declared in a more persuasive tone than the others had managed. "You will achieve nothing with this. If one of you is after the estate, then whoever remains will fall under suspicion."

He stepped out of the line to look at them. "Whatever clever stratagem you have stumbled across, I will have seen it before. If you

94

plan to plant evidence or provide yourself with a perfect alibi, then let me tell you now that I will see through your scheme. If you intend to incriminate someone else to save yourself, it will not work, and I will be there on the day you hang for your crimes."

Grandfather was ambivalent at best when it came to the matter of capital punishment. The fact that he had raised this point showed just how intense the case before us really was.

"It must stop," Hosanna said when her siblings could do nothing but glare wordlessly at her, "but it won't."

She turned and exited with that same curious slowness, as though she no longer had the energy to move any faster. She left more than just an absence. There was a huge gaping abyss where she had previously stood. I believe it was our collective realisation that the killer was not motivated solely by hatred for Abraham or Patience Hindmarsh. Such an explanation was neat and digestible, but with Lemuel's death, the reason for all that bloodshed had become murkier. We had moved down a generation, and all that had seemed solid and knowable had disappeared.

CHAPTER FIFTEEN

From the beginning, it was clear that Elisheba and Ezekiel were the ringleaders at Silent Pool. Their confrontation had been our introduction to the family, but even Elisheba could see that there would be no winners in the game that the killer was playing.

She took a deep breath and tried one last time to appeal to her rival.

"We can finish this, Zeke." She pleaded as she approached her brother. "Just promise that this is the end of it, and we'll forget everything that came before."

I'm sure that she chose such vague language to be diplomatic, but Ezekiel still took exception to it.

"Can you hear what you're saying?" He removed her hands from his lapels one after the other. "I didn't kill Lemuel. We may not have always got on well, but that doesn't mean I would hurt him. How could you think so little of me?"

She turned to my grandfather, and her tone became more desperate. "I'm only trying to find a solution. I don't want to blame anyone. I just don't understand what we can do if—"

"Spare your words." It was Josiah's turn to challenge her. I can't say I'd liked the look of him from the first, but there was something positively reptilian about him as he attacked his sister. "How do we know you aren't saying all this to distract from your own guilt? Perhaps Lemuel killed Father on your orders. Perhaps you killed him to make sure he didn't tell anyone. He was never good at keeping secrets."

"That's disgusting. I wouldn't—"

Josiah walked closer, apparently taking pleasure in the chance to level these accusations against her. "You're deceitful, Elle. You always have been. Father saw exactly what kind of person you were and that's why he turned against you. He realised that you are a back-stabbing, self-interested guttersnipe. You wanted us all to think he was so terrible because you knew that he didn't love you like the rest of us. You even convinced poor Lemuel that he was evil when you're the one who deserves to be locked up." He was close enough to whisper a parting shot. "You were born bad, and you poisoned the whole family. Perhaps Mother saw it too, and so she was the first to die."

Elisheba's soft lips fell open a fraction. It was hard enough for *me* to listen to her brother's theories, so I can only imagine how she felt. After a few more seconds, she collapsed to her knees. There was no one there to defend her. Hosanna had left the scene of their brother's death, and Lemuel had left our plane of existence.

She was all alone, except that she wasn't.

"That's enough, all of you." Lord Edgington glided between them. If anything, it was overdue. "You will go to your studies until it is time for lunch, and you will not say a word to one another unless I give you permission to do so."

Josiah smiled like a schoolboy who was no longer afraid of his teacher, but Ezekiel stepped away to take stock.

"Do you hear me?"

As the eldest child and unofficial spokesperson for at least half of the group, he mumbled a response. "It could be anyone," he said as he sidled closer to the door.

"I beg your pardon?" With all the authority he could muster, Grandfather stepped across to block the way.

"I said that anyone could have killed my parents and Lemuel, too. It could be one of the servants or some vagabond hanging about the place." When suspects were willing to make hypotheses without our help, it certainly made our jobs a lot easier. Ezekiel seemed to accept that nothing was certain, but then his voice rose. "But it is far more likely that our harridan of a sister is the killer. You should arrest Elisheba, Lord Edgington, before she can do it again."

It was his time to slide away from a tackle. He sidestepped my grandfather and disappeared from the room, with his hobbling brother following close behind. The look on Josiah's face reminded me of a gargoyle on one of the towers at Cranley Hall. They were both grotesque and inordinately pleased with themselves. I was coming to agree with Charlotte Elliott that Josiah was the culprit, if for no other reason than my not liking his face.

This would normally have been the time that Grandfather and I inspected the body, but Elisheba was still on her knees in the middle of the room looking thoroughly dejected, and it would have been rude to kick her out.

Grandfather looked at me as if to say, *You're supposed to be the sensitive one. What should we do?*

To which I replied, *Banana weasel chandelier,* as I'm not nearly so talented at expressing myself through body language as he is.

"I'm sorry," the young lady finally whispered in a voice so low that it was almost absorbed by the thick red carpet beneath her feet. That's right. The one very minor positive aspect to poor Lemuel's death was that any blood stains would hardly be visible.

"You don't have to apologise, my child." This was evidently my grandfather speaking, as I rarely use that expression, even when talking to actual children. "It is quite understandable that you and your siblings are disturbed by the events here. I am trying to make sense of them myself."

I offered her my hand and gently helped her up to standing. "Lemuel seemed very pleasant," I said, to have something to say, but this was such faint praise that I felt I should try harder. "I mean that he was definitely different from your—"

Thankfully, she interrupted me before I could say anything worse. I do wish I wouldn't get so nervous at such moments. I swear that I normally know how to form a half-decent sentence or two.

"It's true what Hosanna said; he was the best of us. He had a wonderfully sweet way of looking at the world, and I'll be lost without him. He…" Her eyes became somewhat hazy, and I felt that she was reflecting upon their lives together. I wondered what childhood memory the moment had recalled, but then she came back to herself and seemed more focused than before. "I'm truly sorry for what you witnessed. I would beg you not to judge any of us too harshly, but I think that we're all beyond that point now."

This transformation was quite strange – well, strange even by that day's ridiculously high standards. She no longer looked at the body of her murdered brother but seemed more interested in making sure that we weren't offended by the row we'd seen.

"As I've already told you," Grandfather replied in a warm tone, with just the right amount of melancholy suitable for our surroundings, "there is no need to apologise."

She used the back of her hand to dry the corner of either eye, and then attempted a resilient smile. "I'll be in my studio if you need me." She shuffled away, her long pastel dress trailing behind her on the carpet as she went.

CHAPTER SIXTEEN

"Madness," I said when I felt that we were probably safe to speak. We weren't.

"I beg your pardon, sir?" the passing housemaid poked her head in to ask. She presumably didn't catch sight of body number two (or three depending on how you're counting) as she was looking straight at me and showed no sign of shock.

"I said…" I searched for a word that sounded a bit like madness. "…what gladness. I was just saying how fortunate it is that the police are on hand to investigate your poor master's fate."

She was immediately brought to tears and had to hurry from the room, moaning, "I know, sir. I know. But please don't remind me!"

"Insanity," I tried again and, this time, the chief inspector appeared in the room.

"What was that?" he asked, and I tried the same technique as I had with the maid.

"I said…" I couldn't think of anything that sounded like insanity except for inanity, humanity and manatee. Luckily, my grandfather took over to save me from talking about sea cows.

"Don't be foolish, boy. You can tell the truth to Darrington here." He shook his head, which was disappointing, as I was the cause of his consternation. Yet it also reminded me that I hadn't inspired any such reaction in him for some time. Bravo, Christopher. "We were discussing the madness of the situation before us."

I don't know whether he was about to draw our colleague's attention to the dead man in the armchair but, either way, Darrington had noticed and walked further into the room.

"Another body." He did not sound surprised. "It's so very sad. Lemuel always struck me as a nice boy."

"So you knew the family before this case?" I asked, as I'd had this impression once earlier in the day.

He turned to look at me. "Not the family, Christopher. I know Elisheba. She is a close friend of my daughter's, and she and Lemuel have been to my house a few times."

My goodness! Chief Inspector Darrington had a daughter. I'd

never imagined him existing outside of our cases and now he had a daughter! I couldn't help wondering whether she was a trainee detective just like me who would one day surpass her accomplished old man, just as I wouldn't with Grandfather.

"What do you know about him?" Darrington's former colleague asked.

"Not a great deal more than you can see from the contents of this room." He was more distracted than I'd ever seen him and needed longer than normal to form each reply. "He was a keen runner. Aged twenty-six on his last birthday. He never went to university but did something for his mother's family business." He let out a cheerless sigh. "Yes, he was a nice young man, but not the brains of the Hindmarsh clan. He was terribly close to his mother and, over the course of the investigation into her disappearance, I have learnt that he had little time for his father. Though I believe the feeling was mutual."

Grandfather had observed the scene for long enough and decided that the moment had come to approach the corpse itself. "Whether he killed his wife or not, Abraham Hindmarsh has had a hand in everything that has happened here." He released a sigh to echo his friend's and began to search the body for clues.

"I'd say he was killed with a thin metal wire. Don't you agree, Grandfather?" I asked, as this was the one thing of which I'd been comparatively sure that day.

"Indeed, I do." He pulled open Lemuel's checked sports jacket to feel inside. "But what I find most interesting is the fact that he has been dead for some time. I would think around an hour."

Darrington's boots scuffed against one another as he asked the next question. "And what does that suggest?"

Grandfather had found nothing remarkable on the corpse and sat back on his haunches. "That the killer was eager to ensure that he could commit the crime without interference."

"What makes you say that?" I asked as I looked at the images around the room and realised that one framed photograph on a desk in the corner did not show athletes but a small group of friends beside the lake. Lemuel and his siblings were in the middle and there were two young girls whom I didn't recognise.

"Let's imagine that the same person who killed Abraham killed his son immediately after. It's more than possible that the culprit was afraid he would be found out and arrested, and so he moved on to his next victim as swiftly as possible."

Darrington folded his arms, and I could tell he would draw our attention to a potential discrepancy. "What if there is more than one killer?"

"Then the same still applies." Grandfather's voice often dipped into the register of a schoolteacher when he spoke to me, and it was curious to hear him do this to his former colleague. "As the police are present, the chances of getting caught increase the longer any criminal stays here. You must also consider that, each time someone is killed, the pool of suspects shrinks. All of this means that the pressure is on the guilty party to complete his task as soon as he can without getting caught."

I couldn't see how this would help identify who was responsible for any of the deaths. Whether the brute was in a hurry or not seemed like a moot point to me, but Grandfather was either being unnecessarily thorough in explaining this, or he believed it would turn out to be significant further down the road.

"One thing is certain," Darrington said. "We must do what we can to stop this game, whatever the end result might be. I have already called my superiors to request assistance. The two officers who have already arrived were due to transport the body to the coroner in Guildford. They will sadly now have another passenger when they leave, but I hope to have more reinforcements in due course."

"Surely you could call a whole troop of men here in a jiffy?" I put to him, but he waved away the suggestion with a bearlike paw.

"In normal circumstances, perhaps, but it's a busy day in town today. The socialists are campaigning against the monarchy. The monarchists are campaigning against the socialists, and Fulham are playing Spurs at home. Add all that to a bout of flu that's going around, and it means we're short of men."

"We could just arrest the lot of them," I suggested only half seriously, and they both wheezed at the very thought of it.

"We can't go around arresting whomsoever we please, Christopher," this was Darrington speaking, but it might just as well have been my grandfather. "You have to have a good reason."

"It would keep them safe, wouldn't it?"

"It might," Grandfather conceded, as he had evidently given the matter some thought. "But any one of them could leave here without our permission if he so wished. What I don't understand – what I've failed to comprehend since the beginning, in fact – is why they didn't leave years ago. I'm sure there is a financial explanation, though no one has explained it to us, and so I can't help thinking…"

"Go ahead, Lord Edgington," the chief inspector told him. "Feel free to express any ideas that occur to you. Even if they are only half-formed."

"I just thought that perhaps this is where they've always wanted to be."

Before he could say more, a gong rang for lunch somewhere near the entrance to the house. Darrington was first to the door, but not because he wished to fill his stomach. He had other things on his mind.

"I'll send my officers in here to examine the body and catalogue any evidence. They have murder kits and all the usual scientific equipment they might need. After that, I'll drive to a few of the local stations to see whether I can convince them to spare some constables." He stood where he was for a moment, as though wishing to confirm he had said all that was needed, and then hurried from the room.

Grandfather took some time to inspect the scene. I watched as his eyes travelled over the same photographs and articles that had evidently moved Lemuel enough to cut them out and put them in simple black frames. There was a pair of spiked running shoes behind the door and two crossed tennis rackets fixed in place with nails on the wall above the window, but there was nothing to suggest who had killed the former occupant or why he had been killed.

With a quiet huff of resignation, Grandfather shrugged and left the dead man's study.

We fell into step with one another as we followed the corridor back towards the centre of the L-shaped house. I was trapped in my thoughts for a few moments before I broke the silence.

"I, too, find it strange that a group of siblings who apparently don't get along, and a patriarch whom very few people seem to like, should all remain here together. So I believe you were right when you said that it must have been their choice. I can't imagine how their father could have kept them here, and I noticed something in Elisheba's

104

expression this morning when Ezekiel strangled her; this is all good sport for the Hindmarshes. Even the killings haven't knocked them off their game entirely. The two remaining boys took great pleasure in putting their sisters in their places. And it's impossible to say whether the emotions that Elisheba displayed are genuine or designed to throw us off her trail. Perhaps she is the most capable player of all."

The entrance hall was empty by the time we got there, and so we kept walking until we found a large wood-panelled, wood-floored and wood-ceilinged dining room a little way along the opposite corridor. It was far more in keeping with the Arts and Crafts aesthetic of the exterior of the house than many rooms we'd seen. The windows were of elaborate stained glass with images of birds, vines and angels mixed in with family crests. There was what looked like a richly illuminated medieval painting secured to one wall, but it must have been modern, as it included a family tree that ran right up to the present day. The names of the five siblings were at the bottom, and previous generations had small skulls painted beside them to show who had already died. Someone would definitely have to make a few amendments before long.

In the centre of the room, there was a rectangular table in the same wood as the floors and walls. Elisheba was the only other person who had arrived, and the relative emptiness of the room made the huge table look unnecessarily extravagant. She barely glanced at us as we took our seats and, within a minute or so, her remaining siblings appeared with similarly taciturn expressions on their dejected faces. They sat as far apart from one another as it was possible to get, and I wondered just how uncomfortable this lunch would turn out to be.

"Good afternoon, Lord Edgington," the butler addressed the guest of honour at the head of the table and presented his napkin with a flourish.

"Good afternoon, Blunstone." Grandfather was more restrained than the excitable servant, who looked as though he was savouring the prospect of serving the Marquess of Edgington.

Sitting diagonally opposite my beloved forebear, I turned my attention to the four siblings. Hosanna was the person I was most interested in observing. I hadn't expected to see her after the emotional exit she'd made. I suppose that her hunger had won out over her grief, but this inevitably led me to question for whose benefit her words beside Lemuel's corpse had been. Whatever she had felt before, she now sat oddly silent but stared at Josiah as her teeth bit at her lower lip. Her brother stared back defiantly, clearly aware that he was being watched.

Elisheba was at least consistent. She was just as desperate and desolate as she had been when we'd last seen her. She looked like a woman who could find no hope in the world, and I wondered whether she understood the situation better than anyone.

It would fall to Ezekiel, ever the diplomat and his father's son, to make some stab at conversation. "I've always loved this room. I believe it was mother's favourite, too. She was the original influence for much of the decoration in the house."

Grandfather was about to reply, but it was at this moment that Charlotte Elliott appeared in the doorway and, with the hesitation of a person who doesn't feel truly at home wherever she is, came to sit down at the table. I felt from her expression that she must have been told of Lemuel's death.

"Father decided to change things recently," the eldest boy continued. "He said that he would rather have something modern that looked modern than something modern that was made to look old, isn't that right, Cousin?"

Her head flicked in his direction as though she was moving away from a flame. "I… yes, that's correct. I've done what I could to bring your father's ideas to life."

"You mean you've helped the old monster to erase as much of Mother's presence here as he possibly could. He'd already started the process of removing her long before he dragged her body away." The change in Hosanna was remarkable, and I regretted doubting that her earlier responses were anything but genuine.

"It's not Charlotte's fault," her sister said, but Hosanna was past the point of being polite.

"I'm not saying it is. I'm saying that I was a fool to imagine our father being anything but a vicious swine." Looking up at the ceiling, she opened her eyes wider. "To think that I have tried to be fair to him my whole life. I tried to be the reasonable one amongst us and never take sides. In the end, he was just as bad as poor Lemuel and Elisheba have always said."

"Steady on," Josiah responded, and I saw once again the spite and fury in him to which Charlotte had attested. "There's nothing to say that

Father laid a hand on Mother. There's nothing to say she's even dead."

Blunstone had returned with a maid to serve the first course and, on seeing that they had stepped into the middle of an argument, he stood perfectly still. With the wiggle of one finger, Grandfather told him to go about his task. We were but spectators, and there was really no reason not to enjoy some refreshments while we watched the fight.

"How can you be so duped and inoculated, even now?" Hosanna demanded. "Why can't you cast aside every lie he ever told us and see the truth? Our father was a bad man. He liked to play the good citizen and the noble politician, but he showed us no love. He left the nurturing to our mother but, even worse than that, he knew he was outnumbered, and he did whatever it took to divide us. That was why I tried never to take sides in the first place. I thought that I could be a bridge between you all, but I wasn't strong enough and now look at us."

She was crying again, and it wasn't hard to see why. Everything she'd tried to do for the sake of her siblings had come to naught. I'd told Charlotte that my mother was the one who united our family, but my father, brother and I were never so far apart that she'd ended up stretched as Hosanna had.

Ezekiel still wouldn't pass comment on the situation but continued his attempt at light conversation. "However you look at it, Mother did a wonderful job decorating this house. I believe that she even worked with the architect who built the place to—"

Elisheba's fist cut his speech short as it crashed down on the table. "Stop it! Just stop!" These four short, staccato words were like a volley of gunfire and seemed to ricochet about us. "No one cares about the carpets or the wall hangings anymore. Our brother – our good, kind, innocent brother – had the life choked out of him."

Hosanna took up this thread. "Our mother's body may well rest in a shallow grave, who knows where. And the man who sowed such hatred between us got off lightly." It was difficult to say what purpose this comment served, other than to remind everyone how emotional she was.

"That's enough!" It was Ezekiel's turn to snap. "I'm tired of hearing what a terrible man he was. Tell me this, Hosanna; what did he actually do that was so terrible? He was strict with us, fine. He liked to live in an ordered house, and our mother's emotional ranting never sat well with him. He wouldn't let her out to talk a load of rot about him, but he never hit or caned any of us."

"He didn't need to," Elisheba retorted, and I had the feeling that this was an argument that they'd had on any number of occasions. "His cruelty was of a different kind. He took pleasure in humiliating the weakest of us. It was fine for you at the top of the pyramid, gazing down. I'm sure everything looked wonderful from up there, but you never noticed how Lemuel suffered. Father mocked and laughed at him for not living up to your perfect example. Even you, Josiah, who tried so hard to be like the great Abraham Hindmarsh, received nothing in return but disdain. You are cleverer than any of us, but that wasn't enough for him."

Hosanna had rarely taken her eyes off her youngest brother and now directed a stream of invective in his direction. "He broke and deformed you, Josiah. You know it's true. He did to your spirit what the malady that he passed down to you did to your spine. You may deny it, but even Ezekiel will admit that you were Father's failed experiment. You know what you've become."

This was not the expression to win her errant brother over and, in a flash, he seized hold of his wine glass and threw it across the table. Narrowly missing Hosanna, it smashed into a hundred pieces as it made contact with the wall. A great splash of Bordeaux stained the dark wood as it ran in red rivulets to the ground.

"All I know is that you've lost your mind." He glared back at her, and I sneaked a glance at my grandfather to know what he made of the confrontation. He sat watching quite impassively, but was presumably ready to step in should the need arise.

"Is that what's happened, Hosanna?" Ezekiel demanded, and I saw a shift as the two brothers ganged together to defeat their weaker sibling. "Have the wires in your head come loose?"

Josiah was happy to go along with the argument, even as Hosanna's eyes dropped to the table in front of her. "That must be it! You've lost your mind. You fought with Mother and lost control, so you had to tidy up the body as best you could."

Ezekiel clapped his hands together triumphantly, and there was a vindictive smile on his face. "I thought it was strange that you'd say she was in a shallow grave somewhere. You know exactly where she is, don't you?"

I had to wonder then why they would speak like this with my grandfather watching. Did they not care that such cruelty would single them out as suspects? Could they not see that they were only harming themselves? Or was it a case of simply not caring?

Josiah hadn't finished. "You killed Mother, and Father found out, so then he had to die and Lemuel after that. I thought it had to be Elisheba, as she's always been the outspoken one. She's the one who's supposed to hate us, but it turns out that quiet, restrained Hosanna finally snapped." He let out a burst of crowing laughter, and it even shocked me that he could behave so deplorably after that morning's carnage. "You're insane, Hosanna! That's the only explanation."

It was a horrible moment in a horrible day. The two other girls could do nothing to defend her without playing into their opponents' hands. For their part, the boys evidently enjoyed the suffering they could inflict, and I felt that I'd seen something of this in Abraham before he was killed. They were his disciples, after all. It should have come as no surprise that they would make use of his dubious talents.

Their cousin had been sitting with her eyelids clamped together for several minutes – as though that could shut out the sound – and Elisheba was pale and frightened once more. It looked as though no one was going to stand up for Hosanna, and so it fell to me to do so.

"You muckworms!" I hope you'll excuse my language, but I was really rather incensed. "You think you've proved your point, but you haven't come close."

I paused as everyone turned to look at the one person there who had said nothing until now. Even Charlotte opened her eyes, and I had to hope that I had made up for my previous unpleasantness.

I stood up to make my point more forcefully. "It is easy to invent a story which ties together any number of crimes, but that doesn't make it true. In fact, I think you're the killer, Josiah." I repeated the story that Charlotte had already put forward. "You killed your mother to get your father's attention, but all you succeeded in doing was appalling him. The Abraham Hindmarshes of the world don't like it when their chickens come home to roost. When he realised what a beast he had created in place of a youngest son, he told you how despicable you were. You realised that he would never love you – would never give you the praise and encouragement that you so desperately craved. So you bided your time and then shot your own father through the heart. All you had to do was hide the gun in the lake and return to your piano room after a short break in the music."

This onslaught had left him mute, but I hadn't finished yet. "Lemuel's room is close enough to yours for him to have heard you stop playing. He told you what he knew and so he had to die too. Isn't that right, Josiah?"

CHAPTER SEVENTEEN

I'm not often proud of my achievements. I don't think that I've accomplished enough under Grandfather's auspices to say that I'm a great detective, and I can't imagine what I'll do if I have to get a real job one day. What I can say is that I felt a small upswell of satisfaction as I stood looking down the table at those sniping hooligans. They deserved what they got, and the only thing I couldn't understand was why I'd been the one to give it to them.

Grandfather remained alert and observant, but he hadn't intervened. My defence of the young ladies had led to something of a stalemate, and no one rebutted my unproven claims. Ezekiel even looked afraid of his brother, and I could see that he believed every word I'd spoken.

"There, you see?" I waited for a response, but clearly no one knew what it was they were supposed to see, and so I kept talking. "Anyone can make up a story, though, in this case, I very much doubt mine is true. After all, having killed your father, you would have struggled to make it back to your study so quickly."

A very relieved Josiah breathed out slowly. I was glad to give him a dose of his own medicine and had to wonder how long he'd been holding his breath. As though they had only just noticed that the first course had been served, everyone began to eat their turkey croquettes (on a bed of lettuce with a garlicky French dressing).

I sat down to do the same, and I must say that the dish was top notch. Crispy on the outside, where the breadcrumb coating has met the hot oil of a frying pan, but melting and soft on the inside with hints of bacon and shallot. I could have eaten a whole plateful and soon polished off the four I was given, just in time for the main course to arrive.

Blunstone had a knowing grin on his face as he pushed in a trolley which bore an immense silver cloche. I was hoping there might be a roast chicken underneath, or perhaps a leg of lamb, but when he stopped beside the table and whisked away the cover, there was a pig with an apple stuffed into his mouth – as if his imminent consumption weren't indignity enough.

"Ah, I do enjoy suckling pig!" my grandfather announced, as though we hadn't just witnessed one of the most mean-spirited arguments to which we'd ever been party – including the New Year's Eve when my brother and father both contended that they'd been the first to sit down in the final round of musical bumps.

Whilst the maid served vegetables and sauce, the butler wheeled the trolley closer to the table. With carving fork and knife in hand, he stood facing us as he divvied up the roast beast.

Grandfather certainly enjoyed the display. "In days of old, when the occupation of 'grand carver' was still common, there was no greater moment in such a man's career than the chance to show off his skills at table. There is a real art to the procedure, and I can see that Mr Blunstone knows what is required of him."

The old lord was the only one of the diners who looked happy that the clash had been interrupted by an over-eager butler wielding a knife. Blunstone started on the far side of the animal and deftly cut long strips off the flank before moving on to the legs. It really was an impressive display of knifemanship – if that is a word – though I soon decided that butchery was not the most exciting form of performance.

I must confess that it was a tasty lunch, and the atmosphere improved a mite or two as we tucked into some crispy yet fluffy roast potatoes, along with crunchy carrots, peas that popped in my mouth, and tart applesauce that mixed exquisitely with the meat and gravy.

The conversation never recovered, but the atmosphere for the next half hour was slightly less frosty. I was just beginning to relax – the Sauvignon Blanc wine may have had a hand in that – when my grandfather spoke, and I understood why he'd been reticent until now.

"What made Lemuel so innocent?" he asked no one in particular, and our five dining companions looked at one another as they decided who should answer.

Ezekiel could not be accused of having excessively good manners, but at least he gave the floor to his elder sister. "After you, Elle."

Elisheba continued to peer around the group in the hope that someone else might accept the responsibility. Hosanna was not in a state to do anything more than quietly fume. Josiah still looked angry. Charlotte was scared as usual, and Ezekiel had already passed up the chance to speak.

"He was born kind and grew better as he aged." The surface of Elisheba's eyes became moist as she spoke, and she occasionally had to stop, perhaps to remember that his lifeless body was just yards away from where we sat. "I often think back to one moment when he was a little boy. I must have been ten, and he was three years younger. He spent a whole week making a present for the anniversary of our parents' marriage. I don't remember what it was, but—"

"It was a painting of the family," Hosanna said, her words barely passing her tightly pursed lips. "He borrowed the materials from me."

"That's right! A painting." This memory seemed to spark several more in Elisheba's head. "He read one of your books about what it takes to be a great artist and discovered that the really good ones paint layer upon layer to create the image in their heads. Well, Lemuel was no Old Master, but he put so much thought and love into his work that when Mother saw it, she cried. She was truly so touched by the effort to which he had gone that she couldn't hold in her emotion, and she cried before us. I don't believe I'd ever seen an adult in tears before, and the moment stayed with me."

"And then Father came into the living room, glanced at the painting and declared that it didn't look like any of us." Hosanna skewered her potato with her fork. "That's what I remember most about it." It seemed that all the negativity towards her father that she had suppressed for years had finally risen to the surface.

The two boys exchanged glances that were hard to read, but when the silence returned, Grandfather refined his question. "Perhaps what I should have asked then was not what made Lemuel innocent, but what do you believe makes you bad?"

"Bad?" Charlotte asked as though the word had woken her from a trance.

"That's right, my dear." My grandfather smiled with all the sincerity of a hungry crocodile. "Corrupt, immoral, dishonest, I'm sure you all understand my meaning. And now perhaps one of you can tell me why, when Hosanna stood over his body, she proclaimed that he was the only one of you who was worth a thing."

Hosanna had faded out of the room once more. If I hadn't known better, I would have guessed that she was drunk or doped or some such. She closed her eyes slowly and dreamily and, when she opened them, she continued staring straight ahead at her younger brother.

"There is no reason," Josiah rushed to respond. "She was overcome with emotion and was talking nonsense."

"You would say that," Elisheba muttered under her breath, as though she wanted to refute his claim without starting another argument.

"Leave it, Elle," he snapped. "It will only make things worse."

"I very much doubt that is possible," Hosanna intervened with a despairing laugh. "Mother and Lemuel are gone. We've lost all the good things we ever had. Why should we worry about ourselves anymore?"

"Because life goes on!" Josiah was becoming more desperate, and though his words were vague enough not to give away a great deal, I had the sense that there was a double meaning to what they were saying. "Everything that has happened today is terrible, but life continues. We can leave here today and still have a future. It would be stupid to throw away all we have for no reason."

"That's not the first time you've said that." Elisheba placed her clean spoon on the end of her finger so that it balanced there like the scales of justice. "But how many times can we put our own needs before anyone else's? How often must we sacrifice what is good and fair for that which serves us best?"

"Don't do it, Elisheba." Ezekiel had a touch of orange in his hazel eyes, and they really caught aflame as he glared at her. "I swear, if you do anything so stupid, you will be the one who suffers."

The smile on her face was close to the one I'd seen when her brother had tried to strangle her, and I knew she would go through with it. She sat up straighter in her chair, pushed her clean plate a few inches away from her and broke a pact that had been made many years earlier.

"We are killers," she said quite calmly. "We are all of us killers."

CHAPTER EIGHTEEN

When I was a boy, I once saw a magic show at the London Palladium. At the top of the bill was the legendary escapologist, Harry Houdini. Handcuffed, straitjacketed and hanging upside down, he made his way out of a tank of water, and I have rarely seen a more awe-inspiring feat of human endurance and skill. But the moment that night that I think back on most often occurred right at the beginning.

There was a young English magician there called Brian Godfrey. He was the first on the bill and a large part of the audience hadn't even taken their seats yet. There was something rather shy about him as he made a mess of his first card trick and stuttered through his routine, and the only responses he got from the audience were jeers and laughter. I didn't know it at the time, but it wasn't just the sleight of hand in his act that was meant to fool us. He was playing on the idea that, unlike Houdini, he was out of his depth.

With each trick he performed, Godfrey's skills improved, and the illusions became more elaborate. The jeers soon turned to gasps, and he finished his performance by inviting a member of the audience up onto the stage to select a card. This seemingly unoriginal spectacle was turned on its head when the house lights were extinguished for a few seconds and the magician inexplicably appeared at the back of the auditorium. He ran down the aisle towards the stage, and the whole theatre erupted. It was almost inconceivable that this mumbling, bumbling amateur had transformed before our eyes into an expert prestidigitator.

After his act, there were black-face minstrels and operatic singers. A husband-and-wife duo on a bicycle recited limericks, and the Flying Banvards put on the most sensational aerial act with high wires and trapezes way up in the air above the stage. But even when the night came to its glamorous conclusion, and I was watching the "King of Handcuffs" himself, I thought back to Brian Godfrey in his shabby suit and unpolished shoes, and I marvelled at what he'd done. It was not just the tricks he'd performed, but everything that went with them. I was only twelve at the time, but I realised that night that sometimes, with illusionists at the very least, it's the things you don't see that are most impressive.

My grandfather clearly realised this, too. As we sat waiting to hear Elisheba's confession, I finally understood why he'd acted so peculiarly. He'd barely said anything at the start of the meal before rambling on about how to carve pork. Yet, beneath it all, he was judging the atmosphere in the room, holding his tongue to begin with and then pulling our suspects' strings at the right moment. The most skilful magician I've ever seen is not Brian Godfrey or Harry Houdini, but a man who spent forty years as a Metropolitan police officer studying the people of London to work out how the human mind works.

My grandfather was one of the greats. I don't know how he'd done it, but all of a sudden, Elisheba was telling us what we needed to know.

"It happened almost a decade ago. When we first moved here, there was a small boat that someone had abandoned beside the lake. Ezekiel fixed it, Hosanna and Lemuel painted it, and we used to spend our summers sailing around in circles as though we were pirates or explorers. Our mother encouraged us to make friends with the children who lived nearby and so we invited them to come with us sometimes."

"I won't stay here and listen to this tosh." The account had been so sweet and calm up until now that I hadn't expected Josiah to react so violently. He'd been sitting in silence finishing his main course but chose his moment to throw down his cutlery and toss his plate onto the floor.

He shot to his feet but stopped to point at his sisters. "Whatever these two tell you, it's a lie!"

Elisheba waited until the sound of his stomping had carried off down the hall. When she started her account again, it was as if nothing had happened.

"There were two girls in particular with whom we often spent time. They were our vicar's daughters, and father was desperate to make a good impression in the village, so he approved of the friendship. Martha was Lemuel's age and May was two years younger than Josiah."

Little had changed in the other siblings. It was almost as if they couldn't react while the story was in progress. Hosanna was staring at the spot where her younger brother had previously sat, and Ezekiel gazed down at his plate as though he couldn't bear to look at Elisheba. He obviously knew the story, and it was clear he didn't want us to hear it, but he did nothing to stop her.

"We all knew that Josiah was fond of Martha, but she barely

noticed when he was around. She spent most of her time with Hosanna and me, and I could see how unhappy it made him to be ignored. He went that year from being a sensitive but kind boy to a spiteful brat. He might have tried to win Martha's affection at first, but as soon as he saw how little she cared for him, he changed. He liked nothing more than to tease and intimidate her. He would dare her to do things that he knew she shouldn't and, because she was sixteen and afraid of appearing a coward in front of her friends, she never said no."

"It was an accident." Ezekiel sought to deny in advance of whatever she was about to reveal. His argument might have held more weight if he'd had the courage to look up at us, but he continued staring at the half-eaten vegetables that had long gone cold. Blunstone would normally have brought the next course by now, but he must have heard the earlier ruckus and decided it was safer for him in the kitchen.

Elisheba didn't let anything distract her from the tale. "One night at the end of the summer, we decided to sail the boat across the lake in the moonlight. Lemuel stayed at home as he didn't want to get in trouble, and we knew that Martha and May would never be allowed out after dark, so Josiah made fun of them for being babies. Sadly for everyone, Martha had to prove him wrong. The sisters sneaked out of their house and came here to meet us. If it had ended there, we'd have forgotten all about it, but Josiah was in a particularly nasty mood that night. It was as if he wanted to punish her for not loving him, so he piled one dare on top of another.

"He'd stolen a bottle of brandy from our father's cabinet, and he demanded that we all drink it. He kept handing it to Martha and, no matter how much I reasoned with her or begged him to stop, she never said no. I watched her become increasingly drunk, but I didn't take the bottle away, and Ezekiel and Hosanna just thought it was funny. Even little May drank some, and when the brandy was finished, we got on the overloaded boat and pushed off into the black water."

I thought that Hosanna might have stirred on hearing her name, but she made no acknowledgement. She looked just as hurt and miserable as when she'd been shouting at her brothers some short time earlier.

"We aren't killers," the eldest Hindmarsh brother tried again. His confidence had dissipated and, for the first time that day, the arrogance that was at the very heart of him had gone missing. "Whatever went on that night was an accident."

"Let her finish," Hosanna said to cut him off. "We should have admitted all this a long time ago. So at least let her finish now."

When the resultant silence held, Elisheba moved on to the final part of the tale. "We went out to the middle of Silent Pool, and it was… nice. Josiah seemed to relax and enjoy the warmth of the midnight air. The girls were jokey and silly, and Martha chatted away to Ezekiel as though they were best friends. That must have been what upset Josiah as, with a look on his face like someone had just insulted our precious father, he issued one last challenge."

"'I dare you to swim to the shore.'" Ezekiel's voice was suddenly full and loud. "That's all Josiah said, and I don't think he should be punished for the rest of his life for it."

"You've always lied to yourself," his sister bit back at him. "Father taught you how. It was the only way that you could reconcile the idea of him as a great man, even as he destroyed everything and everyone around him."

Ezekiel's jaw was shaking, and he had to grit his teeth to hide it. "And you are the worst person I've ever met for telling other people how to live their lives. You think you have all the answers, Elle, but you don't. You're just as much a failure as Lemuel was. You have done nothing of any value. You have been nowhere. You remained here at home not because you loved Mother and Father, but simply to poke your nose into other people's business. It would be sad if you weren't such a thoroughly unlikable person."

She wouldn't be intimidated. She continued straight on with the story. "Martha went into the water without even taking off her dress. I think that Josiah was almost surprised that she did it. I think in a way that he was waiting for her to stand up to him, but she wasn't that kind of person. She tipped herself backwards off the side of the boat and when she looked back up at him, he knew that he would be the weak one if he didn't go in with her.

"We tried to talk them out of it. I pleaded with them not to go, but they wouldn't listen. Martha must have believed she could beat Josiah once and for all. Perhaps she imagined that reaching the shore first would be enough to make him leave her alone. She didn't know him like I do, though. She didn't even see why he was doing it, and so she got into the water and was about to start the race when May said that she couldn't go without her. It was another bluff that went wrong. Martha wouldn't back down, so then, a minute later, all three of them were setting off into the darkness."

She held a hand up to her forehead and bothered her golden fringe absentmindedly with the tips of her fingers. "I watched them disappear. The moon was out, but it wasn't strong enough to see them after they'd gone twenty yards. The rest of us listened to their splashing until it faded away. We waited for what felt like hours to hear that they'd made it to the bank, but instead, we heard Martha's screams and then silence fell across the lake."

Ezekiel occupied a strange double role as both protestor and fellow storyteller. He didn't want to hear any more, and yet he remained there to ensure the tale was told correctly. "As soon as we heard the commotion, Hosanna and I rowed as fast as we could to get there. It was a still night with no wind, so there was no sense in using the sail, but we did what we could."

"What had happened?" I asked without meaning to say a word, and my voice didn't sound like my own. I noticed that Charlotte was listening just as intently as my grandfather and I, and I concluded that she was hearing the story for the first time.

Elisheba had her eyes on her brother as she answered. "When we got there, we found no sign of Martha or May."

It seemed that Hosanna would only answer questions approximately once every five minutes, and she took this moment to speak. "Josiah said that May had got into trouble and her sister had dived beneath the water to look for her. Neither of them made it back up."

"But Josiah was fine," Elisheba responded bitterly, stretching the last word out. "He was there treading water, in view of the far bank. And there's one thing I've never understood about his actions. You see, he never called out."

"Not this again." Ezekiel was still shaking, and he'd found his anger once more. "He didn't mean to hurt anyone, if that's what you're thinking. He wasn't much of a swimmer himself."

"He didn't call out," she repeated, "and he certainly didn't try to help them. If the girls were in trouble, why didn't he call to us? We might have made a difference. We might have saved them, but he just floated there, waiting to see what would happen."

"He could have died himself if he'd gone beneath the water." Ezekiel stood up, but he didn't have the energy to make a dramatic exit. He hung there in space, as if hoping that his mere physical presence might change her mind. "He was scared. That's all there is to it."

"It doesn't matter because we were just as much to blame. We sat in the boat and watched it happen."

My grandfather hadn't spoken for some time but now decided that his contribution was required. "I tend to think of myself as a harsh judge of wrongdoers, but I don't believe that you can really be blamed for what happened, Elisheba."

"You don't understand." Her previously calm voice rose in panic. We were her confessors, and she needed to finish. "It wasn't just that night, it was what happened afterwards. We should have told the truth, but Josiah thought up a story and Father made sure we went along with it. We were to say that we didn't know what had happened, and the girls had gone swimming without us. Father told the local constable himself that we had nothing to do with it."

It was strange to hear someone who was clearly so desperate to convince us of her guilt. I was more used to the opposite – to people saying whatever it took to prove their innocence.

"I watched him at the inquest, and I think he was a little proud. He was such a clever man, for all the good it did us. He knew about the bottle Josiah had stolen and worked out the rest. I think the worst part is that he made a large donation to the church after, as if money could make up for the vicar's loss."

"The way you judge him!" Ezekiel's rage was directed in a channel across the table. "Whatever he did was bad by your high standards. You can't say that he made a charitable donation to ease the vicar's pain. You have to think the worst of everyone. We all saw Reverend Callander that day. He was broken hearted and on the point of despair to have lost his daughters, and so Father tried to make it better."

"If he'd wanted to make it better, he should have made his lying children tell the truth. That poor man lost everything, and he didn't even find out what really happened to Martha and May in the final moments of their lives because we all protected Josiah instead of doing what was right."

"Did he blame you?" Grandfather asked when it seemed as though the story was over. "Did the vicar accuse you of knowing more than you'd said?"

Ezekiel looked terribly frightened once more, and Hosanna turned to her sister to see how she would react.

"Of course he did. He said at the inquest that his daughters would never sneak out of the house without someone coercing them. He talked for so long about the good girls that they were, and no one had the heart to interrupt him. He knew that there was more to it than we'd told the police, but he couldn't prove it, and it hurt him even more."

CHAPTER NINETEEN

Grandfather and I were the only people still at the table by the time dessert was served. Normally this would have made me happy – more rolled treacle pudding for me. Hurray! But the circumstances that day, and the sad scene we'd witnessed between the siblings at lunch, had robbed me of my appetite.

"Is it really possible that the killer is someone outside the family?" I put to my mentor when I was sure that not even a passing maid was within earshot.

He considered the possibility for a moment, his thinking face very much engaged. "I believe it is. It seems likely that Abraham's killer exited the lounge through the open window."

"Oh, yes, of course," I said, because I am a fibber, and I hadn't made this connection until now.

"I thought it unlikely that there was enough time for one of the Hindmarsh children to shoot him, and then run back to the studies on the other side of the house in order to be inside so soon after the shot. In fact, it was that which prevented me from selecting the likely culprit before now."

Before I could ask another question, Blunstone appeared at the door with a tray of digestif cocktails. They were, like many cocktails to which I'd been subjected over the years, a ghostly pale cream colour, and I was sure that this was the work of our dear Todd.

"Your man suggested that this is the stimulant that you require, Lord Edgington. He informs me that it is an American drink known as 'The Last Word'." The butler gave us both a glass and left the five remaining servings on the table to go undrunk. He bowed and exited the room, but the conversation couldn't continue because we were both reflecting on the rather unique beverage we were imbibing.

"There's definitely gin in it." I winced a little, just as another flavour hit me.

"And I believe I can taste Chartreuse," Grandfather said, and I believed him because he knows far more about such things than I do.

Waves of flavour passed over my tongue. We'd moved on from the acrid sting of the first spirit to something sour and herbal before a definite note of sweetness popped like a bubble all over my tastebuds.

"Cherry!" We both declared at the same moment, and Grandfather would go further. "Maraschino liqueur, if I'm not mistaken."

"I couldn't have imagined enjoying such a combination," I had to confess, "but Todd has really outdone himself this time."

Grandfather held up his glass to the scarlet light that came in through the stained-glass window, and his previous good humour seemed to fade.

"The Last Word," he murmured rather ominously, and I was reminded of what I wanted to ask him.

"Do you really think that this Reverend Callander could be our man?" I injected a healthy dose of scepticism into the question, and he surprised me with his answer.

"There is no reason why he shouldn't be. We know he lives nearby and has an excellent motive for murder. It would also explain why someone would kill both Abraham and Lemuel."

He took a swig of the drink, and I tried to copy but wished I hadn't. I'm more of a sipper than a swigger.

As my throat recovered, I felt that I'd found a discrepancy in his response. "But Lemuel wasn't there on the night that the two girls drowned."

"Yes, but the vicar would surely suspect the whole lot of them of lying. He wouldn't know that Lemuel had stayed in his bed." He tutted to himself, and his bright grey eyes dimmed a little. "It's all so squalid and sad."

I thought he would suggest a plan of action, but nothing came.

"Might you have some idea for how we might find out whether the vicar might…" I was aware that I'd said *might* three times by this point and made a note not to say it again. "Or rather, how can we determine whether the vicar is to blame for the killings?"

Blunstone had arrived to remove the dessert, which I did manage to find room for after all. We finished our drinks, pulled back our chairs and left the room.

"I do think it's unlikely," he eventually responded, thereby contradicting what he'd told me just a minute earlier. "But we can't rule out the possibility that a man of the cloth would murder someone." He gave me a wink at this moment to remind me of a case gone by.

"However, we must investigate every clue that comes our way. Tell Todd to prepare the car. I will see you at the rear of the house once I've given the staff here instructions to keep an eye on the remaining members of the Hindmarsh family."

We had just reached the curiously decorated entrance hall and, to my surprise, he spun around to return to the drawing room to speak to the butler again. He really was a funny man in a funny mood. I'd grown used to his eccentricities over the years, but he still had the power to catch me out.

"Good afternoon, constable," I said to the man at the door. He once more looked excited to be addressed.

"My name's Argent, sir. How may I be of help to you this fine afternoon?" He had an eager tone of voice and stood up very straight as he awaited his orders.

"My grandfather and I are leaving the estate to interview a witness."

His smile only grew. "Excellent! That's the very thing to do if you wish to solve a crime. I've often said that you cannot catch a killer without interviewing witnesses." I would imagine that he was approaching forty, but he had the mannerisms of a much older man. "Do you require me to come with you in case an arrest should need to be made?"

I was sorry to disappoint him. "That's very kind of you, but I don't think it will be necessary. I'm sure that my grandfather will tell you when he passes this way, but your most pressing responsibility is to monitor the remaining occupants of the house."

"You mean you want me to stay here?" He'd become quite nervous. "Alone?"

I tried to find a way to respond that would reassure him. "Not alone, exactly. The servants are still tending to their duties. And Miss Elliott, Abraham Hindmarsh's niece, seems very nice indeed. I'm sure you'll do a tip-top job."

He worked his lower teeth over his top lip as he sought a response. "Yes, sir. Of course, sir. In which case, the only problem I can foresee is that all four of the Hindmarsh siblings recently passed this way on their way about the grounds."

"The grounds?"

"That's right, sir. All four of them. They passed this way and two of them disappeared into the trees beyond the lake over there, while the others went around the back towards the gardens. I asked them where they were going and each of them said they were off for a walk."

"And you didn't think of stopping them?"

He fiddled with the bronze button on his breast pocket. "No, sir. No one told me to stop anyone. My only instructions were to stand here and take note of everyone who entered the house. That, sir, is exactly what I've done... except when I popped to the kitchen for some tea."

"Ah..." I was tempted to point out the limitations of this task but decided that he wasn't the sort of officer to trouble with nuances. "Well, keep up the good work then, Constable Argent."

"That I will, sir. That I will."

More than a little mystified by his attitude, I left the house behind. I couldn't imagine that he was the type of person who became a police officer in order to right the wrongs of the world so much as to follow orders and bank his pay at the end of each month. I'm sure such officers had their uses, though I couldn't imagine what they were.

It turned out that my path to the car would have more than a couple of familiar faces along it. First, I found Delilah and Samson gambolling together, and I realised just what a puppy Delilah still was at times, though she was apparently well into her third decade of existence. I was tempted to invite our lovable beast along on the excursion, but she was having such a wonderful time with her friend that I didn't like to interrupt.

I stood watching and soon realised that I was not the only one.

"Life looks so easy for them," I heard a voice say, and it was so close by that I could almost believe it was in my own head.

I turned to see Josiah sitting on a cast-iron bench just a yard to my right. He'd been so still and quiet that I hadn't noticed him there.

"I didn't mean to scare you," he said, more as an explanation than an apology. "I didn't expect anyone else to come here."

He was sitting in the centre of a semi-circular bed of rose bushes, each of which was growing around a metal frame. There were no flowering heads on them and, looking more closely, I could see that a gardener had recently cut them back.

"This is a nice spot to sit and think," I said to have something to say, but the dogs had run off again and this was no longer quite so true.

126

"I suppose so. I just needed to get away from everybody."

Grandfather was very good at engaging people in conversation in such a manner that they didn't realise he was digging for information. I, on the other hand, was not.

"Would you happen to know anything about all these wretched kill—" I began, and fortunately he interrupted me.

"What Elisheba said about Father at lunch wasn't true, you know?" His glare was as intense as I'd seen it, and he seemed to be biting the inside of one cheek. "He did love me. He loved all of us, and he was an exceptionally good father."

I believe he was trying to convince himself of this rather than me. I was a brick wall against which he could bounce the things he most wanted to hear. I noticed that he hadn't denied that he was the killer. If I'd been in his situation, that's what I would have done. But, like a tragic hero, he was still preoccupied by his hubristic obsession. Abraham Hindmarsh really was everything to Josiah. I believe that he would have sacrificed his freedom to show how much he loved his father. What I couldn't say was whether he would have killed to do so.

"Families are complicated," I replied noncommittally. "I've always believed that the really strange ones are those in which everyone gets along perfectly."

I thought he might laugh at this pithy observation and tell me I was spot on, but there was no joy left in the man. He was a walking shadow, motivated by a sole driving force. Before his father died, it had been the prize of a hard-hearted man's love. And now that he was gone, Josiah desperately wanted to prove that such a feeling had existed.

"I miss him more than Mother or Lemuel. Perhaps no one has convinced you yet, but he was a marvellous man." There was a sparkle in his eyes and a sort of pride about him as he described his fallen pater. "His very presence was magnetic; a sense of electricity filled the air whenever he entered a room. It was like being in the presence of royalty. That's how I felt about it, at least, and I know that Ezekiel would agree with me. The others will tell you a whole load of tommyrot about what a brute he was, but I never saw that side of him. I could only see a great man who devoted his life to doing incredible things."

I was tempted to interrupt this propaganda, but I imagined that he would run out of steam if left to chatter.

"He was the youngest ever Parliamentary Under-Secretary of State for Foreign Affairs. Did you know that? The Foreign Secretary clearly saw just how much potential my father had and shot him up the ranks in no time." His muscles flexed as he spoke, and his head bobbled about as though he were still impressed by the facts that he had long since known. "I like to think that he would have become Prime Minister before long. And considering the humble background from which he sprang, that really is an impressive feat."

He could have blathered all day, and I could see that the time had come to interrupt. Now, there were two obvious approaches to this. I could have lent him a sympathetic ear and agreed with everything that he'd just said with the aim of extracting some valuable information he otherwise would never have shared or... Well, I had a feeling that such a sly tactic would not work on the intelligent, slightly manic man in front of me, and so I went for the second option.

"You know, Josiah, if this were a mystery on the stage, everyone watching would think you were the killer. You're anti-social, and quick-tempered. You lost your composure at the slightest provocation several times today, and all in all, I have no reason to doubt that you would be capable of killing a member of your family."

To my surprise, it seemed to work. He didn't get angry or push me away. He simply looked back with a smile on his face. "Oh, really? Please, tell me more."

"Very well." I had to recall the other evidence of his guilt that I'd compiled through the course of the day. "You were the last to appear when Lemuel was murdered, perhaps in order to distance yourself from the crime. The way in which you talk of your father sounds as though you're trying to convince us that you would never murder him, when no one has asked you to do any such thing."

"And Mother?"

"Of course, your mother... Well, from what I remember when we first came here some weeks ago – at which point your father wouldn't admit us to the property – you were the one who discovered her abandoned vehicle. Your fingerprints were all over the car and, as has been suggested on several occasions, you may well have killed her when seeking your father's good opinion."

I was amazed that he hadn't launched a defence (or a fist) at me, but then it is often easier to hear home truths from someone who does not come from the same home as you.

"The truth is, Josiah, you've grown up in your more impressive relatives' shadows and never fulfilled the objectives you set yourself. You idolise your father but are in no position to follow his path. You are a warped, frustrated young man whose only love is for the person who failed to love you back."

"I see." As he sat there, his demeanour remained strangely passive, and it was impossible to have any sense of what was going through his mind. "Thank you for telling me what you really think. I suppose that must make me the killer."

"Not at all," I quickly assured him. "I would say that the most likely suspect has only turned out to be guilty in one or two of the many cases I've investigated with my grandfather. If anything, all those things I just listed mean that you're the least likely to have killed anyone." Of course, if what I'd just said was true, that would paradoxically make him the most likely, which in turn would make him the last person who would have committed the crime, which therefore suggests that… Well, I think I've made my point.

"And while what I said is accurate," I continued, "very little of it can be presented as hard evidence of your guilt."

This hadn't made him any more cheerful, and he released a dismissive snort. "It doesn't matter anyway. The game is over. The tale has been told, and it's become increasingly clear to me that this family is cursed. You don't recover from something like this. We won't go on to have normal lives. Wherever we are, people will whisper about us. *There goes the murder family,* everyone will say, and we'll never escape from this terrible chain of events."

"Yes, but chains can be broken," I felt I should remind him.

"Maybe." He smiled his cold smile again and wearily pushed himself up to standing. "Or maybe not."

I knew that I should say something more to him, but nothing came. Advising a man who had lost his mother, father and brother in quick succession in a series of horribly violent deaths was beyond me. *Cheer up,* or, *Try to find a silver lining* would have sounded awfully trite. He had every right to grieve. My main concern was how he would go about it.

He wandered off along the neat garden paths that scrolled and wound towards the wild woods that hemmed us in on all sides. For a moment, as I watched him in the distance, he looked like a man lost in a labyrinth, and I had to wonder whether anyone would be able to help him out again.

Samson and Delilah reappeared as I set off to complete my original task. They were a rather wonderful palate cleanser after the gloomy conversation I'd just endured. Delilah was attempting to pick up Samson by the scruff of the neck, and he really didn't want to go along with her plan. They were dear, sweet creatures, and it did me no end of good to watch their game for a few moments.

"Hullo there, Todd," I called once I'd found the spot where the Napier was parked. "I suppose you've heard all about the events of this morning?" This was a horrid turn of phrase, and I immediately regretted making a series of killings sound like a village fête.

"It's terrible, Master Christopher." He always knew the goings on in the houses we visited. I had to conclude that his master had trained him to befriend various employees wherever we went in order to stay abreast of any important news or – perhaps more helpful – any juicy gossip. "The cook told me that violence has been promising to break out since Mrs Hindmarsh went missing. She's told me some terrible stories about her masters' children, too, though she seems to like old Abraham well enough."

"It's a perplexing case," I had to admit. "It would be much easier if we knew for certain whose view of the dead man… or rather, the first dead man… is closest to the truth. Having spent some time with his children, I can now say that no one here is particularly saintly, so we must question the reliability of everything we hear."

"I would expect nothing less, sir."

Todd nodded, and I stood waiting for whatever was supposed to happen next before remembering that I had a message to impart. "Grandfather asks that you prepare the Napier for a short trip."

"Very good."

Before I could say anything more, the man's master had appeared. "There's been a change of plan, Todd." His cane swung forwards and back as he navigated a circular flowerbed to reach the former carriage house where Todd had parked our car. "I'll drive. I'd prefer you to

130

stay here to keep an eye on things. Whatever led to the two murders, I believe it remains unresolved."

Unlike the constable at the door, Todd was never intimidated by the assignments my grandfather gave him. He nodded, held out the keys, and stepped away from the unnecessarily large vehicle.

"I will do my best, M'lord."

"You might want to start in the woods and gardens," I suggested. "The siblings dispersed about the grounds after lunch, and I just bumped into Josiah, so the others won't be far away."

"Oh, and Todd…" Grandfather rested an arm on the roof of the car as he spoke to his factotum. "Be careful. I wouldn't want you getting hurt."

Our most reliable servant just smiled. He was rarely a verbose fellow, but he could say a lot with a cheerful look. This one said, *Don't worry about me, sir. I know what I'm doing.* And I had to believe that he really did.

Grandfather had just started the engine by the time something important occurred to me.

"Wait a moment. Do you know where the vicar lives?"

He was distracted by a meter on the dashboard and didn't initially respond. "What's that?" I was about to repeat myself when my words finally reached him. "Ah, you're right. I don't." He tapped the circular tiddlypush, and the needle jumped into place. "Run and ask the butler. There's a good boy."

CHAPTER TWENTY

Once I had obtained the necessary information, we were ready to leave Silent Pool. It's hard to describe the sensation as we drove along the overgrown path and off the Hindmarsh family's land. It felt as if a spell had been broken. We emerged from the thick tree cover and onto the country lane outside, and I could breathe more freely again. I had to wonder if the very place was cursed. First Martha and May had drowned there a decade earlier, then Patience had disappeared, Abraham had been shot and Lemuel strangled. I was glad to escape for a short spell, though it was hard to imagine our destination being a great deal sunnier than where we'd just left.

There was a hamlet a few miles from Silent Pool with little more than a church, a village shop and a few houses dotted around them. The house where the vicar lived was a pretty cottage with roses climbing up one wall and the others covered in creeping vines, their leaves changing colour in time for the autumn. The barrier of green was turning yellow and brown, and the red brickwork underneath peeked through here and there.

Grandfather knocked on the front door and stood back to await entry. There was still no answer after a minute had passed and so he tried again.

"Who's there?" a voice eventually came back to us, but the door didn't open.

"My name is Lord Edgington," Lord Edgington replied. "We're here to speak to you about—"

He was interrupted by some shuffling and perhaps a spot of mild cursing. Whoever was there sounded as though he'd banged his toe, but then the door finally swung to, and a man in a floor-length cassock appeared.

"I'm dreadfully sorry," he told us. "I was having a bath, and I didn't think you'd want to see me in my birthday suit." He pointed to a crumpled towel on the floor behind him and smiled a truly welcoming smile. "One of the good things about being a man of the cloth is that the cloth in question is very easy to throw on in a hurry."

"You know, I'd never considered that," I replied, finding his joviality infectious. "Perhaps I'll have to reconsider my future career."

He was a short, round man with a matching round face and bright eyes that peered out at us from behind a pair of clip-on spectacles. If someone had asked me to draw a picture of a vicar, I doubt that the result would have looked very different.

"That's the spirit!" He laughed a full-throated laugh and then stopped as if suddenly aware that there was something he hadn't done. "Can I invite you in for tea, perhaps?"

He didn't have to ask twice, and we were shown inside to a comfortable sitting room with just enough chairs for the three of us and a roaring fire in the grate. It didn't occur to me until I was sitting down with a warm cup of tea and an oat and raisin biscuit that he hadn't asked us why we were there.

"I suppose you must get people turning up on your doorstep all the time," I put to him.

"No." He took a moment to reflect on the matter. "Not so often."

"But you recognised my grandfather's name at least?"

"Should I?" With each question he answered, he laughed a little more.

I turned to my mentor in the hope he would know how to begin this interview, but he looked just as amused by the situation as the vicar. He normally hated it when people didn't know who he was, but this time was an exception.

"Well, I..." I tried again. "Or rather, we... You know? This really is lovely tea."

With this simple, amiable comment, I had got out of my responsibilities and forced my grandfather to take a turn. He didn't seem to mind.

"I believe what my grandson is trying to ascertain is why you would allow us into your house without knowing the reason we are calling."

Reverend Callander raised one finger in preparation for his answer, then had second thoughts. "Ooh, I think I have some shortbread in a tin somewhere that I haven't offered you." He got up to search for the promised biscuits and I wished that everyone we interviewed avoided questions in such a fashion. He soon returned with the sugary offerings and an answer. "If you're knocking at my door, I can only assume you have a good reason to be here. Whether you are a lord or a laundry woman, all are welcome."

Grandfather looked a little puzzled by his attitude and decided to reiterate his credentials. "Well, I *am* a lord, but more importantly, I am a detective. I imagine you have heard about the disappearance of Patience Hindmarsh?"

I should have kept a notebook with me to write down all of his clever interviewing techniques. From the off, he was picking which information to share and which to hold back. He'd mentioned the missing matriarch but not her murdered husband or son.

"I was terribly sad to hear about that," the vicar replied sincerely. "Patience wasn't a regular church-goer here at St Thomas's. In fact, I hadn't seen her about the place for some years, but I remember her as a very kind woman."

If he were harbouring hatred towards the family who had, at the very least, been witnesses to the death of his daughters, he did a good job of hiding it.

"That is the impression that we have been given by her family," Grandfather replied before taking a slow sip of tea. I believe it was too hot for him, as he released a sharp breath immediately after. The dangers of tea are manifold and rarely discussed. "I was formerly a superintendent of the Metropolitan Police. An old colleague of mine asked us here to assist with the investigation."

In that cheery, innocent way of his, Reverend Callander kept watching the detective for a short time before asking a question of his own. "Have you had any success?"

Lord Edgington turned to his grandson as though he couldn't decide how to answer. It was a reversal of our normal arrangement, and it left me quite discomposed.

"I can't say that we have," he finally replied. "It is a complex and puzzling case and, though we've developed any number of theories as to what could have happened to her, we are yet to find the key piece of evidence that will help us resolve the mystery."

This brief response didn't sound like him. It sounded like a politician making excuses for a mistake. It sounded like the senior detective who has failed to solve an important case and subsequently allowed the killer to go unpunished. My grandfather was normally an exceedingly honest person, to the extent that he could be quite rude, and this tricky form of speech didn't suit him.

"If there's anything I can do, you need only ask," the vicar continued. "I know that the situation has had an impact on the local community. People are worried that whoever was responsible for the attack on Patience – if that is what happened – could strike again here."

The two men nodded to one another and sipped their tea. Judging by his closed eyes and bitten lip, Grandfather burnt himself yet again.

"As you say, we do not know for certain whether Mrs Hindmarsh was attacked, but I believe that is now more likely." He still hadn't mentioned that day's killings and was waiting for the man to make a mistake.

"Oh, is it?" The vicar frowned and put his cup down on a small table beside the fire as though preparing himself for bad news. "How dreadfully sad."

I believe that my grandfather and I shared the same thought for a moment. It was difficult to know whether we were dealing with the world's most convincing actor or simply a man who knew nothing about the recent events at Silent Pool.

"Yes… Yes, it's most sad and…" There was a brief hesitation, and I'm sure that Grandfather was debating how much to reveal. "…I'm sorry to say that there has been more violence this very day."

Crossing his arms, the vicar leaned back in his chair and looked concerned. "So it was as we feared then. That is terrible, truly terrible. May I ask what has happened?"

"Abraham himself has been murdered." I thought I should contribute this much to the conversation, and it still gave my grandfather the opportunity to hold back the news of Lemuel's death, which is exactly what he didn't do.

"Swiftly followed by the middle boy, Lemuel. It is a great tragedy."

"A great tragedy indeed," the vicar echoed, and I searched his words and his visage for any hint of artifice.

Perhaps sensing that we had been outplayed, or that the pleasant man in front of us was as unaware of the situation as he seemed, Grandfather switched his approach.

"I thought I would come here because men in your position tend to know what people are really like. I often tell my grandson that the foremost rule of a good detective is to consider everybody's involvement in a crime, not merely the usual suspects."

The vicar winced a little and shuffled in his seat so that grandfather had to correct himself.

"I don't wish to imply that you had anything to do with the murders. I merely meant that good people like yourself are often more aware of what's really happening in a small town like..." His words faded. This was presumably because neither of us knew the name of the town we were visiting.

Again, the vicar looked as though he were trying to understand what we wanted. He really was a masterful foil for the old detective, and so I leaned forward in my chair to bridge the gap between them.

"To put it simply, we would like to know your impression of the family."

The vicar let out a brief laugh and reached for his cup once more. "I see, I see. And I'm very happy to share what I know, but I must remind you that I've seen very little of them since the first year or so they were living here. I can tell you that, for a brief time at least, Mr Hindmarsh made a real effort to be a member of the community. He was a good politician in that sense, for all that they are maligned. He and his wife got to know the locals and learnt everyone's name."

It was hard to believe he was speaking in such a calm manner, considering what we knew about his daughters.

"Do you know what changed?" I asked when Grandfather still didn't step in. "Why did they start off so warmly only to hide away from the world?"

He put one extended finger up to his chin and considered the question. "I truly haven't an answer for you. I was in the middle of a difficult period at the time and— You see, just before the Hindmarshes moved to the area, my wife died quite unexpectedly and, the following year, our two daughters drowned in Silent Pool."

It was my turn to be dumbfounded. He spoke in an open and honest way of what I was sure would be a dark secret. I didn't know how to respond.

Luckily, my grandfather took up the slack. "I am so sorry. I have lost children myself and I can only offer my condolences. Mine were both adults at the time, but the pain never goes away."

The vicar nodded his thanks. "That is very kind of you to say,

Lord Edgington. It was a terrible time in my life and, for a while, I came close to losing my most precious gift." His smile straightened itself out for a moment and he explained his thinking. "I found myself questioning my faith when Martha and May died. I couldn't understand what had compelled them to leave this house in the middle of the night to swim alone together, but, in time, I came to realise that I was asking the wrong thing. If I knew what really happened to them, it wouldn't make me feel any better. It wouldn't bring them back to me, and so what good would it actually do?"

If the conversation had been difficult to conduct before now, this question was almost impossible to answer.

"I know just what you mean. As the Good Book says, '...be ye kind one to another, tender hearted, forgiving one another, even as God for Christ's sake hath forgiven you.'"

I thought the vicar might have shown his appreciation for Grandfather's quotation from... one of the books in the Bible, but he just closed his eyes and bowed his head to absorb its message.

Grandfather sucked his cheeks in before changing the topic. "I'm afraid I must ask you more about the Hindmarshes. We have heard mention of Abraham's fierce temper. His own children have said they feel that the family itself is rotten to the core. Did you find that at all in your dealings with them?"

The vicar raised his eyebrows in surprise. "I really did not. When my girls died, Abraham sat where you are and apologised wholeheartedly for what I had experienced. He sent a donation to the church as well, though any rich man can throw his money around. It was the visit that stayed with me. He went up greatly in my estimation that day. And it was those small gestures – the times when ordinary people rallied around to support me – those were the things that made a real difference."

For the first time in the conversation, it was clear that there was something he wasn't saying. His positivity suddenly sounded forced.

"That's a lovely story." Grandfather did not sound particularly moved by it. "However, I must tell you that everything we have uncovered suggests that his family are not the upstanding, harmonious people that Abraham claimed that they were. My feeling is that the killer could well be one of them."

Again, Reverend Callander seemed comfortable in his silent response. He sat motionless, his teacup in one hand, the saucer in the other. I believe that he was telling my grandfather that, as no question had been asked, he was under no obligation to provide an answer. It was the kind of thing that my wise companion did to me every day, and it was rather nice to see the tables turned.

"To be perfectly honest with you," Grandfather said, as he had no other option by now, "we had heard about your daughters before coming here, and I wondered whether you held the Hindmarshes responsible in any way."

I thought that the vicar would get angry or ask us to leave, but if anything, he seemed relieved that we had come to the point. He belatedly blew on his tea and took his time to respond. "I've already told you, it does no one any good to hold on to the past. Blaming the Hindmarshes or their children for what happened could provide no comfort. Aside from the fact that they were somewhere nearby when it happened, I've no reason to suspect them."

I looked at my grandfather then and willed him not to reveal what Elisheba had told us over lunch. Reverend Callander was right; knowing the sad truth would do him no good, and this conversation would only recall past suffering. I don't know if I'm an unwitting clairvoyant, or my grandfather had simply come to the same conclusion, but he did just as I'd silently begged.

Instead, he asked, "Have you any knowledge of anyone in the area who might have held a grudge against the family?"

The vicar shook his head. "I haven't but, as you may have discovered, one or two of Abraham's sons have put a few noses out of joint over the years. I never saw anything untoward myself, but I've heard talk of their rudeness and arrogance. My girls thought they were marvellous, though. For the year before they died, I heard about nothing but the fabulous Hindmarshes."

He made them sound like a variety act and I couldn't help smiling for a moment.

"All of that money, and none of them know how to be happy." In a trice, his tone had changed. There was a sombreness to it, and I thought perhaps he could only maintain his carefree mask for so long before the memory of what he'd lost came back to him. "You know, the Bible teaches us that we are all sinners, but the difference between a good man and a truly wicked one is often that good men not only learn from their mistakes, but they also learn to forgive those who have wronged them."

I couldn't say whether he was talking about the Hindmarshes or people in general now, but it was hard to disagree with him. Abraham and his clan had every privilege, and they'd only held on to what was bad in life; the vicar had lost everything and found a way to be happy.

He set his cup down for the last time and managed to re-engage the warm and welcoming persona that he'd previously maintained. "I hope that answers some of your questions."

His smile was a thing of wonder. Perhaps it was his training or his unfaltering belief in something bigger than the three of us there in that small parlour, but he seemed to radiate hope.

"You've been very helpful," Grandfather told him, and I could see that he was still holding back some of the things we'd come there to say.

As we walked towards the exit, I noticed a framed photograph on the mantelpiece of a family that had once existed but was now no more. Father, mother and two daughters stood at the front of a church, full of joy. The father was in his vicar's robes, the mother was dressed in a simple pastel frock, and the girls wore the exact same clothes as in the picture on Lemuel's desk. Martha and May looked like kind children. They would have been a few years older than me if they'd lived, and I wondered whether we would have been friends.

Would you mind confirming that you really didn't kill any of the Hindmarshes? I didn't ask their father because I didn't have to. Although he probably had a greater reason to seek vengeance than anyone else, I think we'd known from the beginning that he wasn't to blame.

That isn't to say I regretted our trip to the vicarage. It was good to remind ourselves that not everyone in the world is selfish and bloodthirsty. Reverend Callander shook us both by the hands and we left the cosy home. Our brief time there was the perfect counterpoint to the calamitous place we were about to revisit.

CHAPTER TWENTY-ONE

Grandfather confirmed my thinking as we made our way back to the car. He stopped at the door to our funereal car and looked up at the picturesque cottage set in its wonderfully rambling garden.

"Either he is unaware of the part that the Hindmarsh children played in the death of his daughters, or he is pretending that's the case for his own sake." He pondered this dichotomy whilst I cranked the engine.

"So we still can't eliminate the possibility that he is to blame for the killings," I said, hoping that I was wrong.

"No, we can't, but I don't see it myself. Why would he have waited for so long to get his own back? And why murder Patience first and then come for the others today?" He shook his head sadly and got into the driver's seat.

He had long since given up on persuading me to drive, though, now that I am twenty, perhaps I should be brave and confront my fears. Perhaps it's time I got back behind the wheel. Not today, of course, but at some point in the future, when the moment strikes me.

"Furthermore," he said, much like a teacher explaining a difficult problem, "if he were set on wiping out the family, it would be odd to find him at home when we came here unannounced. He would surely be back at Silent Pool, lurking in the bushes and only approaching the house when the time is right to make a killing – unmetaphorically speaking."

There wasn't a great deal to say to this. I climbed aboard the stately car, and we drove back to the Hindmarsh estate, digesting our thoughts (and our biscuits) in silence. I was trying to remember the questions that I had asked myself earlier in the day in order to decide whether I had been able to answer any of them.

I could now say that the killer was able to move about without anyone seeing him by climbing through windows. But that was hardly the strategy of a master criminal. If someone had happened upon him as he clambered in or out, the game would have been up immediately.

As for the sound that Lemuel and the others heard outside their studies... well, I still didn't have a clue what that was. I also couldn't say whether Charlotte Elliott bought Samson the dog as a perfect distraction from her crimes, and I was nowhere near deciding who had killed whom and why. So, as far as progress goes, I hadn't made any, but I did have a question to ask my grandfather.

"I don't suppose you know how long the average golden retriever lives, do you?"

He glanced at me without moving his head. "Yes, I do."

"Oh… And could you tell me how long that is?"

"Yes, I could." The old rascal laughed under his breath.

"Grandfather!" I complained, and I didn't sound like a twenty-year-old man who was making his way in the world. I sounded approximately six.

"Very well. The average pedigree golden retriever will normally live for a little over a decade."

"Oh." I was a trifle bemused. "In which case, Delilah isn't twenty-three, is she?"

He turned his head for this. "What on earth do you mean, boy?"

"I mean that the Delilah who was alive when I was little isn't the same dog as the one who's accompanied us here today."

"Ah. You've realised, have you?" He didn't wait for confirmation. "I really didn't mean to trick you. You see, the first Delilah died during a period of my life in which I lacked the courage to see even my closest family. Your grandmother had bought that wonderful hound for me, and they had both been such an important part of my existence that their deaths, one after the other when you were six or seven, brought even more darkness to Cranley Hall. For several years, I hardly saw anyone other than your mother, and a few members of staff. So when your mother finally convinced me to allow your family to visit, you came barrelling into the room full of smiles and wonder and asked where Delilah was."

"I think I remember that. I must have been fifteen or thereabouts."

He turned back to the road. "That's correct. And your mother, who is a singularly manipulative, persistent and magnificent human being saw her opportunity and said, 'Don't worry, Chrissy. Delilah had to spend the night at the vet's. She'll be back here very soon.' I thought the whole matter would be swiftly forgotten, but the next time you came, she brought a nine-month-old golden retriever with her and made you believe it was the same dog you'd known in your infancy."

"Delilah Two?" My words came out in a whisper.

"That's right. And a few months later, your mother convinced me that Delilah shouldn't be the only new arrival at Cranley. Before I knew it, a joyful and curious boy was living at my house every weekend. It's hard to know whether it was having that lovely dog about the place, or it was all down to you, but in time I emerged from my self-imposed exile, decided to throw a party and… well I believe you know the rest of the story."

"Ah…" I fell silent then and must have looked a little crestfallen.

"I'm sorry that we lied. It was never my intention to make you think that dogs live forever. Delilah One had a good innings, though, and there's nothing to say that this Delilah won't do the same."

"It's not that," I replied, managing at least half a smile. "I'm just a little sad that I could be so dim. After all, a nine-month-old dog isn't even fully grown. I must have believed what I wanted to believe."

"Now, if that mystery has been solved to your liking, perhaps we should concentrate on the goings on at Silent Pool." As he said these words, he turned the steering wheel and pulled onto the wooded pathway that led to the house.

It was a breezy, cloudy day with the odd burst of sunshine, but under the trees it was awfully dark for the early afternoon. The branches overhead had become entwined like two plaits on a young girl's head. It was a little unnerving, and this feeling was enhanced by the sight of a figure dashing across the path in the distance. It happened so quickly that it was easy to imagine that my eyes were playing tricks on me, but I'm certain that's what I saw. The idea was reinforced when a man in a green waistcoat came into view ten seconds later.

"Todd," I shouted to him, before Grandfather pulled the car to a halt.

Our faithful retainer had come to a stop beside the path and seemed to be quite exhausted. "I was walking through the forest, looking for the siblings as you suggested," he said between deep breaths. "I heard someone in the trees behind me, but before I could get a good look, he'd run away."

"Get in, man!" Grandfather called, and Todd immediately mounted the running board to hang off the vehicle. This sparked a smile of quiet appreciation from his master. "If whoever you saw is on his way to the house, we might be able to cut him off there."

It had been a while since Grandfather had an opportunity to

drive recklessly, so you can be sure that he stepped very firmly on the accelerator. We positively shot off along that shady track which wound through the forest towards the lake. The place was still when we arrived there and the only person in sight was P.C. Argent, who was at his post at the front door.

Getting out of the car, I noticed a rather eerie noise coming from somewhere in the house. It sounded like someone was wailing with tortured laughter, and it was quite inappropriate for that day, let alone that particular moment in time.

"Has anyone passed this way in the last few minutes?" Grandfather asked the officer, having left the car on the stone terrace in front of the building.

"Very good, Constable." Grandfather nodded and entered the house at pace before Todd and I followed close at heel.

The sound I'd heard was louder now, but it had changed somewhat, and I caught a snatch of someone singing.

> **"He laughs upon point duty.**
> **He laughs upon his beat.**
> **He laughs at everybody when he's**
> **Walking in the street."**

The song was unmistakable but, as we crossed the entrance hall and took the corridor which led to the sibling's studios, something about it filled me with dread. I believe that even Todd was a little disturbed by it, as he hung back behind his master and seemed to shudder as we left the bright hall to go deeper into the bowels of the house. I couldn't help feeling that whoever had put the record on was mocking us.

> **"He never can stop laughing.**
> **He says he's never tried.**
> **But once he did arrest a man**
> **And laughed until he cried!"**

Grandfather entered the gloomy space off which the cell-like rooms led. I could already tell that the loud music was coming from Josiah's study and, by this point, I believe that even my grandfather was frightened. I slipped past him to lead the way, put my hand on the door handle, pushed it open, and…

144

"Woo ha ha ha ha ha ha ha ha,
Woo ha ha ha ha ha ha ha ha ha,
Ah ha ha ha ha ha ha ha ha ha!"

The record turned on the Victrola orthophonic phonograph and Charles Jolly kept singing 'The Laughing Policeman' but there was no one inside. Josiah's room was empty except for the medium-size grand piano that only just squeezed in on the diagonal. I had to wonder how they'd got it in there in the first place and decided that the house must have been built around it.

We walked deeper into the room, but there was little to see there. Beside the ever so technological record player, there was a wooden crate of records with various classical concertos and piano pieces at the front and more modern, novelty songs towards the back. I noticed discs which said Mozart, Bach, Verdi, and "When Father Papered the Parlour" by Billy Williams, but nothing else stood out.

"A piano but no pianist," Grandfather mused, and he sat down at the instrument and flexed his fingers theatrically.

Now, I feel I should mention that I had never seen my grandfather at a piano before. In fact, I hadn't even heard it said that he knew how to play, so it came as some surprise when he started a fast, dramatic piece full of rhythmic vigour, with parallel chords leaping energetically around the piano. Todd was standing in the doorway, as though to guard us as we hunted for clues, and couldn't resist a smile at his talented, though peacockish, employer.

I know approximately as much about classical music as I do about bricklaying, but I was sure I'd heard the piece before. And after ten seconds or so of playing, Grandfather explained what it was.

"It's by Pyotr Il'yich Tchaikovsky," he revealed, and I am happy to say that I had indeed heard of the fellow. "It is his eighth opus. Widely known as 'Capriccio in G flat Major'. It's always been my favourite piece to play. You might say it's something of a party trick."

"I thought you were as musical as I was," I admitted, and he looked a little disturbed, then signed off the brief performance with a flourish of rising arpeggios leading up to one of the highest notes on the piano. For some reason, the final note didn't sound right, and so he pressed it twice more with the same discordant result.

Todd frowned at the unsatisfying noise. "You'd think he'd keep his piano in order, if he's so devoted to his music."

Before Grandfather could reply, we heard a sound coming from the room next door, and the three of us instinctively moved to investigate what had caused it. There were only a few rooms we had yet to enter, and Grandfather stopped to knock at the first.

"Come in?" a voice travelled back to us.

We were once more in that tense situation of having to open a door without the faintest idea of what could be on the other side. For all we knew, there would be another body to discover, or perhaps this was where the Hindmarshes kept their dragon. For a moment, I imagined that generations of the family had been forced to guard an ancient beast, and the three people who had died were sacrifices to their supernatural ward. I'm not saying that I expected to see a dragon there. I only mean it was a possibility which, inevitably, went unrealised.

"How can I help you all?" Ezekiel asked as he sat in a butterfly chair in the bay window, reading what looked like a rather dull political treatise on something or other.

"When did you get back to the house?" Grandfather demanded. "The constable on duty told us that the four of you were in the grounds and that you hadn't returned."

Ezekiel uncrossed his legs and sat to attention. "The constable is at the front door. I went for a short walk and returned through the door beside the kitchen. Have I done something wrong?"

"Did you see anyone while you were outside?"

He wrinkled his brow. "No, I don't think… Actually, yes. I saw Hosanna sitting beside the lake. She was looking just as morose as she was at lunch."

"Did she see you?" Grandfather's tone suggested that he didn't hold out much hope for a useful answer.

"You'd have to ask her that. Why? What's happened?"

"Nothing whatsoever," I replied. "Though we'd like you to leave the room for five minutes while we…" I was about to say nose around, but I don't think that would have gone down well. "… investigate a hypothesis."

What a wonderful word hypothesis is. It really does help conceal the fact that you haven't a clue what you're supposed to be doing.

"Very well. I have nothing to hide. I'll go and tell Josiah that he should keep his music down."

He closed his pamphlet and spun it carelessly onto a small table at his side. Grandfather nodded his thanks as our suspect left.

We may not have found another body (or a dragon) or turned up any particular evidence, but it was interesting to have a peek inside Ezekiel's room to see what his main passion was. We knew nothing of Elisheba yet, but Lemuel was a runner and Josiah a musician. Hosanna painted, and it turned out that Ezekiel liked nothing more than his own father. The walls were covered in newspaper clippings and half-page profiles of Abraham Hindmarsh's career.

There were articles on the speeches the now deceased politician had given to parliament on international trade, and pieces on the relevant laws his department had introduced. He'd had a meeting with the French Foreign Minister, Aristide Briand, about sales of British pork to the continent and even attended conferences at Lord Darnley's magnificent residence at Mentmore Towers. Of course, none of that immediately explained why the man had been murdered, or whom Todd had just chased across the estate.

Grandfather slapped his thigh – though not in a comical way, I hasten to add. I believe it was a sign of exasperation. "More evidence that is unlikely to lead anywhere." He approached a picture of Hindmarsh shaking hands with an African dignitary. "I hadn't fully abandoned the idea that we would find a political motive for all this. I would like to believe that the killer is not someone within the family, but the chances keep growing slimmer."

I refused to be so negative and had a question for Todd. "Do you think that it could have been Ezekiel whom you saw in the woods?"

"The man who just left, you mean?" He put his hand to the back of his head and considered the possibility. "I'm afraid it's hard to say. He really was just a blur through the foliage."

"Can you show us where you first spotted him?" I asked, already moving towards the door.

"With pleasure, sir."

Grandfather looked dubious that this would do any good and decided upon a worthier use of his time. "You will find me in Patience Hindmarsh's study. I am keen to discover exactly why she hated her husband."

With that, he slipped from the room and along the corridor, as Todd pointed the way outside.

CHAPTER TWENTY-TWO

"Why do you think they do it, sir?" my dear friend asked as we crossed the formal garden to access the wild woods. I know that the main reason Todd spends time with us is because it's his job and Grandfather pays him, but I don't think it's inaccurate to describe him as a friend. I jolly well hope he is as, if we exclude canines, my only other friends are busy at university or touring Britain with a theatre troupe.

"Sorry, do what?" I replied.

"Murder one another? These posh folk who have all they need: how do they summon the savagery to be able to cut the life from someone? I really don't understand it, even now."

I had to think before answering. "To be honest, I have never spent enough time considering the matter. We are normally so busy trying to identify a killer and understand his motivation that I rarely have the time to ask how he has the gall to go through with his crimes."

"It boggles the mind."

I suppose it's my grandfather's training that has made me so reluctant to leave a question unanswered, and so I tried my level best to reply. "There are different motives, of course, but if we put aside love and jealousy, the most common reason is surely greed." I licked my lips and began to feel more confident about my theory. "You might see a rich man like Abraham Hindmarsh and think that he has everything he wants, but he would disagree."

"Not anymore, he wouldn't," Todd mumbled through a cheeky grin.

"You're right there, and it would be nice to think that, as the killer stood before him and pulled the trigger, the victim realised the error of his ways. But my point is that everything people think is relative to their own experiences. The Duke of Hampshire probably doesn't feel rich after visiting the Marquess of Cheadle Hulme and realising that he has a smaller fishing lake and not quite so grand a collection of Ming vases."

"I think I do well enough on six pounds a week, thank you very much. And I'm sure that my mother doesn't need any more vases than the one she's got."

I liked his view of the world, but he'd missed the point I was trying to make. "Yes, but if you've grown up with lots of vases and you see someone with more vases than you, perhaps you would feel differently. Perhaps you'd do whatever it took to get more."

He looked truly baffled for a moment. "I'm sorry, Master Christopher, but I really can't imagine that. To be perfectly honest, we don't have enough flowers round our house to need so many receptacles to put them in."

I gave a brief laugh and tried to correct my analogy. "You have a point, Todd. What I'm really trying to tell you is that the more some people have, the more they want. When you combine that with a propensity for violence or a lack of basic morals, then murder becomes more likely."

"That's something I've never understood before." We'd come to a narrow passageway between two neatly trimmed hedges, and he paused to let me through. "You see, if you have the money to escape from whatever is happening in your life, there must be a better choice available than killing someone."

We'd reached the track that Grandfather had driven along to get to the house some fifteen minutes prior, and Todd began to retrace his steps. There were several Singer Junior 8 cars passing, and I waved to the chief inspector in the first vehicle. Once they'd gone, we disappeared back into the forest. It was at moments like these that I most enjoyed having Delilah at my side, but she was having a much-deserved day's rest. I love to go darting through the trees with her in search of clues, and so I chased after Todd just as eagerly as she would have.

A minute or so later, we came out in a large clearing. There was no sunburst overhead as the sun was also on holiday and only popped by when it really had to.

"This is the place." Todd turned on the spot to get his bearings. "I'd come the way we've just walked and must have stopped right here when I heard a sound over by the bushes."

He pointed again, and I could see exactly where he meant. There was some tall grass and a few spiky plants that looked like monkshood. It wasn't the right time of year for them to be in bloom, but the shape of the leaves was quite distinctive and always reminds me of the cross of Saint James. We walked over to see whether there were any footprints, but apart from the verdant plant, there was nothing to find.

150

"I must have walked fairly close to him and not noticed," Todd said, his voice flat and disappointed as though he felt he'd let us down. "By the time I realised I wasn't alone, he'd taken off."

"Do you remember any detail that might help? His hair colour? The clothes he was wearing."

He shook his head. "It was all just a blur. In the first instant, I thought I'd stumbled across a deer, but then I saw more movement farther into the woods, and I knew it was a person. I went after him as soon as I realised, but there was no making up the ground."

"Which does suggest it was a man you were chasing," I told him, and I was glad that my grandfather wasn't there as he would probably have contradicted me. Despite his absence, I still felt I should defend the idea. "Women's clothes and footwear are less suited to running for one thing, and I've seen how fast you are."

"It is possible," he replied in as cautious a tone as any I'd heard his master use. He really was a very wise fellow, and I'd often wondered why Grandfather hadn't trained him to be his assistant. Perhaps he prefers me because my services come free of charge.

I looked down at the spot where he'd seen the mysterious figure and noticed that a few branches were bent and broken. Sadly there was no sign of snagged clothes or hair, as Sherlock Holmes would have found and swiftly identified. Grandfather kept saying that we had too much evidence, but I would argue that the evidence we had was all the wrong kind.

I imagine we would have given up and gone back to the house, but we heard voices nearer the lake and moved to investigate. I could tell from that first moment that they didn't belong to the Hindmarsh siblings. They were too deep, for one thing, and I heard Chief Inspector Darrington shouting in reply.

When we emerged once more from the woods, I saw three pairs of officers in the distance walking around the border of the lake. Their superior was following slowly behind with his eyes to the ground, as though he'd dropped something.

"What's the matter?" I called to him, and there was no warmth in his expression as he looked back at me.

"Elisheba says she hasn't seen Hosanna for some time. We've spent the last five minutes looking around the house without luck."

He jerked his thumb back over his shoulder, and I noticed Elisheba on a bench in front of the building. She looked quite distraught, and her cousin was standing next to her, trying to calm her down.

"We'll help you search," I told him, and Todd accelerated away.

The constables had made good ground, and two of the pairs had passed through the treeline to search in the woods. Darrington preferred a slow, careful approach. He stopped occasionally to peer into bushes that, if you ask me, were too small to conceal a person, but then cases aren't solved on bodies alone. There could have been anything there to lead us to Hosanna, and you can be sure that the chief inspector would have found it... eventually.

Perhaps a little luckily – in that I felt obliged to walk at his speed but was eager to aid the others in their search – one of his constables poked his head out from cover to get the chief inspector's attention.

"Sir," he called, "you had better come quickly."

It turned out that Darrington could run when it was needed. He found a burst of speed and, removing his cap so that it didn't fly away as he went, he soon reached his officer. The constable held back a large bush of brambles for us, and I had to duck to avoid it scratching my face. There were plump blackberries there, just waiting to be picked, but my watering mouth would have to wait.

Delilah had lost her friend and was sitting in a dark patch under a hawthorn tree. I could already tell that she'd found something, and I wondered whether she'd seen the police officers and done what she could to help, or it was just by chance she was there.

There was a limp bundle beside her, and a constable was kneeling down to inspect it. He looked up at the chief inspector as we approached and spoke in a nervous voice.

"Sir..." He had to stop to clear his throat. He was around my age and can't have been on the job long. "Sir, the victim said something to me before he died."

We were standing over the body by now and I caught a glimpse of Josiah's face staring back at me from the ground.

"What did you hear, lad?" Darrington replied, and the anxious young officer was shaking as he answered.

"He said, 'It wasn't Father's fault.'"

CHAPTER TWENTY-THREE

The Hindmarsh family wasn't like any other I'd encountered. We'd investigated nasty characters before, but everything about this day felt bleaker and less redeemable.

Before we found Josiah's body, I would have placed a bet on him being the killer. He had been the angriest, most bitter sibling from the start. We knew he would have done anything for his father, and I had considered a number of narratives that would link the killings to his obsession with the great man and his desire to please. Now that he was dead, there would be nothing so simple to explain away the carnage.

A knife had cut through Josiah's white shirt, and the blood had soaked in around it. The pattern was really not so very different from the one I'd noticed on his father several hours earlier. He had followed his example in death, as in life, but I still couldn't say why either of them had been killed.

His was the third dead body of the day at Silent Pool. And it was easy to imagine that the attack on Patience was the killer's prelude to a full-blown massacre. My grandfather had made me read old case files on famous Victorian killers like the West Ham Child Killer, Jack the Ripper and the Thames Torso Murderer. As well as leaving me with nightmares for several months after, the accounts gave me the sense that such criminals often had to build up to their most famous barbarities.

You don't wake up in the morning and decide to be a violent person. Most killers will have shown signs in advance of who they will become, and perhaps that explained what happened to Patience. Perhaps she argued with one of her children, and he lashed out. I could just imagine the crime unlocking some dark element within him, and it was only a matter of time before he struck again.

Or perhaps my brain was searching for an explanation that didn't exist.

Grandfather and the two specialist officers we'd seen that morning returned to examine the body for clues. The knife that killed Josiah looked as though it was used for hunting, but there was nothing else of interest to discover. My grandfather stood staring at the scene, and I practically heard his brain whirring, even as the traumatised young constable was comforted by his sergeant away from Josiah's motionless body.

"What about Hosanna?" Elisheba demanded when we broke the news of her second dead sibling of the day. She was in her own room beside Hosanna's art studio, and Ezekiel had just arrived with a cup of tea to calm her down.

"It's your brother that—" Grandfather began.

"I don't care about Josiah. I'm sorry, but it's true. I do not care about that savage boy. I'm sure that whatever happened to him was his own fault."

"Go easy, Elle," Ezekiel demanded, but she was in no mood to listen as she dumped spoonfuls of sugar into her cup.

"You heard what I said." She glared at my grandfather and issued a command. "Find my sister. I can't lose her. I just can't."

She burst into tears then, and I saw the pain that was flowing through her. Admittedly that might sound impossible, but I'm willing to bet that you've never been in the presence of a young lady whose family were steadily being eradicated before her eyes. The one good development in the last hour was that there were now enough officers present to guard the remaining Hindmarsh children, not that we knew where all of them were.

"Don't tire yourself unnecessarily," Charlotte told her frantic cousin before Grandfather made his own attempt to calm Elisheba.

"Nothing either of us can do or say will bring back your brothers or your parents." I didn't say it was a very good attempt. "But I can promise you that Chief Inspector Darrington and his men are doing all that they can to find Hosanna."

She held his gaze for a moment longer and then collapsed back into her chair. In the hush that followed, I looked around Elisheba's studio. I had to wonder whether their parents had assigned them their interests. Each of them had such clearly defined pastimes that it struck me as odd.

Elisheba, it seemed, was passionate about flowers. On a worktable in front of the window, there was a press with a large selection of already dried petals and full roses nearby. There were many examples of her work already on display about the place, including an enormous, framed piece above the mantelpiece which used vibrantly bright purple flowers to depict the lake and its surroundings. It was interesting that

154

she had managed to capture the scene so clearly using just petals and leaves, but it was immediately recognisable. Looking further around the room, I noticed jars with foliage drying and various tools and gloves for handling plants.

I'm not the most artistic person myself, unless you consider my impression of my grandfather to be an art form, but I must say that something about flower pressing has always seemed very peaceful to me. That said, it clearly wasn't enough for Elisheba just then, and so Grandfather sat down next to her and spoke in a soothing tone.

"Can you tell me exactly what happened since you left the dining room at lunch?"

She looked at her cousin, perhaps hoping that she would answer for her. "Tell me, Charlotte," she begged, "is this really the best use of our time? Shouldn't we be looking for her? Shouldn't *they* be looking for her?" She explained who *they* were with a flick of her eyes in our direction.

"I think you should answer Lord Edgington's questions, Elle," her kindly companion responded. "I really think—"

"Yes, that's enough from you. Thank you, Charlotte," Ezekiel interrupted. "This is a family matter, and if anyone should advise my sister, then it should be me."

Elisheba was so distraught that she didn't even notice how rude her brother was being. Knowing the precarious place that she occupied in the house, Charlotte nodded and stepped back. I could see the same thread of sorrow in her as I'd noticed during our conversation in the garden. I believe she would have snatched up Samson for a comforting hug, but he was back outside with Delilah and could provide no such support.

Ezekiel stood beside his sister with a consoling, or possibly controlling, hand on her shoulder. "You should answer the question if you feel it is the right thing to do."

Since we'd told them about Josiah, I'd noticed that Ezekiel was doing all he could to appear kind, co-operative and generous, which was quite the opposite of the picture I'd had of him before. If he felt any great sadness at the loss of his closest brother, he certainly didn't show it.

Elisheba nodded and her interviewer held his hand out to encourage her. She took it in hers and finally answered his question. "I left the house shortly after we finished lunch. You can ask the constable at the door if you don't believe me. Was it half-past three by then? I can't say for certain, but it was around that time."

"Continue, my dear."

I'd felt like saying something very similar, only a little less patient.

"Yes, of course." She looked at her small, soft hand in Grandfather's great, large, wrinkled ones and recalled what happened next. "I followed the edge of the water to a path I often walk when I want some time to myself. There are pretty flowers there in the summer, but it's too late for them now. Just before I entered the woods, I saw Hosanna beside the water's edge. She was sitting on the branch of a willow tree that overhangs the lake, just like Ophelia in the Waterhouse painting. I called to her, and she seemed to hear, but she didn't respond. She stared at me blankly, then turned to look at her reflection."

"Did she appear to be in pain or suffering in some way?" I asked, as something about her description was alarming to me.

"No, no. She looked distant or perhaps worried. But then, considering everything that has happened here, it's hardly any wonder. I suppose that is why I didn't go over to her. I wanted to be alone, and I imagined that she did too. Charlotte's little puppy started following me, and I shooed him away. So you can imagine how I must have been feeling."

"Of course we can, dear sister," that fraud Ezekiel cooed, and the more he took on this new persona, the more confident I was that he was our culprit. If he wasn't a killer, he was at the very least a fawning sycophant, which is a lesser but still serious crime in my book.

"Where exactly did you see your sister?" I asked, as she was prone to discussing trivialities when we needed precise information.

"She was close to the herb garden. I've often sat there myself to enjoy the view over the lake. I told the constables this when they started looking for her."

"That's very good, Elisheba." I was so used to hearing my grandfather prod and needle our suspects that it was always odd to hear him turn so gentle. "But what happened after that?"

"After that..." she said to herself as though she needed prompting. "After that, I noticed Josiah through the trees. He had a positively evil look on his face, and I wish that I'd gone to see what he was doing there, but I was preoccupied and instinctively took a path in the opposite direction."

"Did you hear anything unusual at the time?" Grandfather asked, presumably accepting that she had now told us all that she'd seen.

"Nothing. I went on a circuit all the way around the lake and came out in the gardens a while later."

"Did you see Todd, our servant?" I asked without explaining why I needed to know, but she just shrugged.

"I don't believe I saw anyone." She blew on her tea and took a long sip before adding a final spoon of sugar. "I came back through the house, and after a short time sitting at my desk here, I realised that Hosanna hadn't returned. I had been thinking of her the whole time and felt terrible that I hadn't done more to make certain that she was all right. She had looked so utterly wretched at lunch, and I knew that if I didn't do anything to help her, no one else would."

At least Ezekiel didn't have the impudence to contradict this. I hadn't seen him express much love for any of his siblings, and he'd done nothing but attack Elisheba before putting on this pitiful display.

"So you went back to the lake." Grandfather tapped her hand three times with his index finger as though to help her along.

"Yes, I returned to the spot where I'd last seen her, but she'd gone, and so I entered the woods and went to—" Her voice broke once more, and she turned to her nearest companion for solace or perhaps guidance.

I believe she must have been looking for Charlotte, but there stood her duplicitous brother. She glanced out of the window instead and tried to compose herself.

"Take your time, my child." Grandfather always knows when to push our witnesses forward and when to give them space to think.

"Thank you."

Charlotte nipped over with a clean handkerchief, and Elisheba silently repeated these two words before continuing. "I tried to find Hosanna, but I couldn't, and so I returned to the house just as James... or rather Chief Inspector Darrington had arrived with a number of officers. I explained what had happened, and they began their search."

Grandfather didn't speak again immediately. He leaned back from her and put a finger to his lip. "I have one last question for you." He paused, and I wondered if he were picking over his words so as not to offend or alarm her. "Can you tell me in which direction Josiah was walking when you last saw him? Was he heading deeper into the woods or…"

"Towards the lake. He was definitely walking towards the lake."

"Thank you, Elisheba." He smiled a sad smile.

Although a sombre mien is a prerequisite of the job, this expression was perfectly judged. My grandfather is a jolly old soul, but he rarely smiles in full. He shows his amusement through laughter, and his snow-white moustache often does a good job of hiding his emotion the rest of the time. In fact, I could count on one hand the number of times I'd seen his lips stretched wide and his cheeks dimpled.

He rose, nodded to the three young people and motioned for me to follow him outside. At the door stood the young officer who had heard Josiah's last words. He bowed as he saw the famous detective.

"Constable, I have a task for you. You are to take Ezekiel Hindmarsh and put him in one of the upstairs bedrooms. Guard that door, let no one in or out, and I will send another man to look after his sister. The most important job you have today is to ensure that no one else is murdered. Do you understand?"

He showed no apprehension this time as he accepted the assignment. "Perfectly, sir. I will do my best."

Grandfather cuffed him around the shoulder encouragingly. "I know you will. Keep your wits about you, and all will be well."

We were to have a similar conversation with an emotionless, near-silent constable we found in the entrance hall. Elisheba and Ezekiel would be safe for the time being, but Hosanna was still missing, and I hadn't a clue how to find her.

Some inspectors had arrived from Scotland Yard and were receiving their orders from Darrington. Outside, I could see men dotted here and there around the gardens and off through the trees. As we followed the path that Hosanna would have taken before Elisheba saw her, Grandfather confided in me in a quiet voice.

"You do realise that Josiah was found close to the very spot that his sister just described. I'm worried for Hosanna, I really am. I foolishly hoped that the killer had completed his task when Lemuel died, but this horrible game just won't end."

I had to wonder how many times I'd asked him not to use the

word *game* to talk of murder, but perhaps it was more accurate than I'd ever realised. That day, the killings happened in batches, just as wickets often fall in a cricket match. There'd been two in the morning, and then another run of them in the afternoon.

Little Samson was oblivious to sadness. He leapt up to scratch my previously clean white slacks, then bit at my shoes as we walked along. He was an animal, designed only for fun, but his new friend was older and more in tune with those around her. Delilah rushed up to nudge him off me, and there was a sad look on the two dogs' faces as we hurried away.

Even as we arrived at the shallow water where Hosanna had previously been seen, we heard the calls from the officers who had reached the far shore. I was tired of the Hindmarsh family. Tired of their arguments and arrogance, but most of all, I was tired of death.

We trekked around to them, and in the light of the afternoon, the water of the lake was as clear as the sea in photographs of foreign beaches. I'd read pirate stories that describe the turquoise water of the Caribbean Sea, and seeing the shallow spot where Hosanna now floated reminded me of that.

CHAPTER TWENTY-FOUR

We sat on a raised bank and said nothing. Darrington arrived soon after we had, but he wouldn't break the silence. I don't know how my grandfather felt just then, but I was close to giving up altogether. It was not merely the senseless violence that we'd witnessed at the Hindmarsh estate that had brought me low; it was the feeling that we should have been able to prevent it. Life was too precious to allow such tragedy to transpire.

I sat beside my grandfather – the man who had secured the confession of the Dartford Butcher and identified the Charing Cross Spider less than twenty-four hours after her most daring crime – but the great Lord Edgington didn't have the energy for what came next, and neither did I.

"At least it ends here," he muttered and threw a stone way out into the middle of the lake so that the ripples travelled back in our direction and all around. "One thing for certain is that I will not allow the two remaining siblings within ten miles of one another after today."

"We can't force them," I responded and wished that I hadn't, as this comment drew two simultaneous disapproving looks from the most experienced detectives I was lucky to know.

"It's simple," Darrington said, but he spoke in the same half-resigned, half-disbelieving tone as his old colleague. "We'll just have to deport one of them. The boy's the likely culprit. Elisheba has always struck me as a decent young woman, so it was probably him."

"What a good idea!" Grandfather clapped his hands together and looked a little brighter. "Yes, that should do it. We'll send him off to the colonies. Is that still legal?"

I decided not to mention any potential problems with their plan, as it was clear that they were only pretending that any of this would work.

"It doesn't matter either way." Darrington threw a stone of his own, but it went pinging off a rock and into the bushes without a sound. "I'll have a word with someone whose name would mean nothing to you but who has the power to arrange such things. He'll make sure it gets done without the public being any the wiser."

This comment reminded me that Darrington had friends in high and ever-so-secretive places.

"Mark my words," Grandfather began most sagely, "sometimes the only solution is the most radical one."

I decided that, if they were allowed to talk nonsense, I could too. "Very well, but Ezekiel could slip back here easily enough. What with long-distance liners and international flights, it wouldn't be so difficult for him to find his way home again."

"Then what do you suggest?" Grandfather raised his eyebrows in anticipation.

"One of those markings that sailors have."

"A tattoo," Darrington replied, and he scratched the top of his arm as though an old war wound had started to sting.

"That's it. We'll make him get a tattoo of his name… on his forehead. That way, he can't pretend to be someone he's not and come back to kill his sister."

"An excellent plan." Grandfather did something unusual then. He put his arm around me to express his affection. Normally, I was lucky to receive a pat on the back or a squeeze of the shoulder, and I had to wonder whether he had been drinking.

"Of course, the only problem," I began, and they both groaned at me, "is what will happen if Ezekiel is innocent."

Darrington couldn't see any issue with this. "What does that change?"

"Well, if he's innocent, and Elisheba's the one who's been killing everyone, then she could go over to Australia, or where have you, and murder him. It's not as if our culprit is particularly worried about getting caught. Carrying out a massacre with the police right there on the scene to stop him suggests a fearlessness that borders on insanity."

"Then it couldn't be easier." It was Grandfather's turn to present a truly stupid solution to an admittedly tricky dilemma. "We'll tattoo them both, send one to British Ceylon and the other to the Pitcairn Islands."

Darrington looked puzzled, but not because everything we were saying was farfetched. "Where are the Pitcairn Islands?"

"Right in the middle of the Pacific Ocean. It's the perfect place to get away from the world. And you can be sure there are no long-distance flights that will whisk Ezekiel back to Britain. You'd be lucky to get off there on a cattle boat."

Darrington sighed as if to say, *Wouldn't it be nice if the world were that simple?*

"Enough of this," I said as I got to my feet. I turned back to them and offered them both a hand. "You can daydream after we work out which of the siblings is to blame."

"I suppose it's still possible that one of the staff is responsible," Grandfather posited.

"It seems unlikely, unless they're all in on it." Darrington was a big man and needed quite a heave to get him up to standing. "My officers have interviewed them, and each has an alibi for at least two of the murders. They were together in the kitchen for much of the morning and would have been busy with their duties."

"It could still be the cousin," I said, though I didn't want this to be true.

Grandfather froze to imagine a scenario in which this was possible. "Yes, it could." He looked a little more enthusiastic than before, but his positivity soon faded. "We'll have to ask where she was for the last hour and see if anyone can confirm it. The only way she can gain from the killings, though, is if every last one of them dies, and then she'll be the only suspect left anyway, so I doubt that will be the motive."

"And don't forget that she has a lovely little puppy," I said out loud for some reason.

Oddly, no one chastised me for it, and both men let out short, cynical laughs.

"If only the world were that simple," Darrington said, to echo the very thought I'd previously had.

In that moment, Grandfather's face fell further, and he looked like a depressed basset hound. "That's enough procrastinating. We owe it to Hosanna and the others to do our job."

He turned to face the lake where two officers had already removed their heavy jackets and waded out into the water to reach the body.

"Very well, gentlemen," Darrington told them. "Bring her closer."

She was around five feet beneath the surface and had sunk to the lake floor just like any stone. The two men had to hold their breath to access her and then did what they could to pull her over to us.

When they made it to dry land, they turned her onto her back, and her dark hair splayed out around her head. In a sad twist, she looked more elegant and remarkable than she had when alive. She looked every bit the artist, and her colourful dress was all the more dramatic for its darkened pattern.

"There are wounds on her body," I noticed. I could see holes in her dress going up the sleeve and there was a definite cut on her neck and right hand.

"They're clean cuts and look as if they were made with a knife," Grandfather declared. "I don't think that's what killed her. They're not big enough."

One of the officers examined the fabric for cuts in order to confirm the theory, but there was no sign of a major wound.

"So she was drowned?" Darrington concluded. "But wouldn't the constable at the front of the house have heard her splashing about in the water? It is no small feat to drown someone quietly."

To be perfectly honest, I wouldn't have put it past Constable Argent to have been searching for refreshments at that moment, but I took his point. "Why drown someone if you have a knife? Surely stabbing would have been a simpler method to dispatch a victim."

"You're both quite right," Grandfather replied in that mysterious manner of his, which always made me think that he had discovered something vital. He would never have told me even if he had, but I had to hope this was the case.

"What does it all mean?" Darrington asked, and I thought for a moment that we might find out after all.

"It means that we have another contradiction to unpick. From the very beginning of this case, we have come up against paradoxes and enigmas. We started with a murder without a body and now have four more victims, an apparently invisible killer and no clear theory to explain what has happened. I have letters from the second victim's lover, a manifesto from Patience Hindmarsh which explains exactly why she hated her husband, and the warring camps within the family have been reduced to their two furious generals."

He hadn't taken his eyes off poor Hosanna for some time. "And now the one person who appeared to be at least somewhat detached from this maelstrom of violence has been killed just like the others."

I really do wish there was a clock in my mouth to stop me from speaking for a good minute after my grandfather has. Sadly, there is not. "At least we have fewer suspects to consider."

He looked suitably appalled. "In which case, Christopher, what do you suggest we do next? Should we release the two remaining members of the family so that our suspects are further reduced?"

"That's not what I meant, Grandfather. You know that I was merely seeking to show that, for all the horrors we've witnessed, we are now in a far better position to identify the killer."

This did nothing to placate him. He threw his hands in the air and walked back along the water's edge towards the house. I thought he was going to give up entirely, but then he turned around to address me once more. "Very well. As you can apparently see the case more clearly than I, what should be our next course of action?"

I paused for a moment – not quite a minute, but long enough to ensure that what I was about to say wouldn't horrify him. "I think it's simple. We return to the house and interview Ezekiel and Elisheba one after the other until we find a discrepancy in their stories. The killer is bound to make a mistake, and then we'll know who's guilty and who's not."

"Well, yes." He stopped walking and released a long breath. "That does sound like a sensible plan."

CHAPTER TWENTY-FIVE

Chief Inspector Darrington went ahead of us to break the bad news to Elisheba, and Grandfather and I walked back more slowly to give him time.

"Did you read Patience's diary that we found in her study?" I asked, as this had been playing on my mind ever since.

"I did." He didn't say anything else for a moment, and I thought he was going to play that infuriating game in which he will only answer direct questions. "It seems the problems with their marriage started in earnest when they moved here a little over a decade ago. There were a number of factors which upset Patience. As the oldest of the three boys, Ezekiel was sent to France to fight in the war. It was just before he left that Reverend Callander's daughters died in the lake."

I allowed these details to file themselves away in my generally disorganised brain, but he had more to say.

"She grew to hate Abraham because he refused to show any emotion at his own son's participation in one of the deadliest wars in history. Meanwhile, his only reaction to the two girls' deaths that fateful night was to make sure that they didn't reflect badly on him. That was the real reason he helped his children to conceal the truth. I found her commentary quite insightful; she believed that her husband's every action was for the benefit of his career and not the family. She even said that he had insisted on antiquated religious names for their children to give the impression that he was a pious man, when in fact he'd rarely set foot in a church since they were married."

He stopped talking as we navigated a stone statue that was between two curved flower beds. It was another mythical god – Zeus (or possibly Jupiter, I can never tell the difference). He had a great bushy beard and an intense stare. Perhaps it was just the light passing over his face, but as he pointed his lightning bolt (or possibly thunderbolt, I can never tell the difference) down at me, he looked just like the former doyen of the Hindmarsh clan.

"What I found most interesting in her criticism was not the reasons she hated Abraham, but the way in which she expressed herself. She writes of the uncontrollable sorrow she felt after they moved here and says that he locked her away so that she wouldn't embarrass him in public. I knew there would be an explanation for why they retreated from the local community. I'd felt that the vicar was reluctant to tell us something when we saw him earlier, and I believe this must be it. Perhaps she made a scene in the street one day and Abraham forbade her from leaving the house. Perhaps she told the vicar of the guilt she felt over the deaths of Martha and May."

If his eyebrows did not exactly inch, then they at least quarter-of-an-inched together. "Abraham Hindmarsh forbade her from owning a car and even physically locked her in her room sometimes when she threatened to run away. She was essentially a prisoner here, but her only real failing was the depression that came upon her after that difficult period in her life."

A pang of sadness stung me then, and I found a connection to the other victims. "If that was enough to affect a grown woman who only knew half of what went on here, imagine the impact it had on the five impressionable children who remained. Lemuel wasn't on the boat with the others, of course, but he would still have been affected by his siblings' experience of tragedy."

Grandfather pointed across at me in agreement. "It may not lead us to the killer, but Patience's account certainly helps us understand what happened to this family. If one of the remaining pair is responsible for some or all of the killings, we can now see how they could have become such monsters. Imagine what you would be like if your father had locked your mother away from all outside human contact. He treated the staff well in order to ensure that no one would report his behaviour. No doubt he told anyone who asked that she was a raving lunatic who couldn't control herself. Husbands have been doing such things for millennia. When existing marital power breaks down, they require another form of hegemony to subjugate their wives."

He had become quite distressed by this and ran his hands through his long silver hair to move his fringe from his eyes. I had never known that he was such a free-thinker. This kind of talk would have been considered quite radical just decades earlier – and perhaps it still is in certain quarters today. I was proud of him, as always, for championing the underdog in the face of a callous world.

"So there's no doubt about it then," I hastened to say. "Abraham

Hindmarsh was the very knave you envisioned from the beginning. Did she say anything about her sons? Did she mention why Ezekiel and Josiah sided with her husband?"

"That was another interesting part of her account. It was clear that she loved her sons and daughters equally, like all good parents should. I know from experience that we may have children who are a treasure to claim as our offspring, and others who unnerve and alarm at every turn, but when we set them side by side, it is impossible to say that we love one more than the other."

The house came into view as we left the formal gardens behind and walked across the terrace. He was still speaking when we caught sight of the constable in the distance.

"Events in the Hindmarsh family were more volatile and extreme than anything I myself experienced. Patience had two children who were so indoctrinated by their father that any criticism of him led them to lash out like vipers. She didn't blame the boys for believing the lies he fed them. He was a manipulative but charming man, and they were innocent when he first sowed the seeds of his control."

The scheming and machinations that had occurred reminded me of the books I'd had to read at school about aristocratic European families from the Middle Ages. Among the Borgias, Capets and Plantagenets, betrayal and intrigue were a way of life, and rivals were forever plotting to steal the crown or seize wealth and power. They made what we'd seen at Silent Pool look quite moderate.

"Lovely afternoon," Constable Argent commented in an inappropriately carefree tone, and Grandfather looked despairingly at him as he entered the house. The poor, slightly useless constable dropped his head, and I felt a little sorry for him.

"As it happens, I have a question for you, Constable," I told him, and he perked back up again.

"Whatever it is, I'm your man."

"Can you tell me whether you heard any splashing on the far side of the lake within the last hour or so?"

"Splashing? What, in the water?"

"Yes, splashing." I was afraid I might have to define this word, but he scratched his chin and appeared to understand.

"No... no, no, no. I didn't hear any splashing. I heard a sort of plopping sound at one moment, but I didn't think anything of it."

I considered digging deeper into his recollection, but I could tell it would do no good, so I merely thanked him and stepped into the house.

"Any time, Mr Prentiss," he called after me. "Police Constable Rodney Argent is at your disposal."

"Christopher," my grandfather called from the top of the impressive double staircase in the entrance hall. "Up you come. Quick smart." As he spoke, the young constable who had been charged with guarding Ezekiel descended, and I had to assume he'd been relieved of his watch.

I enjoyed running up that curving wooden structure. It was rather like the staircases I'd seen in historical sagas about the American Deep South. In films like 'The White Rose' the grand families there have wonderful colonial mansions. They also tend to have slaves, which is terrible, of course, but I really do admire their staircases.

"I've had men looking into various details concerning the family," Darrington told us when we reached a plain white corridor that I calculated was just above the studies and studios on the ground floor. Further along the hall, the constable we'd assigned to keep an eye on Elisheba was standing with his eyes dead ahead and his arms behind his back.

"What have they discovered?" Grandfather was his usual inquisitive self again.

"For one thing, it seems that someone was siphoning off money from Abraham's account. There was a standing charge of ten pounds withdrawn weekly. The bank is closed this afternoon, so we can't find out anything else, but it started six months ago, and it may be related to the crimes."

"Could the money have been sent to his mistress, Nancy?" I suggested, though I thought it unlikely he would have left such obvious evidence of his misdeeds.

"There was nothing about that in the letters she wrote him." Darrington stood up straighter, as though discussing such sordid topics required even more decorum. "From what we understand looking at the family accounts, he kept her in fancy hats and nights out to the theatre by paying her triple the salary of a typical secretary."

Grandfather looked a little distracted, so I continued. "Then what about the account to which the missing money was transferred?"

170

"All we know is that it belonged to a person called J. Smith. Have you come across anyone with that name?"

Grandfather shook his head. "No, but it does sound like a perfectly discreet pseudonym. And ten pounds is a small enough amount that, unless he was particularly careful with his accounts, Abraham might not have noticed it. I wonder…" He floated away with his thoughts again, and I wished I could be a spy in his brain.

"There's something else I have to tell you, and I'm afraid it's not good news." Darrington put one arm against the door jamb and had to pause for breath. He had looked more tired as the day wore on, which, considering how experienced an officer he was, tells you all you need to know about the case we were investigating. "There are journalists on the property and the news of Abraham Hindmarsh's death will be in the evening papers."

"How could they have found out?" Grandfather asked, though I didn't think it was much of a problem.

"Someone here must have spoken. I imagine it was one of the staff, but a constable looking to make a few bob for a tip to the press isn't out of the question. The good thing is that the press don't know about the other murders, and they can't come up to the house without our permission. The officers on duty will make sure of that."

I just had to hope that dear P.C. Argent wouldn't be given this responsibility.

"There's nothing we can do about it now," Grandfather said with a certain hurried excitement, as though he were anticipating what came next. "It's time to interview the first of our remaining suspects."

CHAPTER TWENTY-SIX

Darrington put his hand out to let us pass, and I opened the door for them to go ahead of me. This led to an unnecessary degree of politeness from the chief inspector, who insisted he should be the last to enter the bedroom that we had requisitioned for the interview. I eventually consented to go first and found myself in a large room painted in dark browns and deep greens. I had the feeling that whoever had decorated it was influenced by the wild woods beyond the gardens.

The room was made darker still by the stained glass on the windows, which depicted Saint George fighting the dragon. There was a wide archway built into one wall, with three large wardrobes accessible behind it and, on the other side of the room, there was a chest of drawers and a ceramic chamber set. The bed was small, hard and austere, and the eldest and now sole remaining Hindmarsh brother was lying half on, half off it, looking particularly bored.

"How long do I have to be in here?" he asked, whereas I would have expected an innocent man to enquire as to whether we had discovered who was to blame for the murder of at least four-sevenths of his family. "You could at least have laid on refreshments."

Trapped and boxed in as he now was, I noticed in him something of the whininess and self-pity of his youngest brother. Ezekiel could no longer play the cool and unruffled politician that he wished to become. He was in trouble, and he knew it.

We stood in the middle of the room and waited for the interview to begin as Darrington nipped back outside and returned a minute later with two chairs. Grandfather positioned his directly in front of our suspect and I gave up mine to the chief inspector. I'm more of a floater than a sitter. I'm like a hawk – or perhaps a falcon or an eagle – who hovers around the conversation and strikes at (hopefully) the right moment.

"You'll be kept here for as long as it is necessary. We found Hosanna's body in the lake and wish to make sure you are safe. For the moment, this is the best we can do."

"You think that Elisheba's to blame, don't you?" His nostrils and pupils all seemed to flare at the same moment, and he put his hand to his forehead as though he couldn't believe what he'd just heard.

"She did this. She did all of it." He certainly sounded shocked, but I wouldn't put too much stock in that. We'd met the most incredible liars over the years, and I had a feeling he wasn't up to their standards.

"She couldn't have killed your father," I was quick to tell him. "She was with us when it happened."

He wasn't very subtle in his approach and modified his claim against her. "Then it's just as we said this morning; she got Lemuel to murder Father, and then killed him, too. Josiah would always have been the next to die, but why Hosanna? That doesn't make sense. Unless…"

He was lost in his thoughts for a moment, and so Grandfather pulled his chair even closer to the bed upon which Ezekiel perched.

"As my grandson told you at lunch, it is easy enough to make up a story. As detectives, we are interested in facts. We are looking for hard proof that your sister is the one who plotted against you all. Theories are not enough." That wily wolf had done nothing to contradict the suggestion that we had set our sights on Elisheba.

In other circumstances, I might have told Ezekiel that, when theories are not enough, hypotheses sound more impressive. I wisely kept my mouth shut, and he responded in time.

"What can I tell you?" He looked from one to the next of us. "I'm as much in the dark about what's happening here as anyone. The only thing that occurs to me is that I'm still alive. As soon as father was murdered, I thought I would be next."

"Because you're known for causing arguments and division in the family?" Darrington suggested in a gruff tone. I felt that he was taking the investigation more personally than he normally would. It only made sense for him to want to protect his daughter's friend, but we couldn't ignore the possibility that Elisheba was the guilty party.

"No, because I was his constant defender. I believed in my father and tried to follow the good example he set. If someone hated him enough to steal into this house and murder him, then the killer would surely feel the same about me and Josiah but bear no ill will towards Lemuel or Hosanna."

"Weren't you just saying that you were convinced your sister is to blame?" I paused to underline this contradiction. "Elisheba wouldn't need to steal into the house to kill anyone; she was already here."

Ezekiel hesitated. All the certainty – or, perhaps more accurately,

174

arrogance – that had characterised him for much of the day was gone. "I don't know what I mean. I assumed at first that it had to be someone from outside of the family. It's nice to believe that your nearest and dearest have no wish to kill you using increasingly violent methods."

It was Grandfather's turn to point out another discrepancy. "Yes, that would be nice to believe, wouldn't it? However, from the very beginning, you've put Elisheba forward as the killer. Wasn't that why you fought with her this morning?"

There was a flash of Ezekiel's usual over-confident persona. "She's my sister. That's just how we are together." He shook his head dismissively, then returned to his primary concern. "So was it Elisheba or not? Have you worked out *anything* about the killer's motives?"

I didn't like to step on toes, and Darrington probably felt the same way, so we both waited to see what Grandfather would say.

He observed Ezekiel in a rather contemplative manner and slowly turned his head from one side to the other. "We know that your father was not the saint you made him out to be. We know that he had a mistress in London and that his solution to your mother's depression was to lock her up in—" He stopped himself then and looked about him. "Well, in this very room, I imagine. Was this where your parents slept?"

Ezekiel made no sign of having heard but gave a short, sharp nod, so grandfather continued.

"From what I've discovered, your mother was unfairly treated by your father. Have you got anything to tell me that could contradict that perspective?"

"I know the real man who Abraham—"

"We don't want platitudes and empty words. I told you; we need facts. So what do you know that could prove your father was a good man and not the abusive, philandering misogynist that he seemed?"

Ezekiel looked more unnerved with every question he was asked. It was hard to believe he could last through much more of the interview without crumbling. Grandfather, on the other hand, was only getting started.

"I've never said he was a saint," the young pseudo replied, perhaps instinctively casting his eyes to the heroic depiction in the window to his right. "Few great men have spotless reputations."

"You're saying that it is acceptable to ride roughshod over the corpses of your enemies if the goal you have set for yourself is more important?"

Ezekiel's head immediately snapped back to look at my grandfather, and he seemed upset to have to listen to such accusations. "What corpses? You're making him sound like a monster. He was the one who was killed today. And his fiercest critic – the woman who has spent years arguing with him and putting him down— Elisheba is still alive."

"Your mother may well be dead," Grandfather told him in a crisp burst of sound. "And I've seen nothing to rule out the possibility that he was responsible for her disappearance. There was blood all over the car she'd been driving, and it was the same rare AB blood group that we know your mother had." I don't remember hearing this before, so he was either making this up to drive home his point, or I hadn't been paying attention. "We also found traces of her hair inside, and there is no doubt in my mind that she was the person who bled in that car. So what happened?"

"I don't know what happened!" Ezekiel's response started softly but grew.

"Oh, come along. You just told us that you were the member of the family who was closest to your father. You must know what went on between them. Was she threatening to leave him? Is that what happened?"

"You disgust me!" It was certainly an unexpected reaction to the question. "People like you will make up whatever you like to tar an innocent man. You rebuked me for inventing stories, but what are you doing now?"

Grandfather would not relent. "I'm asking questions. Now answer them. What happened before your mother disappeared?"

Our suspect looked at me and I could see how afraid he was. "I can't say it."

Gosh! I hadn't been expecting such a response. I really thought that, if there was anything to get out of him, Grandfather would have done it at lunch that day. Ezekiel was both stronger and weaker than I'd imagined. He'd kept his secrets until now, but they were about to spill out of him.

"Of course you can." Grandfather gave him a few moments to compose himself. "Your father is dead – that much is certain. He can't be disappointed in you anymore. Whatever hold he had over you has gone, and you are free to tell the truth."

Our suspect gripped his stomach as though the very thought of revealing his father's secrets made him sick. "You don't understand, do you? You really think that I've been damaged by him, and now I'm finally liberated. It's pathetic how you've come here to judge us when you can't comprehend how lucky we were to be raised by such a man. I don't call him great because I was his son or for the things he achieved as a politician. I worshipped him because he deserved it."

Grandfather smiled then. I can't say whether he was happy to have an opponent who was willing to fight back, or because the very ideas that Ezekiel had expressed were amusing to him. All I know is that he sat there and smiled.

Clearly incensed by the reaction, our suspect rose from his chair and stormed to the window. "I've read plenty about you in the newspapers. Did you know that?" If this was supposed to intimidate us, it didn't work. "Even my father spoke of 'the legendary Lord Edgington' and all the impossible cases you've solved, but I must say I find you a rather common sort. I'd imagined you sweeping in here in the garb of a stage magician and making the killer magically appear like a girl dressed in sequins, but there's nothing so special about you."

I did consider pointing out the flamboyance of grandfather's amethyst-topped cane, not to mention his propensity for wearing top hats and long coats, but the man in question spoke before I could.

"Which means your father knew who I was." His voice was so calm and soft that I'm sure the furious figure in front of the window had to strain to hear. "Is that why he refused to allow me onto the estate until today? Did he want to wait until the evidence of your mother's murder had been safely cleared away?"

"He didn't kill her!"

"Did you?"

"No, of course I didn't. I loved her despite her faults. She was a drunk, and she'd never known how to hold her tongue. You should have seen her with a half-empty bottle at her side and a cigarette hanging from her lips as she coughed out her lungs. She was a disgrace, but I had no reason to hurt her. None of us did."

"Except for your father."

The allegations and contestations shot back and forth across the room.

"He wouldn't do that. He loved her in his own way. I know he did."

"He didn't love her." Grandfather looked away from the suspect as though he wanted to spit in contempt. "He told me himself that she didn't fulfil her matrimonial obligations. She couldn't be taken to functions or interviewed in The Lady about their idyllic home life. Patience Hindmarsh was only a disappointment."

"She wasn't. He loved her." The anger that surged through Ezekiel suggested that he could have kept shouting for ever, but he stopped himself and his voice dropped to an enraged whisper. "That's why he kept her here instead of seeking a divorce. She wasn't an easy person, but he loved her."

"She wasn't an easy person, and that's why they argued on the day she disappeared."

Ezekiel stared back in dismay. He must have believed that he could keep this from us. The fact that we knew the truth really shook the ground beneath his feet.

"That's right. Your sister told us that she heard it through the walls," Darrington told him in that rough, direct tone that he sometimes employs. "She said that your father threw something at your mother. Were you there to witness it?"

"Yes, I... No, I mean... I wouldn't say that they argued." He had already contradicted himself. He was too tense and het up; he didn't stand a chance against two such experienced interviewers (and the dopey-looking chap standing near them).

"You are such an obedient son, Ezekiel." Grandfather was soft and understanding again. "Your father told you not to reveal what really happened that morning, and so you haven't said a word. But your life is in danger now. There is a path of violence that has led from that very moment to this one. So tell me what happened when they argued. Tell me what happened to your mother."

Ezekiel had turned his eyes from the man who was interrogating him and seemed to focus on a point in the middle of the room where there was nothing but empty space. "She was so angry with him. She knew about his secretary. It wasn't as if he did a great deal to hide the affair, but she'd smelt perfume on his shirts and found receipts for

178

clothes that certainly weren't presents for her or my sisters." He almost sounded proud of his father's disloyalty, as though he hoped to grow up and behave in just the same way. "There were some nights when he didn't come back from London. He had a whole other life away from her and, when she found out, she..." Even knowing what he knew – even after everything he'd seen that day – he struggled to say the words. "She said she would do whatever it took to get away from him."

"And that's when he threw the plate at her. Is that what you're saying?"

It had been hard enough once and, with tears already varnishing his round cheeks, he could only nod.

"What happened next? Did you see her go?"

"No."

I almost didn't realise how caught up I'd become in the emotion of the scene, but rather than standing mutely as I'd been expecting, I went closer to talk to him. "You have to tell us, Ezekiel. We can't connect all the pieces together unless we know. Did you see her leave the house?"

"No, I didn't." He paused to think and breathe. "When Father threw the plate, his face was so angry that I thought he really might murder her, and so..." He looked up at the green ceiling of the room then, and I wondered whether he was begging his mother for forgiveness. "... and so I left. I ran into the woods and stayed there for hours. I lay on my back and stared at the leaves swaying in the wind, and I tried to forget what I'd seen."

"Was there anyone else in the house at the time?" Grandfather stood to move into his field of vision once more.

"Not as far as I know, though you told me that Elisheba was here. I know that Lemuel and Hosanna were out together, and Josiah was up in the city."

"Did you hear the car leave?"

"I... no, I don't think so. I was too far from the house for that." Ezekiel sat down on the windowsill and put his head in his hands. I can't say I blamed him for becoming so distressed.

"Your father told you not to tell the police what you'd heard." Grandfather weighed up every word he spoke. "Isn't that right?" This drew another dejected nod from Ezekiel and so he continued. "He told you to lie to us, and no one here knows what happened after that."

"It doesn't mean he… You can't prove that Father had anything to do with her disappearance."

"Face the facts, man," Darrington put to him. "They argued. You left. Your father had kept his wife locked up here for the last decade. There's no way he would have let her abandon him. It could have ruined his career, and so he took her out in the car, presumably with the pretence of driving her to the station, but instead he drove along a deserted path and murdered her."

This version of events sparked a few different questions, and one of them would be voiced by Ezekiel just as it was forming in my head. "That doesn't explain why the car crashed. And, for that matter, why wouldn't he have killed her in the woods itself? It would have been easier to hide the evidence."

Darrington was calmer now and responded in his usual steady tone. "We are just trying to understand the sequence of events which led to—"

"Don't you think I've tried to do that?" Ezekiel immediately started pacing. His previously pressed shirt was crumpled and stained from who knows which moment of a terrible day. He looked half-crazed as he shot back and forth. "Don't you think that I've gone through every permutation of what could have happened? Nothing makes sense anymore. Nothing."

I thought that Grandfather might try to charm him again, but instead he calmly walked under the arch with the three wardrobes and began to open doors and drawers to see what they contained. The rest of us stopped what we were doing to watch.

"What are you looking for?" Ezekiel asked as the eccentric fellow closed the first wardrobe and moved on to the next one.

"I'll know when I find it." He looked like a tailor selecting materials from his collection, but he soon stopped after examining a third drawer at the bottom of the piece of furniture. "Your mother's clothes are all in the wrong places. Some of them are muddled entirely, and the last items that were put back here are folded far less neatly than the rest."

"Which means?" Darrington's face turned sterner as the interview reached its conclusion.

Grandfather went back to his search, and so I explained. "Someone put them back in a hurry. It evidently wasn't your mother or a member of the household staff." I waited a few moments to be sure of myself. "If she'd packed a case to leave, and then your father had murdered her, he would have brought the clothes back here so that it looked as if she had never gone."

Ezekiel didn't say a word. He had one hand on his stomach and one on his head and wouldn't look as Grandfather turned around to us with a piece of white cotton in his hand. Tucked at the very back of one of the drawers, he had found something far more incriminating than a few poorly folded blouses mixed in with Patience Hindmarsh's socks. Even from across the room, I could see that it was a lady's handkerchief, stained with blood.

CHAPTER TWENTY-SEVEN

"It might help us solve the first murder, but what about the rest?" I had to ask once we were out in the corridor again.

"One thing at a time, Christopher." Grandfather was clearly computing every possibility that had arisen from our discussion. "If Abraham killed his wife and hid the body, then our initial hypothesis still stands. We've seen no evidence of an outside hand in any of the crimes. The staff haven't reported anyone coming and going, and we've had an at least partially competent officer on the front door throughout the day."

"So it must be someone in the family," I said.

"Which means it's probably still Ezekiel." Darrington would need to say more than this to convince us. "I accept that it's still possible that Elisheba is to blame, but we know she couldn't have murdered her father, and, at the very least, the attack on Lemuel would have required no insignificant amount of strength. Therefore, Ezekiel is the likely culprit." He wiped his hands against the side of his navy blue trousers, perhaps hopeful that the case was solved.

I'm glad that I didn't have to be the one to point out the limitations to this solution. Grandfather walked over to him and, looking the man dead in the eyes, said what had to be said.

"I know you are fond of Elisheba. I'm sure that, in other circumstances, I would have found her a sweet and charming person myself. But we must put aside our prejudices and concentrate on the evidence. You can't say that she didn't kill Lemuel just because she's a woman. And the fact that she is innocent of her father's murder does not mean that she couldn't be responsible for the subsequent crimes."

"That would imply there were three different killers!" Darrington tried to keep his voice low, but the nerves running through him made it difficult. "Abraham killed Patience, one of them murdered the father in revenge and then Elisheba did the rest. It sounds quite insane. You're saying there are five murders and three killers in one family."

"We must talk to Elisheba to see what she can tell us." Grandfather held the man's gaze and waited for him to find some composure before turning towards the bedroom in which our final suspect was being held.

The rock-like constable was still staring into space as though he hadn't heard a word anyone had said. The two senior officers filed into the room ahead of me, but I stopped to congratulate him.

"You really are doing an exceptional job," I said as he sidestepped unemotionally over to Ezekiel's room to guard the other door. "Keep up the good work."

He did not respond in any way, which I took as another sign of his dedication to his duties.

"Have you discovered anything new?" is the right question to ask when you see the pair of senior officers (along with one myrmidon) who are investigating the case of your family's slaughter. Elisheba's eyes were red with tears, and I could only imagine how the news of Hosanna's death had affected her.

Grandfather's moustache wiggled for a moment before he replied. I would love to be able to tell you that the movements of his facial hair hold a specific meaning, but if there is one, I have never been able to identify it.

"Not that we can share just yet. Although it does appear increasingly likely that your father knew more about your mother's disappearance than he ever admitted."

She got down from the high bed and breathed out loudly. "You should have believed me from the beginning."

"Now, Elle," Darrington said, and he sounded as though he were talking to a daughter of his own. "No one has doubted you at any moment. But as Lord Edgington will have already told you, an opinion is worth far less than a fact."

Perhaps feeling it would be better for a more neutral detective to lead the interview, he retreated to a corner and allowed his old colleague to take charge. In turn, Grandfather motioned for me to step forward, and I rather wished that Delilah were there so that I could at least attempt to defer to someone. I doubt she'd have done a particularly thorough job – and she would surely have spent a lot of time on her back, hoping that the suspect would scratch her tummy – but it would have been nice to pretend that I was not the lowest rung on the ladder.

"Thank you for seeing us, Elisheba," I said, then cleared my throat as it delayed my having to form a sentence for an extra five seconds. And, yes, five seconds is a long time to clear your throat and, yes, by

184

the end of it, it was quite obvious that I was merely putting off the inevitable. "I hope you've been comfortable here whilst you waited for us to return."

"There is very little than can make me feel better." There was such sorrow in her pretty brown eyes just then that I wished I had come to the point already. "Since the chief inspector told me about Hosanna, I feel as though my every last organ has been ripped out from within me." She must have heard the sound of her own voice then, as she softened her message just a mite. "But you are very kind to concern yourself with such things."

There was a rather springy-looking armchair positioned in front of the window, and I pointed to it so that she wouldn't have to remain on her feet. She reluctantly accepted the invitation, and all of this took up at least another minute, by which time I had some idea of where to start. Oh, and in case you were wondering, this room was decorated in a similar fashion to the one next door, but instead of brown and green, the walls were yellow and the ceiling red, so that it reminded me of a desert sunrise. Not that I've ever been to a desert but... Well, I think you understand my meaning.

"Elisheba," I began. "We spoke to you this morning about the day your mother disappeared. Correct me if I'm wrong, but you were in your study, where you pursue the pastime of pressing and arranging flowers. You heard shouting and a piece of crockery being smashed. Do you remember anything more that happened after that?"

She bit her lip and tried to concentrate. "I'm sorry, I really don't. The house fell silent, and I didn't think anything more of it until a few hours later when I realised that my mother wasn't at home."

She had brushed over a whole section of that afternoon, and I needed to focus on the details we were missing. "Are you certain? You didn't, for example, hear anyone driving away?"

She thought again. "I didn't, but the cars are kept at the back of the house and my study faces the lake at the front."

I looked at my grandfather, who was leaning with one elbow on the marble mantelpiece and one brogued foot on point behind his other leg. He did not volunteer any help, so I kept going.

"Ezekiel said that your other brothers and sister were out that day. Is that true?"

"It is. They returned around suppertime, which was when I noticed that Mother was missing. She had barely gone as far as the woods in years, which is why her absence was so remarkable."

"So you didn't go to comfort her after the argument?" Grandfather couldn't resist asking this, and I didn't mind it one bit.

Elisheba looked down at her hands. "I'm afraid I didn't. I very much wish I had, of course. I've thought of little else since, but arguments are far from a rare thing in this house, as you will have observed."

"Did you notice where Ezekiel was?" I was about to tell her exactly what he'd told us, but something my grandfather had probably already told me popped into my mind and I heard the maxim, *Let them hang themselves with their own rope,* repeating over and over again in his voice. It was rather irritating.

"I thought I'd heard him when they were first arguing. But then I didn't see him again until the evening. When we noticed that she wasn't at home, we split up to look for her around the estate. It was Josiah who found the abandoned Bentley on the side of the lake farthest from the house."

"Did you go there to see the car?"

She held in her response for a moment to recall the events of three weeks prior. "Not immediately. I was still looking for her in the woods at the time. I believe that only Father and Josiah inspected the scene that night."

It felt as though we had discovered all we were going to about Patience Hindmarsh's last day at Silent Pool, and even Grandfather looked eager for me to move on. We'd spent our whole time with Ezekiel discussing his parents, though, and I felt perhaps the initial burst of violence had eclipsed everything that came after it.

"Coming back to today, can you tell me whether you have developed any idea for why someone murdered your three siblings?"

She took a deep breath and rattled off her thinking. "First, I imagined it could be connected to what happened to the Vicar's daughters, but different motives have been churning around in my brain since then. I've started to wonder whether someone is after the estate. Perhaps Father upset a local landowner who wants to buy the place cheaply once we're all gone. Or maybe there's a political motivation; isn't it possible that his enemies set out to destroy him by killing his whole family? Perhaps there is even a foreign government involved. Unless of course—"

I had to interrupt, not least because she had begun to speak so fast that I was having trouble understanding everything she said, but also as Grandfather had considered and dismissed these ideas himself. "Do you think that any of these explanations are likely?"

She breathed out again despondently. "I don't know. I really don't. But I decided that I could either try my best to think of an answer or sit here remembering the sight of Lemuel's dead body and imagining what my poor sister went through before she drowned."

I felt great sympathy for her, but she was still a suspect, and I needed to get to the truth. "For most of the day, you've been blaming Ezekiel for everything that has occurred. Do you no longer believe that to be the case?"

"I didn't blame him alone. I said that Josiah had a hand in the murders, too. He's always been the more vicious of the pair, but they were in their own little club ever since they were old enough to conspire together. They've seemed like assassins-in-waiting for decades. Father trained them that way."

"What I need to know," I said, pausing then to choose the right words, "is what evidence there is to prove he's the culprit. I'd like to believe that this whole terrible affair was directed by Ezekiel and not you, but we've found very little to prove it."

"He's cold and ambitious. If Father was the worst of us, then Ezekiel has lived his life as a close copy."

"That isn't evidence." I knelt down before her to speak more directly. "You must know that claiming someone has a nasty personality isn't enough to arrest him." Though it was the kind of conclusion I'd regularly formed on our early cases, and (less frequently) that very day.

"Have you forgotten that he tried to strangle me this morning?"

"Of course I haven't. And I'm not denying he's an aggressive person. But I need you to think back through your day and try to remember one particular moment in which Ezekiel's movements corresponded with the killer's. I need you to think of something that we don't already know."

She closed her eyes and did just this. "I was with the three of you when Father was murdered." She gave a healthy pause between each comment, as though recalling notes she had memorised for a school exam. "And then, after Lemuel died, Ezekiel came in and made a big scene about overcoming our differences and not pursuing a violent path. But there was no honesty in it. He was only saying such things because he wanted us to ignore the possibility that he could be the killer."

"Yes, but where was he before that? Did you see or perhaps hear something that could prove relevant?"

Her eyes still closed, she took her time, as though she were attempting to re-enter a dream. "I listened to the sound of a window opening… it was either Josiah's or Ezekiel's. I'm sure of that because theirs are the only rooms to the right of mine. And then, immediately after, I heard footsteps outside. I didn't look at who was there because I was reading and thought it was one of your lot."

This was what we needed, and I tried not to get excited but urged her to keep going in the same calm, supportive voice that I generally fail to perfect. "Josiah and Hosanna were killed next. Where was Ezekiel (and where were you)?" I thought but didn't say these last four words, but she answered them anyway.

"I went for a walk after lunch. I couldn't stand to be in the house with all my memories of Mother. It was too tragic." I was about to remind her of the question, but she got there without further prompting. "I stayed in the garden for some time, then walked once around the lake. I came back into the house through the door beside Father's office. You can ask Charlotte for confirmation, as she saw me coming along the corridor there. When I got to my study, there was no one around, and so I sat looking over the work I'd recently done. I find that flower pressing helps me to relax."

She tucked a lock of golden hair behind her ear and, just for a moment, it reminded me of one of her pictures made of bright buttercup petals or laburnum. She was more animated when discussing her hobby than she had been before, but she soon lost her enthusiasm as we reached the part of the story that we really needed to hear.

"When I was in there, I heard something unexpected. Someone came running along the corridor and stopped in Josiah's room to start the phonograph. It produced the most dreadful racket. I didn't have the strength to tell whomever it was to be quiet, though, and so I sat at my desk, listening to a madman's laughter and watering my dried flowers with tears. A minute or two after that, I heard your voices, and I realised you were talking to Ezekiel."

"There was no other noise between the record starting and our arrival? No one could have walked past your room in that time?"

She looked more hesitant now, as though worried she might say the wrong thing. "No… I don't think it's possible. The music was loud, but I would still have heard someone walking past."

In an instant, my whole body tingled. I was finally confident that we had our man.

CHAPTER TWENTY-EIGHT.

"It has to be him," Darrington proclaimed with great relief as we returned to the corridor to talk.

"It has to be him," I repeated as it gave me a joyous feeling to know that, after everything that had happened, we could put a stop to the killer's plans. "Perhaps he even killed his own mother. He was there at the time, and his story about walking off to the woods to do nothing for hours struck me as unlikely."

"I agree." A half smile troubled Darrington's normally dead-straight lips. "He might have killed Patience, thinking that his father would take the blame, and then, when the dust had settled, he began to get rid of the rest of them. It was all for the inheritance. It's always for the inheritance! We should have known."

I had to fight to hold in a yelp of glee. Or rather, I failed entirely to hold in a yelp of glee. "He killed the father first, knowing that no one would suspect Abraham's golden child. Next was Lemuel, as he was the most naïve and wouldn't put up a fight. The final two were more difficult, but perhaps he encouraged them to go out into the woods and then picked them off in quick succession."

Darrington had been unable to stay still until now, but he came to a sudden halt just in front of me. "Precisely, my boy! Precisely. And if we hadn't done what we did when we did it, he would have got to Elisheba too. He saved her until last, knowing that she was the cleverest of the lot."

He put his hand out to me, and I took it. I felt terribly proud of the work we'd done and kept shaking it until we both looked along the corridor to the spot where my grandfather was saying nothing whatsoever.

"Oh, don't mind me," he muttered. "I'm just thinking things over before we confront our dead-on, guaranteed, no-doubt-about-it culprit."

I couldn't say why his half-hearted response upset me so, but it did. I tried to ignore him and go back to our celebrations, but I couldn't lose the feeling that everything he had just said was a lie.

"Would you like to present some problems with our theory?"

"Me?" he replied ungrammatically. "I have nothing to say on the matter. I'm merely compiling the evidence we require in order to prove, beyond any doubt, that Ezekiel killed five people in his family."

"Beyond any doubt?" Darrington had picked up on the old fox's tone. "But you just said that he's the 'no-doubt-about-it culprit.'"

"Yes, I did, didn't I." He shook his head and smiled. "And he is. He really is. I suppose I'm only questioning things because it all seems rather too convenient, don't you think?"

"No, I don't think," I said, which only caused him to laugh again. "Oh, you know what I mean, Grandfather. I don't believe that there can be any doubt or question or uncertainty that what Elisheba just told us points to Ezekiel as the culprit."

He bowed his head respectfully. "You are quite right. Everything she said pointed to her brother, which is, you must admit, rather convenient for her."

I could see that, on some level, he was right, but I still tried to prove him wrong. "She knew about the record which he put on the gramophone. She knew that we spoke to him. If she were off killing the others at that moment, how could she have guessed what we were doing?"

His jaw moved left and right, then left again, tugging his moustaches along with it like passengers on a roller-coaster as they are pulled around a wooden mountain. "Well, as you ask, she could have had a spy."

"A spy?" Darrington was as perplexed as I was and looked as though he was about to reveal his frustration at a thoroughly frustrating man.

"That's correct. Someone here in the house who could keep an eye on matters and provide her with otherwise unknowable information in order to strengthen her alibi."

"Your cynicism amazes me, Edgington," the chief inspector exclaimed. "I know it is our job to question the unquestionable…" It was easy to tell that he was my grandfather's former protegee when he said things like this. "…but there is surely a limit to just how mistrusting we should be."

"You're quite right," Grandfather surprised us both by agreeing. "I sometimes have to hold myself back from doubting every last element of an investigation. I am a cynic, and it is hard to forget the myriad cases in which culprits have fashioned layer upon layer of subterfuge in their attempts to outwit me. But if you honestly believe we have enough evidence to charge Ezekiel Hindmarsh with the murders of his family, then I bow to your judgement."

"He is the only person remaining without an alibi for any of the crimes," Darrington was right to point out.

"And he was surely the person whom Todd chased through the forest. Why would he have run if he didn't have something to hide?"

Grandfather had covered his mouth, and it was hard to read his expression. He didn't react for the count of five but then removed his hand to speak. "Yes, that is all true. I accept your judgement, and I believe it is time to put the accusations to our suspect."

The ever-pernickety detective had tested our case and found that it held water... not that actual cases tend to hold water. I suppose if you sealed the inside of one with bitumen, that should do the job. Though it might not be the best substance if you wanted to store anything cleanly inside it. Over all, my point is... Well, bitumen? Marvellous stuff!

"It has to be him," I whispered as we returned to the first bedroom with a spring in our collective step.

Ezekiel was in a chair beside the bed. He sat hunched over and barely raised his eyes to look at us.

"We know you'd been out in the woods just before we visited you in your study earlier," I said as soon as the door was closed. Why I had decided that I should be the one to level any claims against him, I cannot say. I also realised that, out of context, this didn't show that he was a killer, so I kept going. "You put 'The Laughing Policeman' on in Josiah's room to distract us when we came looking for you. That gave you the chance to regain your composure and pretend you had been there for some time. In actuality, you had killed your brother and sister and would have calmly returned to the house if our man Todd hadn't spotted you and given chase."

His only response was to wheeze. It was a curious defence.

"Answer the man, or I'll arrest you this minute and see how you like the cells at the nearest police station," Darrington warned, but Ezekiel wouldn't open his eyes, let alone respond.

"Pure arrogance." Grandfather looked angrier at this than anything we'd seen that day. "The silent treatment will do you no good, my boy. You need to accept the trouble you're facing."

Ezekiel finally mouthed a response, but it was too weak to extract any sense from it and, a second later, he fell face-first onto the floor.

CHAPTER TWENTY-NINE

"Constable," Grandfather immediately shouted as Ezekiel retched and flailed. "Call for a doctor. I believe this man has been poisoned."

"That wasn't supposed to happen," I murmured, unsure of how to help.

Darrington was more alert than I was and dashed forward to assist my grandfather in his ministrations. They placed him on his back and tipped his head up to face the ceiling, as most doctors recommend these days in an emergency.

"What's wrong with him, Grandfather?"

He was looking into the man's fluttering eyes and didn't respond for some time. "I can't say. His lips have a slight blueness to them – which might suggest he had been attacked with chloroform, but he has been isolated here for too long for that. His breath is short, but his heartbeat is slow, and so digitalis is out of the question. And I would have expected vomiting if that were the cause. When was the last time we saw him consume anything?"

Darrington looked uncertain, and so I tried to answer. "At lunch, I suppose. He brought his sister a cup of tea after Hosanna's body was found, but I don't believe he drank any himself."

"That's around three hours ago. I…" Grandfather put his hand to his head in desperation. "I really don't know what he's consumed, and if we can't work it out, we can't save him."

I hated to see him so desperate and felt I had to do something, so I ran to the basin on the other side of the room, doused the hand towel that I found there in water and brought it back for Ezekiel's brow. To my knowledge, cold compresses don't have any detoxifying properties, but it would at least keep the man cool as he thrashed about and his stomach performed somersaults.

I heard the sound of footsteps in the hall. The household had evidently been alerted to the situation, as Charlotte Elliott and the butler appeared in the doorway.

"What can we do to help, sirs?" Blunstone asked in a pleading tone.

"I don't know!" Grandfather's voice reached a new peak. "I just don't know what to do for him."

"The doctor has been called," Charlotte told us. "But if it really is poison, might milk or water dilute its effects?"

Grandfather sat back on the floor – his energy depleted. "Anything is worth a try, but if someone has given him a lethal dose, then there's very little we can do."

She ran off with a new sense of purpose, and I knew exactly how she felt. No matter what she might have thought of the victim, she didn't want to see him die. Just then, an idea came to me that I hoped might work.

"I'll be back as soon as I can," I told them and dashed from the room.

The silent, burly constable was back in front of the door to the neighbouring bedroom, but he wordlessly stepped aside when I approached.

"You poisoned your brother, didn't you!" I shouted to Elisheba as I entered the room. "Tell me the truth. This was your doing."

She was lying on her side on the bed looking sleepy, and didn't say anything at first.

"Please, I'm begging you. If you did this, you have to tell me what you used. If he dies, you will be the only one left, and that means the police will arrest you for his and who knows how many other murders. We'll find the evidence of what you've done."

"I didn't..." she said, but then her words tailed off.

In my typical Christopherish way, I'd done my best to avoid imagining that either of the pretty girls were to blame and become so fixated on the fact that Elisheba was with us during the first murder that she'd always been low on my list. But now I needed to prove that she was the likely suspect if there was to be any hope of her telling me what I needed to know. I searched through every scrap of evidence we'd accumulated, but the best I could think of was...

"Flowers! They're your great passion, aren't they? You would know which ones are poisonous and how to handle them. The police will use that against you in court, but I promise I will do all I can to help you once I've saved your brother."

"I can't..."

"Was this all about money?" I tried instead. "Were you the one stealing from your parents' bank account? If that is how this started, then it truly is a tragic state of affairs. So tell me the truth and redeem yourself. Tell me what you used to poison your brother!"

Having seemed drowsy until now, her eyes suddenly focused upon me. "I'm so sorry, Christopher… It was you."

I waited in case she had more to say, but nothing came. "What does that mean, Elisheba? How does that explain anything? What have I got to do with any of this?" I was really shouting by now, but she closed her eyes and, with a soft smile on her face, seemed to fall asleep before me.

I stepped closer and shook her by the arm. Her eyes briefly flittered open, but there was no sign of consciousness. She had drifted off into a deep, apparently peaceful sleep.

"Grandfather!" I shouted. "Grandfather, come quickly. I think Elisheba's been poisoned too."

Charlotte had returned with a bottle of milk from the pantry, but rather than going to see Ezekiel, she stopped in the doorway where she now stood screaming.

When Grandfather arrived, he didn't know who to comfort first. We swapped places, and he went to see the new patient while I put an arm around her distressed cousin.

"Are they the same symptoms that Ezekiel has?" I asked as he commenced his inspection.

He opened her eyes, listened for a heartbeat and checked her muscles by raising her arm and dropping it again. "No, they're quite different. Her heartbeat is fast and irregular, but I still don't know what's caused it."

He stood back to watch as her hands drew down to her stomach and she retched. She looked barely conscious but was presumably still in immense pain.

"Will she die?" Charlotte asked, as Elisheba's breathing became more ragged, and I resisted the temptation to get a wet towel.

Grandfather looked back at us, his face a picture of distress. "I simply cannot say."

The local doctor arrived within the hour, but he was no toxicologist and was just as much at a loss as any of us. Darrington telephoned the hospital in Guildford for advice, and they sent their specialist in a car, as there was nothing we could say on the phone that could definitively identify the cause of the poisoning.

For a short time, believing that this man would come and fix everything, we had hope. But before he could reach us, the siblings' symptoms worsened. Ezekiel was comatose for some time, and though Elisheba seemed to gain lucidity for short periods, it never lasted. The ordeal her body went through was simply too much. It is not just the venom passing through the body that kills. The subsequent effects are so intense that the heart eventually gives up the fight.

In the end, brother and sister died within a few minutes of one another, and the house at Silent Pool fell truly silent.

CHAPTER THIRTY

Twilight had fallen over the lake, and the trees in the woods moved with quiet co-ordination, as if they knew exactly what had occurred, but would keep the secrets of the dead. The atmosphere in the house had turned stagnant; it felt as if the place had been prepared for sale and there was no longer anyone living there.

Even Samson was less lively than he had been. He either sat on his mistress's lap in the sitting room, as she stared out at the darkening world through the window, or he huddled with Delilah on the carpet nearby. There were uniformed officers darting about in search of evidence, and Darrington went to interview the staff to see if any of them could explain how the two final victims had been poisoned, but they were as oblivious to the goings on as they had been all day.

It felt at that moment as though the murders had been carried out by a ghost. Perhaps there was a parallel story to our own to tell – one we hadn't even glimpsed. In this other tale, Patience Hindmarsh was driven mad by an unseen force. She tried to escape it and crashed her car before being killed. The evil spirit was appeased for a short time, but then its bloodlust returned, and it came for her relatives. Had each of the children been picked off by the phantom, leaving only the spectral figure of Charlotte Elliott to wander the halls of the Hindmarsh property?

The answer is no. Of course that isn't what happened.

The fact is that someone picked up a gun and shot Abraham through the heart. Even in the outlandish tales of Sheridan Le Fanu and M. R. James, the ghosts who exact revenge on their (literally) mortal enemies tend to do so via fright and paranormal abduction rather than resorting to pistols and knives. The killer was made of flesh and blood – that was one thing of which we could be certain.

Grandfather disappeared from the house without a word when the coroner came to remove the final bodies, leaving me alone with the woman I could only assume was the heir to the Hindmarsh fortune.

"Are you quite all right, Charlotte?" I asked when we'd been sitting in silence for the best part of an hour.

She looked at me as though she hadn't previously realised I was in the room. "That is not the expression I would use, but you needn't worry yourself on my behalf."

"I am sure you miss your cousins a great deal, especially Elisheba."

At the mention of the final victim's name, she looked down at the dogs, who had now fallen asleep where they lay. "I don't know what I will do without her. She was the one person in my life who I felt must truly love me."

The detective in me wished to point out that she had previously praised her uncle's kindness, but I wasn't that cruel. "You are young, and you will surely inherit this wonderful estate. You can build a life for yourself now and have a family of your own."

I'd tried to sound optimistic for her sake, but she looked away once more. "I would give it all up to have them back."

I realised that there was little I could say to comfort her, so I excused myself and left the room. Darrington was in the entrance hall talking to one of the inspectors from Scotland Yard, but he sent the man away when he saw me.

"Please tell me you've found something useful, Chief Inspector."

He shook his head even before I'd finished speaking. "I wish that I could, Christopher. All we know is that the staff can't have had a hand in the killings unless they were in on it together and co-ordinated their stories, which makes little sense. They'll be out on their ears if the new owner decides to sell the place or hire different staff."

I dropped my voice to ensure that Charlotte couldn't hear through the doorway to the sitting room. "Have you discovered who inherits now that the family is dead?"

Darrington pulled on his coat as though he wanted things to appear more respectable before discussing such a grubby topic. "As we suspected, Miss Elliott is the only remaining heir. Patience Hindmarsh had no family, and Abraham's one sister – that is, Miss Elliott's mother – died a few years ago. Charlotte will get the whole estate, the family business and all of its holdings and interests."

These words burrowed deep within me, and I felt a sudden surge of pain. For a moment, I imagined that I would be the next to die, but I hadn't really been poisoned. The idea that the girl I had very much not wanted to be the killer was to blame might have felt like venom, but I would live.

Darrington closed his eyes for a moment so that his fine white lashes interlinked. I knew how fond he had been of Elisheba and could see that he was suffering, but he was a dedicated officer and would not let this distract him from his job.

"I must oversee the investigation here but do tell your grandfather or one of my men if a new idea strikes you."

"Have you seen him?"

He was already looking through the window towards the lake. "He escorted the local doctor out of the house. I believe he's still out there."

I didn't thank him or say goodbye. I just nodded and the look on his face told me that he would not rest until the killer had been apprehended.

The temperature had fallen outside, but it was warm enough for moths, flies and midges to come out in their hundreds. I stood on the doorstep and watched them gliding through the air above the paved terrace. Abraham Hindmarsh, the patriarch of a now extinct family, had collected moths. He had gone out with a net on nights like this to trap them. I don't actually know how collectors kill their specimens – I doubt they hit them on the head, despite what I previously claimed – but that's what he did. He exterminated the creatures that he admired and put them on display in his office.

Was the real killer a collector? Did he want to complete the set of the whole Hindmarsh family and so went through them one by one?

I looked into the dark woods and wondered if we'd got everything wrong from the beginning. I considered whether there really could have been someone hiding out there. I would have been more positive about this theory if we'd found evidence of a better living suspect than Reverend Callander. Instead, all I had were doubts, question marks and the still very present, very physical fear that, whether she had killed anyone or not, Charlotte would be the one to hang for the crimes.

I watched my grandfather as he stood at the edge of the water. He was so close that his leather brogues must have been wet, though I doubt he would have noticed. He was perfectly still, standing in the silver moonlight that shone past him to turn the lake to mercury.

When he hadn't moved for a whole minute, I went to talk to him.

"Good evening," I said, because you have to start difficult conversations somewhere.

"Good evening, Christopher."

I was worried that neither of us would think of anything else to say, but he turned to look at me, and the words poured out of him. "We must feel no shame for not solving this case." I doubt that he believed this and was sure that he was only saying it for my benefit. "*Yet*! I should have said that we haven't solved it yet. There is still a solution available to us if we know where to look."

"I'd say there were still many solutions available," I replied. "The problem is that none of them is particularly likely. Whenever I thought I'd come close to identifying the killer, my chosen suspect was murdered, and I had to start again."

"I know just what you mean." He kicked a stone, and it went skipping over the water before sinking without a sound. "As I told you earlier, we have too much evidence to consider. There are too many motives at play, and the culprit never showed his face. If there is someone on this property who killed the family without being spotted, he has done a remarkable job. All day long, I've been watching for out-of-place footprints or traces of an intruder, but I've found nothing."

The cold was starting to penetrate my thin summer clothes, and I shivered before replying. "I have tried to isolate significant elements of the case in order to judge them dispassionately, but I didn't get very far. I considered the possibility that Elisheba was the person taking money from her parents. You see, for a moment when Ezekiel first got sick, I felt that she had to be responsible. I considered Josiah's last words when he said that it wasn't his father's fault, and I wondered whether he could say that because he knew Elisheba was the killer. Perhaps he saw her before she stabbed him and assumed that she killed their mother, too."

"Last words… like the drink that Todd made us." He breathed out and shook his head as though dispelling certain thoughts. "As for your idea, it is a possibility. However, I think it likely that Elisheba told us the truth. Her account of what she heard from her study when we found Ezekiel matched closely with what I remembered. More importantly, it would have been difficult for her to stab Josiah and drown Hosanna without getting splashed with blood or soaking wet. She went back and forth to the house, too, so her time would have been limited."

He looked up at the break in the clouds where the moon was peeking through. "It's just as you said, as soon as one likely culprit presented himself, we found something that ruled him out."

"You know, we've only been investigating this case for half a day. Just because our main suspects are dead and we don't have any clear theories for what really happened, it doesn't mean we have failed."

He let out a short laugh and looked down at the point where the water met the land. "When you put it like that, I can see that I should be more optimistic."

I hated to see him so worn down by a case and felt it was my duty to think of a solution. The chances of this seemed slim, as I was currently just as helpful as when we'd first investigated crimes together. Of course, it was during that very green period that he decided I should become his assistant in the first place. So perhaps my halfwit rambling back then helped distract him just enough to find the answers we required.

Rather than hold my tongue, I said the first thing that popped into my head. "You know, we can't know for certain that Abraham's secretary didn't come down here this weekend with murder in mind."

"What on earth are you saying, boy? The police will have eliminated that very possibility."

That wouldn't stop me. "But isn't it possible she was working hand in hand with the vicar whose daughters died?"

"No, it's not."

"Then have you considered the fact that Patience Hindmarsh's body was never found and, as far as we know, she's the mastermind behind everything. She may not just have hated her husband but her children, too. Maybe she planned all this to escape from them and will turn up in a hotel somewhere, pretending that she had amnesia or some such and can't remember how she got there."

He looked down his nose at me. "Christopher, you really are a very unusual young man. I'm sorry, but I must say—" He came to a sudden stop. "Hold on for just one second. Don't say another word."

He walked along the bank and ended up splashing into the water where the moonlight couldn't get through. He didn't seem to mind, or perhaps notice in the first place, as when he turned back to me, he was smiling.

"You wonderful fool, Christopher. You knew just what to say, didn't you? You are a genius in disguise."

"I'll try to take that as a compliment."

"Yes, and you know that I meant it as one. You were talking practical gibberish in the hope of sparking some life into me, but what you don't realise is that, even when you try otherwise, you talk a lot of sense."

He immediately took off towards the house. I thought I would have to chase after him, but then he spun back round to explain himself. "There is one possibility, but I didn't think it feasible until now. You've plotted the points for me, and I admit that it probably sounds ridiculous, but we might have stumbled across the solution."

I just stood there, unable to believe that I was in any way responsible for his success.

"Well, hurry up, boy. There's nothing to keep us out here in the cold. Are you coming?"

He didn't need to ask twice... Well I suppose, in a way, he did, but I sped off after him and soon made it to the brightly lit house that stood out in the darkness like a storm lantern.

"Lord Edgington," Darrington called to catch our attention as we entered the house. "The specialist from Farnham Road Hospital inspected the bodies of the last two victims. Based on the symptoms that we witnessed, and the state in which he found them, he has put forward certain substances that may have been used. Assuming the killer didn't have access to pharmaceutically prescribed poisons, the most likely cause of Elisheba's death was aconitine."

Grandfather looked a little pleased with himself – or rather a little more than he already had. "That is much as I thought. Aconitine, extracted from monkshood, would certainly match her symptoms. The sickness she experienced before death and the convulsions we witnessed very much fitted with such a diagnosis. What about her brother?"

"The doctor said he couldn't tell me unless he was forced to guess."

"And knowing you, Chief Inspector, I'm sure you forced him to guess. So what did the good doctor say?"

Even Darrington had to smirk at this. "He said that it was very difficult to determine, as the symptoms fit a number of different poisons, but if it was obtained from a natural source, it could be the coniine in hemlock, or taxine, which is extracted from the yew tree.

Both plants are likely to grow here on the estate."

A question came to me then, and I presented another mystery. "Why would he have used two different poisons on his victims? Surely it would take time to prepare them?"

Grandfather had his thinking face on as he replied. "Not necessarily. Depending on what poison was used, if the most potent parts of the plants could be extracted, they wouldn't need a great deal of preparation. Not unless he was in a hurry to kill quickly."

"It still doesn't explain why he'd use two different kinds." I muttered this, but he still tried his best to answer.

"Then perhaps he wanted a higher chance of the poison doing its worst. If a doctor had come in time to save them, he would have had to work harder to identify the different courses of treatment required." No longer eager to discuss the matter, he pulled his shoulders back. "Now, if you've finished interrogating me, it is time to face our final suspect."

He marched across the entrance hall to the sitting room and pulled the double doors open theatrically. Still looking as nervous as she had all day, Charlotte Elliott turned to face her accuser.

CHAPTER THIRTY-ONE

The sitting room was one of the three places we'd seen in the house which had already been redecorated in line with Abraham Hindmarsh's desire to bring it up to date. He had left his orphaned niece in charge of that process, along with a number of other tasks in the house, the details of which we had never learnt.

It was more ornate than the white lounge where he had been murdered and more welcoming than the red room in which Ezekiel had almost strangled Elisheba. The walls were a shade of duck egg green that I found rather soothing, and the furniture, while simple and modern, was smooth with rounded edges, not sharp or jagged as we had seen elsewhere. The only detail that was truly decorative or opulent, however, was the pretty young lady sitting in the bay window that gave on to the terrace. Her eyes were red, her cheeks were wet, and she looked just as tragically beautiful as she had that morning.

"I am sorry to trouble you at such a difficult time, my child," Grandfather told her once he'd set the stage for the interview.

There were three chairs there this time, and so I forwent my usual ghostly floating and decided I deserved to sit down. We sat in a neat line facing the window, with Darrington at one end, me at the other and Charlotte straight in front of us.

"I understand that you need to ask questions," she replied. "It's only your job."

"You're very kind." He certainly sounded sincere, though it was safe to assume he was not. "May I start by asking for how many of the murders that occurred today you have an alibi?"

"An alibi?" The word seemed to alarm her. Whereas, for my part, my heart was suddenly beating too fast at the idea that this was our killer.

Grandfather turned his head to the side. "That is, corroboration of where you were at the time someone was murdered."

"I don't think…" she began but couldn't finish, so he prompted her once more.

"Were you perhaps with any of the servants when Abraham or Lemuel were killed? The times of the other murders are, of course, less precisely known, but those two are quite fixed."

"I don't think," she tried again. "I don't think that I was with anybody. I believe I was on my own upstairs for much of the morning and only came down when someone called for me."

"What were you doing upstairs?" Darrington put in. "If you don't mind my asking."

She looked around the room and opened her hands to imply... something that I didn't yet understand. "My uncle put me in charge of decorating certain parts of the house. There is a drawing room on the first-floor landing which is my next task to complete."

"Ah, I see." Grandfather made sure to look at me then and his expression said, *Well, that may indeed be a problem.* "And after lunch, when Hosanna and Josiah died? Can you give us a general idea of what you were doing?"

"I..." She gripped the fabric of her plain white skirt. "Much the same, I'm sure. Until I heard Elisheba crying out for help and went down to her in the garden. I believe you saw me leave the house as you arrived, Chief Inspector."

Darrington confirmed her speculation, and this had little impact on his colleague. Grandfather remained cheery and polite throughout, like a representative of a charitable foundation who goes door to door on Boxing Day asking for contributions to his cause.

"From what I understand of the conversation you had with my grandson this morning, you were invited to live here by your uncle, despite the fact he did not get on well with your recently deceased mother and he despised the man who sired you?"

This was a loaded question if ever I heard one, but Charlotte answered as calmly as she could. "That is correct."

"You did not resent him for treating your parents so callously? You were happy to live here with such a man?" Grandfather raised his chin a fraction. He was a wonderful ham. When I'd first watched him interviewing suspects, I thought that he'd meant every word he uttered, but now that I was more familiar with the process, I could see just how much of it was melodrama.

She could only release a short hum of agreement this time, and to be quite honest, I didn't blame her.

"Upon your arrival, it was only Elisheba who treated you as one of

208

the family. Isn't that correct? I understand that her brothers and sister and even her mother…" He paused as though the word he required wouldn't come to his mind. "…alienated you."

"I don't know what you're suggesting," she replied very primly, but it was obvious that she did.

"Of course you don't – of course not." Grandfather had a Mad-Hatterish quality about him now. This was another of his special techniques. I believe he wanted people to underestimate him and so he pretended there were bats in his belfry. "A young lady in your position cannot pick and choose with whom she lives. It must have been a very trying time."

Had my grandfather started the interview differently, this apparent sympathy might have drawn a response, but Charlotte looked disconcerted and wisely kept her counsel.

"What I can't quite grasp, however, is why, when both my grandson and the chief inspector here spoke to you, you failed to describe the problems that existed in the Hindmarsh family."

"Perhaps I was in no position to say anything."

"Perhaps!" Grandfather clapped his hands together, almost in celebration. "Indeed, perhaps!" He smiled then and turned his head back the other way. He really was playing the mad September hare. "In which case, you did notice that your uncle kept his wife as a virtual prisoner and that two of his children despised him for it."

"I am not blind." Charlotte looked at me then. Whatever she had or hadn't done, I couldn't help but feel sorry for her and offered a small, supportive smile.

"Quite, my dear. I imagine that your eyesight is first rate." Presumably Grandfather would get to the point eventually. "In which case, you were aware of the balance of power in the house and tried to stay out of any drama; is that an accurate summary of affairs?"

"It is."

"Did you sympathise with Patience's situation?"

Again, Charlotte was lost for words and struggled for an answer.

"It's a simple enough question," Darrington told her. "I'm sure that Lord Edgington has no ulterior motive in asking it."

So he was in on that game, too? What a pair of rascals. My grandfather always had an ulterior motive. I don't honestly think I know what the word *ulterior* means outside of the context of everything my grandfather does.

Charlotte glanced down at her slender hands. "Of course I sympathised with her. I do have a heart."

Grandfather continued with his questions almost as if he were ticking them off a list. "You could see that your uncle had a cruel bent and exercised his power over his family in a rather inhumane manner."

Her nervousness had been replaced by something approaching anger. "As I've already said, I am not blind. Her suffering was hard to ignore."

I breathed in sharply. "Then why did you tell me otherwise in the garden this morning?"

Everyone turned to look at me. I hadn't meant to take this so personally, but I'd built much of my opinion of her on the back of that interview, and now I'd discovered that she was lying like... like... well, like my deceitful mentor, I suppose.

"I wasn't lying," she replied ever so softly. "I just didn't want you to think that I involved myself in family matters that did not concern me."

Grandfather gave a short burst of laughter. "Ha! Oh, I am sorry. I didn't mean to sound so cynical. It's simply that I don't believe a word you're saying." I thought he would give her the chance to defend herself, but no. "Your uncle, whom you claimed to love, had just been murdered, and yet you refused to discuss the motives that people here might have had for killing him."

"I haven't done anything." She was becoming more distressed again. Her fingers worked at the buttons on her black cardigan, and her already red eyes looked filmy once more.

"I'll be the judge of that, Miss Elliott." I believe that Grandfather would have gone for a walk about the room to punctuate this speech, but he was still sitting down. After a short, motionless break, he continued with what he was saying. "And I must ask you again why you lied."

She couldn't or wouldn't or no longer had the energy to respond.

"I'd like you to tell me how you really felt about Patience Hindmarsh."

She shook her head, and her jaw fell open a crack, but she wouldn't speak.

"Come along, child. Tell me what really happened on the day she disappeared."

"I can't do it." She looked back up at me, and I had to hold my breath because I didn't want to believe what my grandfather was suggesting.

The imperious Lord Edgington finally threw off the invisible guises he'd been wearing. He was no longer a kindly helper at a charity, nor a muddled hatmaker. He was himself, and it was far more frightening.

"Tell me how you helped her!"

"I beg your pardon?" Darrington and I both said at the same time, and Charlotte continued quaking as Grandfather explained.

"I believe that you arranged the transfer of the money from the Hindmarshes' bank account. It couldn't have been Patience herself as she never left the estate, and I don't believe that one of her loyal children would have done it, or the events that occurred today would have unfolded quite differently. As for the money, you must have taken it with her written permission, or else you wouldn't have been able to access the account."

"You were helping her?" I had to ask.

She held her head up higher. "I did what anyone would have. Patience was treated abysmally. My mother had always told me that my uncle was cruel, but to see it for myself was quite another matter." Plump tears came to her eyes, and I felt she was probably relieved that the truth was out.

For some reason, I was the one to respond to this. "I found it strange that you were the only person here who claimed that your aunt was unkind. You said that she treated you badly because she felt you were an interloper, but not even Ezekiel or Josiah accused their mother of cruelty."

"I had to say that so that you wouldn't know what I'd done. Their bank account was still in her name, but he would have found out if she tried to leave the house. The staff here are the most horrible spies you've ever come across. They idolised him and would never have helped her because he paid them so well for their loyalty. I opened a bank account in a false name for her to use when she finally left, and then we put a small amount of money in it every week. I was worried at first that my uncle would notice, but he was never a man for details."

"That doesn't explain how she disappeared." Darrington rose from his seat and went over to the wall for a bit of a lean. I felt like stretching my legs too, but I think it would have looked odd if we all started wandering about.

"Tell us what happened the last time you saw her," Grandfather ignored the disturbance to petition our witness.

"I really don't know a great deal more than you." She was still nervous and glanced out of the window but turned straight back again.

"Just tell us the part you remember. I'm not asking you to fill in any gaps."

She brushed the long black hair from her face with both hands and closed her eyes ever so tightly. When she opened them again, it was clear that she would try her best to answer.

"I heard the argument they had in the white lounge. Patience had known about his affair for weeks. The day she disappeared was the first time she'd confronted him about it. She believed it would do her good – that she could use it to negotiate her release – but he was furious when she broached the matter. My uncle liked to think that he was cleverer than everyone around him, and he did not like being found out. When he threw the plate, and I heard it crash against the wall, I waited outside the room to make sure that Patience wasn't hurt."

"Did you see Ezekiel?" I asked to confirm his story, and she looked at me once more.

"I did. He ran out a moment later. He went straight for the front door, and I didn't see him again for hours."

"Did he see you?" Darrington was leaning against an unfilled shelf on the wall behind us and would observe the rest of the interview from there.

"I don't believe he did. He ran straight past me without looking in my direction."

Grandfather raised one finger to get her attention. "Continue with what you were saying. What happened next?"

"Ezekiel's escape must have distracted Abraham, as he shouted a few more insults and left the room. The look he gave me as he passed was one of pure contempt, and I knew for the first time how he really felt about me. I was nothing but a nuisance in my uncle's eyes, and I was glad that I'd never trusted him."

She took a moment to steady herself, and this surge of vitriol died back down again. "As soon as he had gone, I told Patience that she had to leave immediately. She said that she wasn't ready. She said that she needed to prepare herself and that it would be better to save more money first. I wouldn't let her change my mind, and I went up to her room and started packing for her."

"There was no case when the police inspected her car," I pointed out.

"Josiah must have found it and hidden the evidence that she was leaving. He wouldn't have wanted anyone to think badly of his father."

"That would also explain why he climbed inside the vehicle," Darrington muttered. "I wouldn't have gone anywhere near it, considering the amount of blood there was."

Charlotte wouldn't be distracted now and kept talking. "We waited until Abraham was in his office and the house was silent. I stole the keys to the Bentley and charted a path to the back of the house without any of the servants seeing us." She looked up sorrowfully, her big brown eyes full of soul and sentiment. "Patience would never have taken that final step without me. The reality is that she could have left at any time once she had enough money, but she would have struggled to leave her children, so I gave her the push she needed. She got into the car. I cranked the motor as quietly as I could and she drove away with a cheerful little wave that said, *We did it. I'm finally free!*"

Her account came to an end and, for a few moments, no one spoke. It would inevitably be my grandfather's job to do so. "But what happened after that? If you saw her drive away, how did her car end up in such a secluded spot? What led to the blood that we found all over it?"

She no longer looked frightened for herself but for the woman she'd helped. "I honestly don't know. I've spent the last three weeks praying that she managed to escape. In truth, I was worried that Josiah had intercepted her, killed her for leaving his father and hidden the body. That's why I told Christopher that I thought Josiah was the killer. He was out of the house at the time of the argument, but he could have seen her driving off the estate, blocked her path and threatened her. He had time to do it all, and he certainly found the car quickly when we went looking for signs of her."

It felt as though we'd met another dead end. We couldn't interview Josiah anymore. All our witnesses were dead. A terrible thought occurred to me, and I wondered whether Grandfather had already considered the same thing. Could that be the reason for the killings?

Were Abraham and his children murdered so that there were no more witnesses to what happened to Patience Hindmarsh?

It was both a tempting scenario and riddled with holes. Luckily, Grandfather thought of a better one.

"Tell us the truth, girl." He changed his form of address as the moment demanded. Charlotte had been "my child", then "my dear" and now she was just "girl." "Did Patience Hindmarsh come back here today to kill her husband?"

"I... No, I haven't seen her since she disappeared."

Grandfather showed her no mercy and pressed for more. "Did you help her kill your uncle?"

The poor young lady looked terrified. "I don't know who murdered him."

"Tell us the truth, Charlotte! Is Patience the killer?"

"No, of course I'm not," came the response from the woman staring in from the doorway. And there stood Patience Hindmarsh.

CHAPTER THIRTY-TWO

I had no wish to be the one to break the silence. I held my breath and whispered in my head (just in case my usual thoughts were too loud) *Don't say anything stupid, Chrissy. Don't suggest that Abraham isn't really dead either and he staged the whole thing to get rid of his children, and don't put forward the ridiculous notion that Patience was in league with Reverend Callander, and together they planned to eliminate the family. In fact, don't say anything at all.*

And because I stuck to this demand, we had to endure fifteen seconds of tension as Patience walked into the room and looked about her as though she had been away for decades. I can tell you just how long this was as I had time to think of approximately fifty more questions, including, *How did she leave the estate without her car? Whose blood was it?* and, *Why is she dressed in the ragged clothes of a vagabond?*

"Is it true?" she finally said, and I could breathe once more.

Grandfather didn't answer but addressed me instead. "Christopher, how many times have I told you not to hold your breath for so long? It isn't healthy." He tutted and rose to speak to our new arrival. "Is what true, madam?"

"Is Abraham dead? I read about it in this evening's paper. That's the only reason I'm back here."

Darrington left his nice, comfortable wall shelf and approached the previously dead woman. "It's true, Mrs Hindmarsh. My name is Chief Inspector Darrington. I'm here from Scotland Yard, and I'm sorry to inform you that your husband has been murdered."

Grandfather was less polite. "Can you prove that you aren't the one to blame?"

It was curious to see in the flesh the woman I had heard so much about. The photograph I'd seen of her was quite distinct from reality. In my head, she'd been a small, mousy woman – a born victim who would cower from anyone she met. In person, she was strong and lithe and rather impressive. Despite her oddly tatty grey coat that was four sizes too big for her, and the torn brown dress that looked as if it had been designed for the meek and mild daughter of a bishop, there was still something innately glamorous about her. She stood with her weight on her back foot, apparently unafraid of the detectives before her.

"That would depend on when he was killed, but I've been with approximately fifty other people in the centre of London for most of today."

I punched my fist into my open palm then, as the last viable route to the truth seemed to have closed. Since my conversation with Charlotte beside the lake, I'd wondered whether my wild idea that Patience was still alive and had killed her family was actually true. When she'd appeared at the house, I was sure that would be the solution.

Josiah's final words had come back to me. He said, "It wasn't Father's fault," which he would have known if he'd seen his mother there alive. If she had an alibi for her day until then, though, there was little chance she was the killer.

For the first time in a long time, Grandfather was speechless. He was so used to leaving our suspects lost for words that I think it was difficult for him to comprehend. I would have done what I could to bring him back to life, but he eventually found his voice.

"Of course. I can see now how foolish I've been." I suppose he must have realised that his own disappointment was nothing when compared to the suffering the woman before us would endure when she found out what had happened to her family. He closed his mouth and didn't say anything for some time.

"Patience, I'm so glad you're alive!" Charlotte ran to her aunt, and the woman embraced her much as a mother would.

"I'm sorry, dear child. I'm so sorry that things happened in the way they did. You must have been terribly worried after the scene I left behind, but I saw an opportunity to disappear forever, and I took it."

"Where have you been?" Darrington asked as he examined her strange appearance. It was not just her clothes that looked out of place on a woman of her standing. Her hair was knotted and unkempt, she wore no stockings on her feet, and one of her leather shoes had a hole in the toe. It was as though she'd come in disguise.

"I was somewhere safe," was all that she would say at first, then Charlotte took her over to the padded bench before the window, and Grandfather rang for tea.

"I'm sorry to rush you, madam," he began once we had all settled back down. "but it's very important that we understand what happened to you on the day you left this house. Most pressingly, I must know whether you were attacked and, if so, by whom."   ·

She waited a moment as the butler delivered a tea tray, and the pair eyed one another cautiously. I thought it telling that Blunstone didn't say anything to her. He did his duty and left the room, and I could only imagine he would hurry back to the kitchen to tell his colleagues the gossip.

"No one attacked me," she finally revealed. "The blood you found in the Bentley was my own. I am dying." She had a proud, high voice and said this as though it was a badge of merit. "In fact, I might even say that I'm practically dead. I was driving off the estate full of hope when my cough became so bad I had to leave the main path. I lost control of the car a moment later, which is why I hit the tree."

Charlotte looked quite heartbroken to learn a secret she apparently hadn't been told, and she held her aunt more tightly.

"I'm sorry, what caused the blood?" I asked, because sometimes I miss obvious things.

"The coughing. I have cancer of the lungs. It came on a year ago, and I didn't need to go to a doctor because I already know what's wrong with me." I suppose this must have explained the alcoholism that had come on a year earlier. She was drinking away her pain. "My mother died of the same disease with the exact same symptoms. It was one of the reasons why I decided I had to leave. I wanted to live the last months of my life away from the man who has stymied and controlled me for so long." In that same haughty manner, she turned to my grandfather. "Did you have the misfortune of meeting my husband, Lord Edgington?"

He nodded, and she shook her head sadly.

"If you can imagine putting up with him for thirty years, I'm sure you'll understand why I accepted Charlotte's help in planning my escape."

"Where did you go after the car crashed?" Darrington asked, to keep her explanation moving.

Patience crossed one leg over the other and thought back to the terrible scene beside the lake. "I was in a daze. I don't know whether I hit my head as the car smashed into the tree or it was the blood I'd lost, but I tried to get out of the car and fell. I was able to walk part of the time and then I'd collapse again. By the time I reached the road, I looked… well, I daren't imagine. Suffice it to say that, when a motorist found me collapsed there, he mistook me for a tramp and offered me a lift to the nearest town. He was going home to London and so I asked him to drive me all the way. It took all the strength I had to convince him that I didn't need to go to hospital."

Even through this humbling experience, I felt that she spoke in much the same voice as if she'd been recounting a trip to Buckingham Palace to take tea with Queen Mary. "When I got to the city, he let me off beside the Salvation Army Mission Hall on Oxford Street. He was a dear, kind man and evidently wanted to make sure that I would be all right after he left me. At first, I found the idea of going inside quite ridiculous, but then I realised that the police would look into our finances and perhaps notice the money that Charlotte had transferred. I decided not to touch it for a month and to hide in plain sight. I swapped my clothes with a poor soul who was in an even worse state than I was. Days later, when the story was all over the papers, no one realised that I was the missing woman. I did what I could to help at the mission and not just take from them, and I was there today when I heard the news of Abraham's death."

She stared straight back at my grandfather, as if to say, *That's my story and I'm not in any way ashamed of what happened.*

"What of your children?" Darrington asked, and I wondered whether he was about to reveal the bloody events of the day.

"I didn't tell them anything, if that's what you want to know." She took a long sip of tea, and I had to hope it wasn't too hot. I'd recently read that hot drinks may be the cause of lung cancer, though the doctors still aren't certain. "I did consider taking Elisheba into my confidence, but I was sure that Abraham would interrogate her and find out where I'd gone. Lemuel would have been no better – he was terribly protective over me and could get quite het up at times. But Abraham was oblivious to just how close Charlotte and I had become, and so she was the only one who could help me."

She put her cup down to squeeze her niece's hand, and Grandfather let out a long, tortured breath.

"And that, as they say, is that." His gaze reached across the room to me and, I must say, I felt terrible. It was not only that we had exhausted our theories for who had killed the – as it now turned out – six victims, but he would surely be the one to break the bad news to Patience.

"Now that you mention them, where are my children?" There was a note of apprehension in her voice to even ask the question.

"Grandfather," I said before he could reply. "Why don't you take the chief inspector to look over any new evidence that his men have found? Charlotte and I will finish talking to Patience."

I believe he must have appreciated this small gesture as, when he tried to speak, his voice was terribly hoarse, and he had to clear his throat. "Very good, Christopher. That is truly kind."

"One of my officers will have to interview you formally at some point," Darrington told her, but he was already at the door and presumably eager to avoid the sad job that I had just taken upon myself.

"Thank you, gentlemen. I am grateful for all that you've done." She was such a formidable person it was hard to imagine that a man like Abraham Hindmarsh had exercised so much control over her. But then strange things happen in families, as everyone knows.

I picked up the chair Grandfather had vacated and, once we were alone, went to sit in front of the returning mistress of the house. Charlotte gave me her hand and, together, we would do what was needed. I can honestly say that, despite every last despicable act we'd witnessed, this was the part of the day that stung the most.

I took a deep breath and began.

CHAPTER THIRTY-THREE

Patience cried for what felt like hours. Charlotte held her throughout the broken tale I told, and she helped to explain certain elements that I hadn't realised before. Of course, what we couldn't tell her was why any of her children had died.

I found it incredible that Patience didn't interrupt us once. She put forward no theories on the identity of the culprit, and she never even asked for clarification. She listened, and she sobbed, and she occasionally buried her head in her niece's shoulder when she couldn't bear it any longer. I told her the story without going into the gory details of each killing. I made sure to repeat Elisheba's last words, in case they meant something to her, but she showed no sign of recognition, and so I moved towards the sad conclusion.

And when I finished, and all three of us were in tears, she squeezed my hand in appreciation.

"Thank you, young man. I don't even know your full name, but I am so thankful that you and Charlotte were the people to tell me."

"It's Christopher Prentiss." For a moment, I did feel all of my twenty years (and four weeks). Perhaps I hadn't developed into the near clairvoyant sleuth that my grandfather was, but I was mature enough to do what I'd just done, and that wasn't bad going at all.

"Thank you, Christopher Prentiss."

I hoped that Patience would cope with the pain she was feeling, but I still had a question to put to her. "Do you have any explanation for what happened here?"

Her expression suggested that she expected me to ask this but had hoped otherwise.

"I do not, but I was worried as soon as I knew that Abraham was dead." She stopped to clear her throat, and I imagine that she was grateful for the interruption. The coughing this produced was so strong that Charlotte had to fetch her a glass of water from a jug in the corner of the room, and a few moments passed before Patience was ready to speak again.

"Abraham stole those children away a long time ago. He tried to turn them against me and would have succeeded if Elisheba and

221

Lemuel hadn't realised what a brute he was. For the last ten years, my five beautiful children have been at war with themselves. Every war has casualties, and Abraham was never going to go without destroying the rest of us, too."

These words may have sounded cold or detached considering what she had just learnt, but I could see how much she was suffering. It wasn't about what she said, or even the way she said it, but something in her manner told me that her heart was more than just broken. It had shattered into a million pieces.

"I'm so sorry," I said when her story dried up. I looked at Charlotte and her together and felt something approaching relief. "I'm so happy that the two of you have each other – that something good can still come of all this. And you mustn't give up just yet. My grandfather knows all the very best surgeons in England. Those clever types are forever finding new treatments and what have you. I'm sure he'll do all that he can to help."

"Of course he will," Charlotte said quite seriously. "I knew the moment you arrived that you would help us somehow."

I didn't know what to say after that. It felt trite to thank them for their time, and so I lent my hand to Patience for a few moments longer, bowed to Charlotte and left them to their mourning.

On stepping outside the sitting room, my very being felt both lighter and heavier than normal. I was glad that I'd completed my task, but I knew the case wasn't over, and the uncertainty of it filled me with dread. Not knowing what else to do, I went in search of my grandfather. A constable directed me towards the siblings' studios, and I found him sitting in Hosanna's art gallery. Well, it wasn't really a gallery, but there were twelve or so paintings on the walls and he was there in the middle of the room, studying them one after the other.

"They're really quite good, don't you think?" he asked in a slow, solemn voice.

It was almost as if someone had been watching us throughout the day and painting pictures of the key elements of our time at Silent Pool. A skilfully executed watercolour showed the house and, beside it, the lake with a small sailing boat laden with people. There were paintings of each of the siblings, their father and mother, and even of the very room in which we stood. It was quite uncanny.

"They were all talented people in their own ways," I replied as I walked up to the painting of Elisheba in the hope that something in her sunny face might tell us what we needed to know. "That's just one of the sad things about their loss. All that potential has been wasted. Perhaps Ezekiel would have become Britain's greatest prime minister. Hosanna could have been the next Renoir, and Lemuel might just have broken the four-minute mile."

"We will never know." He closed his eyes, presumably to shut out the memories of our failings.

"But we will come to understand why they died," I assured him. "We'll find the evidence that explains this whole puzzle."

He would offer nothing more than a non-committal, "Perhaps."

"And if not, you've had other cases before that went unsolved."

He opened his eyes and considered the point. "Not like this one. There has never been a case in which I was on the scene for every single murder and failed to find the killer. He's been laughing at me all day long. Perhaps that was why he did it. Perhaps he thought he'd show me up as an amateur."

"You're not an amateur, Grandfather. You're the man who has outwitted countless other killers who thought they were cleverer than you – the man whose name is known throughout the country and beyond for your successes – and this one case will not define your legacy."

I took a few steps closer in the hope that I might still convince him. "You…"

"Thank you, Christopher. But I can't help feeling I should have done better." There was no emotion in his voice. He was as detached and clinical as ever, but I still couldn't bear to think that he was doubting himself."

"You…" I began, and the word caught in my throat. "You… Oh, my goodness! Grandfather, what did the doctor say could have poisoned Ezekiel?"

He tipped his head back to look up at me. "Hemlock or perhaps extracts from a yew tree. Why do you ask?"

I had already turned to leave but called to him over my shoulder. "Come with me, quickly!"

I shot along the corridor to Elisheba's studio. It was just as we'd left it after Josiah had been killed. Her teacup was still resting on an occasional table in the corner of the room and her cuttings and pressings were as they had been when we'd interviewed her.

I looked for hemlock first as I knew that plant well, and I didn't want to get carried away with the thought that my brilliant idea was in any way brilliant. Finding nothing, I moved on to the second option.

"Yew trees have bright red fruit and soft, needle-like leaves which poke out in different directions, isn't that right?"

Grandfather lingered in the doorway. "Yes. What of it?"

I didn't answer at first as I was pulling open drawers in search of what I really hoped to find there. "So they look like this then?" I held up a small branch from the lower drawer, which had been hastily hidden beneath the tools of Elisheba's art. There were six red berries still left on it, but ten or so had already been picked off.

"That's correct." He stepped into the room at last and sounded a touch more interested.

"Are the berries poisonous?"

"They're not berries. They're arils..." Presumably realising that I wasn't interested in a lesson on horticulture just then, he answered the question. "But no, the 'berries' aren't poisonous. Every other part of the plant is, though, including the seeds."

I stripped off one of the "arils" to see what was underneath and discovered an acorn-like seed casing. They were all missing from the rest of the branch.

"'It was yew,'" I muttered.

"I beg your pardon?"

I can't say how happy I was to see the look of confusion on his face.

"Those were Elisheba's last words. I couldn't make any sense of them at the time. I thought she was saying that it was my fault somehow, but she wasn't saying *you* the pronoun, but *yew* the tree. I asked her what she'd used to poison Ezekiel, and she told me in the very moment before she passed out."

"You little..." The great detective couldn't finish this thought, as he was apparently a little stunned.

"How long does yew poison—"

"Taxine." He evidently wasn't so moved by my brilliance that he would fail to correct me.

"Yes, thank you, Grandfather." I might have sounded a mite

224

sarcastic. "How long does taxine take to have an effect?"

"I would think a few hours, whereas the monkshood she was presumably given acts a lot more swiftly."

"There you go, then. She must have put the ground-up seeds in his wine glass at lunch. She was the only person there when we arrived, and the siblings all had their own dedicated seats at the table. Blunstone was too busy showing off to you to notice a few specks of dust in the glass."

"She was the killer!" Grandfather couldn't believe his own words just then and I'm afraid I had to contradict him.

"In this case, yes. But there are at least three more she couldn't have committed. Her father's, Hosanna's – because Elisheba would have got wet drowning her – and, let's assume, her own. Even Josiah's would have been difficult to carry out and get back here to hear our conversation with Ezekiel."

"Oh, how disappointing. However, if that is the case then…"

He walked over to the cold cup of tea and gave the dregs a good sniff. "The tea must have been bitter, as she added a lot of sugar to it. Do you remember?" He put one finger in to taste it and then winced at the flavour. I personally thought he was mad to even do this, but he knows a lot more about poisons than I do.

I looked around for the plant that had likely killed her, and Grandfather did the same.

"There are purple monkshood flowers on one of the pictures on her table," I remembered. "I saw them when we were in here earlier."

He inspected it and frowned. "Yes, but that looks as though it were made some time ago. There's no sign of the plant itself. In fact, it's the roots of the plant that are the deadliest part. The tiniest fragment could kill." He paused to have a think. I was frankly glad that he hadn't worked it all out on his own to show me up. "Ezekiel gave the tea to his sister, but we can't rule out the possibility that someone else put something in the cup."

"Yes, but don't forget what Todd saw in the woods." I was full of good ideas now. "When we went back to the place where he'd first seen the man running away from him, there was monkshood growing there. I even noticed some broken branches. That is why Ezekiel ran. He went there in search of poison. I suppose it's not surprising that he would know about such things with a sister like Elisheba. You only had to look at the gloves she had for her flower pressing to know that the plants she handled were dangerous."

He smiled, quietly impressed by my observations. "So Ezekiel ran back to the house and turned on the record in Josiah's room to throw us off his scent and catch his breath. He didn't want us to know that he'd been looking for the weapon he would use to kill Elisheba."

I picked up a dry white flower (which I knew to be harmless) and tapped it against my hand as I considered what else we could now determine. "They murdered one another, but why? Did they realise that they were both responsible for the other deaths and so sought revenge?"

The question hung in the air for a few moments before he made an observation. "At lunchtime, only Lemuel and Abraham had been killed. Elisheba couldn't have murdered her father because she was with us."

I interrupted then, as I felt that there was a significant point to which we hadn't paid enough attention. "But Elisheba believed that Ezekiel had to be to blame. He was her long-time rival. He tried to strangle her this very morning, and so she thought that her sweet, kindly brother's murder must have been his doing."

Grandfather hesitated for a moment, then moved on to another of the killings. "You know, I was fairly confident at the time that, if there wasn't an outside force targeting the family, Josiah was to blame for Lemuel's death."

"Do you have any evidence?" My voice came out sounding a lot like his.

"Yes, I certainly do. In fact, I came very close to accusing him on a number of occasions. Over the course of the day, I identified significant clue after significant clue that seemed to lead in one particular direction before my cast-iron hypotheses were undermined. You put your finger on our dilemma when you said that, whenever you thought you'd identified the killer, that suspect was murdered. Perhaps that makes more sense now. We weren't looking for one killer but several."

I agreed with everything he said, but still barked at him. "And the evidence?"

Looking very pleased with himself, he hurried from the room to yet another of the studios. This time, when he arrived at Josiah's piano, he didn't sit down to play but stood at the end of the keyboard and pressed the same malfunctioning note as before. It still made a horrible sound, but he was more positive about the outcome this time.

"Do you know anything about pianos, Christopher?" he foolishly enquired.

"I certainly do not."

"Well, this fine specimen is produced by the Blüthner company of Leipzig, Germany." He pointed to the panel above the keyboard which said, *Blüthner, Leipzig.* "They are considered one of the finest manufacturers around today, and I would expect a boudoir grand like this one to cost one hundred and twenty pounds or more. When he moved to America after the Soviet Revolution, Rachmaninoff himself said that the only two things he took with him were his wife and his Blüthner piano."

"And your point is?"

"My point is that you don't play a piano like this one and allow one of the keys to fall into disrepair."

To make the point even clearer, he took the upper lid of the piano between his two gloved fingers and gently lifted it to reveal the inner workings. Just as he had anticipated, there were only two fine metal wires attached to the key in question, whereas the other high notes had three.

"I believe that Josiah suspected Lemuel or perhaps even saw him killing their father. As such, he came back here to look for a weapon and removed one of the strings in order to garotte his brother. With the crime complete, he hid the steel string when no one was looking. I'm tempted to think that the police will find it if they dredge the lake, not to mention the gun that Lemuel used on his father."

I weighed up what he'd told me and still wasn't convinced. "But someone else could have chosen that weapon knowing that it would incriminate Josiah."

"Which is why I will recommend that Darrington's officers search the internal workings of the piano for fingerprints. If they only find Josiah's prints around the area of the missing string, or they identify one of his siblings, then we will know what happened."

I moved over to the window to look out at the darkness. "Very well, but how can you prove that Lemuel killed Abraham?"

"It's like a line of dominos all on end." I hadn't seen him so happy in days. "One knocks over the other and so on and so forth. All we needed was the push you gave them. You worked out Elisheba's role in the proceedings and the rest is falling into place."

CHAPTER THIRTY-FOUR

He raised his hand to silence me then, though I hadn't actually said anything. Admittedly, I was going to remind him of the need for evidence and he stopped me before I could, but he wasn't to know that!

"As for the proof that Lemuel killed his father…" Instead of continuing with that sentence, he moved us on once more to yet another of the small rooms. A younger Christopher would have complained about all the exercise we were doing, but I was twenty years old now and slightly less prone to whining.

"Tell me how long you think it would take to get here from the white lounge on the other side of the house," he demanded when we reached Lemuel's study. "Running the long way around so as not to be seen by Constable Argent who, as it happens, wasn't on duty at the time anyway."

I estimated how long a normal person would need, and then how long it would take me, and then gave up as I couldn't be sure of my figures. "I really cannot tell you."

Considering that I was the one who'd worked out the trickiest part of the case, he really did seem terribly proud of himself. I suppose he was happy to feel that we were finally close to a solution.

"The exact time is not particularly important, but I know that it would be beyond my ability. I feel that the rather heavy-set Ezekiel would have struggled too, and Josiah had a pronounced curvature of the spine that would have made it quite impossible to get back here less than a minute after the shot was fired – which is a generous estimation of how long could have reasonably passed before one of his siblings decided to come into his room to look for him."

I had to take a gulp of breath then as he'd quite bamboozled me. "Of course! Lemuel was a runner. He had pictures of athletes all over his walls." Another piece of the puzzle clicked into place. "And his window was open when we inspected his room."

"Which may well have been his downfall. He was sitting there, perhaps calmly reflecting on his vengeful crime, when Josiah came with the piano wire to kill him. The avenging brother probably didn't even need to climb inside. He could have reached through the open window and crushed Lemuel's windpipe. That was one way that he could have had the strength to kill his brother; an attack from behind in which his relatively diminutive stature did not inhibit him."

"Wait one moment," I said to throw a spanner into the well-oiled machine of his thinking. "Lemuel heard someone moving around in the corridor before the shot that killed Abraham was fired. His brother and sister confirmed it."

He was greatly enjoying himself and rubbed his hands together. "Yes, but if anyone was listening in at doors, it was him. He knew that we were interviewing Elisheba, so she couldn't be blamed for their father's death, but he wanted to make sure that the others were all in their separate rooms, so as to ensure that they didn't have alibis. With that confirmed, he moved off to commit the crime. He only said that he heard something out in the hall to rule out the possibility that he was the one creeping about."

"Gosh, that's actually rather clever."

"Not really." He grimaced then. "Don't you remember what Lemuel claimed to be doing at the time that Abraham was murdered?"

"He was sleeping."

"Precisely. So how could he have heard a soft sound in the corridor?"

"Gosh, that's really not very clever!" I shook my head as I realised just how easily Lemuel could have been caught in the act.

"Quite. Although, at the time, I assumed this was the hastily composed alibi of an innocent man. It is sometimes more difficult to understand the workings of a simple mind than a complex one."

I couldn't quite follow his logic, because I was thinking of another matter entirely. "Perhaps Josiah caught a glimpse of his brother through the window as he sat playing the piano. Yes, I believe that he knew Lemuel was to blame for their father's death but decided to exact revenge rather than saying anything to the police."

"It's certainly possible."

The dominos were falling, and I didn't want to miss the chance for a second push, even if that does somewhat ruin the metaphor. I desperately tried to think of another piece of evidence that could explain the next two killings. We'd worked out everyone else's – Lemuel had killed Abraham, Josiah had killed Lemuel, and Elisheba and Ezekiel had murdered one another. So who killed Josiah and Hosanna?

I was too slow to answer. Grandfather beat me to it.

230

"Josiah's physical limitations might help us understand who killed him. Remember that Elisheba told us that she saw him walking in Hosanna's direction before they both disappeared. I thought at the time that she'd incriminated her brother to hide her role in their deaths, when in actual fact she was on the other side of the lake, or back here in her room by the time they died."

I felt the comment about Josiah's malformation must have been an essential clue, but still my mind drew a blank.

"Josiah really did go to kill Hosanna after lunch." He savoured this moment and gave me time to make sense of his hypothesis. "She'd been staring at him the whole time we were eating. She must have blamed him for Lemuel's death. When we spoke to her here after the second killing, she said 'It can't have been Lemuel' not, *He shouldn't have been the one to die.* I believe that she'd worked out that he had killed their father and that Josiah had punished him in turn."

"She was distraught throughout the meal because she had realised that at least one of her siblings was a murderer. It's quite possible that she saw Josiah climbing back through his window after killing Lemuel. Constable Argent may have been oblivious to the goings-on here, but that doesn't mean everyone else was."

"Yes, and to prevent Hosanna from killing him or telling the police what she knew, Josiah saw his sister walking into the woods and went after her with a hunting knife."

"But she drowned," I said too quickly before remembering the cuts on her arms and neck.

"Yes, she drowned, but she must have killed Josiah first." He paused to let this reversal sink in. "He came at her with the knife but didn't have the strength to overpower her. Remember, Hosanna was broad and muscular. When he didn't kill her with the first strike, she managed to turn the knife on him."

It was all too much, and I decided to sit down in the chair where Lemuel had been killed. I felt odd and stood straight back up again, but the three seconds of rest did me good.

"So Josiah tried to kill her and failed, then died for his trouble." I breathed in deeply and my eyes opened wider. "He really was a nasty chap."

"From a nasty family." Grandfather walked to the sash window and lifted it higher to let the cool air rush inside.

"But then, if he were already dead – and Ezekiel was searching for monkshood and Elisheba was taking a turn of the lake – who killed Hosanna?" I was loth to have to ask this question and felt even worse to have failed so miserably to identify the clues that had unlocked this puzzle box in my grandfather's mind. Then, just as he was about to give me the answer, the words sprang from my mouth. "Ophelia!"

He leant against the wall as though my very comment had knocked him backwards. "I beg your pardon?"

"Elisheba was reminded of the John William Waterhouse painting when she saw Hosanna beside the lake. In Shakespeare's 'Hamlet', his mistreatment of his prospective wife, Ophelia, not to mention the fact that he murders her father, sends her quite mad, and she kills herself. The same thing happened to Hosanna – not because of love or insanity, but because she couldn't live with the knowledge of who her family really were. She may have already been planning to do it when Josiah came along, or perhaps killing him pushed her over the edge, but I'm sure that's what happened." I had to hope this was the case, as otherwise it meant that Charlotte or one of the staff was to blame.

He folded his arms. I don't think he was particularly impressed. "Let us be clear. You're saying that Hosanna must have committed suicide because she looked like a fictional character from the Elizabethan era who, three hundred years later, was captured in a painting by a pre-Raphaelite artist?"

"Well, if you put it like that, no." I clicked my fingers on both hands and searched for real proof. "But we saw everyone shortly after and their clothes were dry. It would be almost impossible to kill someone in the lake here and not get wet. It's too shallow at the edges. You'd at least have to go in up to your ankles."

He looked dead serious for approximately four seconds before bringing his hands together. "Bravo, Christopher. That is exceptional reasoning." He gave me a round of applause and I felt rather relieved. "I believe that Hosanna killed herself. It wouldn't be easy to do, but if she went down far enough into the depths of the water and waited until her air was exhausted, it's plausible that she would have fallen unconscious before surfacing. That would also explain why her body was found some way from where she was last seen."

"And the plop that the constable heard as Silent Pool ejected her."

"Ah, yes. The constable's plop." He put his arm around my shoulder to steer me from the room. "If only we'd considered its importance."

I couldn't help but smile. "When you think about it, the whole case was quite simple after all."

CHAPTER THIRTY-FIVE

It was midnight by the time we had explained what we'd discovered to Chief Inspector Darrington and then sat down to break the news to Patience and Charlotte. This time, Grandfather took the reins, and something about his telling made the whole thing feel more real. Perhaps it was Patience's pained reaction, or the sound of her sobs, but when we left the sitting room for the last time, a look of peace had come over my wise companion's features.

Darrington gave his officers clear instructions to find the evidence we needed to prove our elaborate theory, but I was confident that we'd got it right. Well... most of it at least and, if we'd slipped up along the way, we could always come back to have another crack at it.

More difficult, however, was having to say goodbye. I was used to these short, intense encounters, but our dear dog Delilah wasn't, and she really didn't want to leave.

"I'll tell you what, girl," I said as she lay down on the front doormat beside her beloved Samson and the pair of them refused to move. "We only live half an hour away. If Miss Elliott doesn't mind, we'll come back to visit sometimes."

"She won't listen. You have to be firm with her," Grandfather told me before giving her strict orders of his own. "Come along, girl. We'll have no silliness. To the car we go!"

Delilah just lay there. She didn't even glance up at her master.

"I'll give you a piece of my steak next Sunday lunch," he tried instead, and the clever creature was up on her feet in a flash. "You see, Christopher. It is just as I said. If you're firm with her, she will always obey." He ruffled his moustache with one finger and opened the door to leave.

Delilah nuzzled her briefly adopted puppy, and then Samson got distracted by something and went yapping around the room for a while.

"I'll miss you too, Christopher," Charlotte told me, which I thought was a jolly nice thing to say to someone you'd only met half a day earlier. "I wish we'd met in different circumstances, but I do hope you'll visit again soon."

She looked at me with a curious mien. It was as though there was something terribly important she wanted to tell me, but she couldn't find the words. I could make neither head nor tail of it, so I shook her hand and hurried things along.

"I'm so glad that you will have the chance to transform this sad place after everything that has happened here." I looked at her leaning against the door frame, playing with the ends of her long black hair, and I realised that I really meant this. "You're a good person, Charlotte Elliott, and I'm sure you'll make a fine mistress of Silent Pool one day."

She blushed and looked away from me. Of course, I wouldn't have said any of this if Patience or my grandfather had been in earshot, but happenstance had thrown us together for a moment on our own.

"Why do you say that?" she finally asked, her voice low.

"Because you've had a difficult life and still have the instinct in you to help people. Whereas your cousins and uncle had every opportunity available to them and turned out to be rotters."

"Anyone would have helped Patience. It was the right thing to do." She smiled then, and I was right in what I'd imagined that morning; happiness really did make her look very beautiful.

I realised that I was still holding her hand. We both looked down at the same moment, and a familiar electrical charge raced through me. I wouldn't discover whether she felt it too, as it was just then that the constable poked his head into the house.

"Sorry, folks. I didn't mean to interrupt. I just thought I'd ask whether I'm still needed."

"My goodness, Constable Argent. Are you still here?"

"My shift finished a few hours ago, but I didn't like to say anything."

I looked him in the eyes and told him what he wanted to hear. "Then I think it's about time you went home."

He smiled, and his cheeks puffed up like balloons. "Oh, you're very kind, sir. Very kind. The wife will be wondering where I've got to. But I must say that it's been a pleasure to work with you and your grandfather today, Mr Prentiss." He looked at Charlotte, then back at me, and with a nod, he turned to go. "Goodnight, all."

Charlotte and I watched him leave, and I felt that he was possibly the worst police officer I'd ever encountered – and I once knew an inspector who killed several people.

236

"It's a good thing that he'll never get a promotion," I told her once he was some way off in the moonlight.

"Why's that?"

"Because Sergeant Argent is a terrible name."

There was no time for her to laugh, as Samson started savaging the curtains and she ran over to stop him. "I'm sorry, Christopher," she called without looking back. "It was lovely to meet you but—"

The dog slipped from her grasp, and she went running after him again. I didn't mind. I was quite content with my minor successes of the day. I may not have solved the case single-handedly, but I hadn't done badly. And besides, I'm only twenty. There's plenty of time to improve.

I found my way along the path that led around the building to the carriage house where Todd had parked the Napier. He was standing at the ready, his gloves in his hand and his chauffeur's cap pulled down on his head to keep out the cold.

"I hear you had a triumphant day, sir," he told me with a wink as he opened the rear door.

"We did what we could." I got in beside my grandfather and the door closed after me with a pleasant thud.

As Todd cranked the engine, I looked at my companion. He had his hand on Delilah's head and was patting her over and over as though unaware he was doing it. I never like to interrupt him at times like that. He was lost in thought, and I didn't imagine I would hear from him again that night.

As we drove off the estate and onto the country lane, I listened to the musical rhythm of the wheels beneath the grand old vehicle. I reflected on the almost unbelievable string of events we'd witnessed and was about to close my eyes for a pre-bedtime nap when the man sitting next to me said something quite out of the blue.

"I'm ready, Christopher." The light from the moon flickered through the trees onto one half of Grandfather's face. "I'm finally ready."

"I beg your pardon?" I believe this was the question of the day.

"It's that family," he answered without really answering. "They were quite possibly the nastiest bunch I've ever come across."

"Luckily, the Hindmarshes are quite different from most of the people we meet," I began, but he spoke right over me.

"Yes, but think of all the cases we've investigated – of the Fairfaxes and the Fontaines, the Rivers family and the Templeton-Swifts. There have been some real horrors, but the Hindmarshes take the biscuit."

"I'm sorry, Grandfather. I'm afraid I don't understand what you mean."

"I mean, Christopher." He turned to look at me and the dappled light shifted. "I mean that with your help, I solved one of the most puzzling strings of murders I have encountered in my career." He gave a gentle laugh and repeated himself. "So what I have to tell you is that I'm ready."

My eyebrows drew together, but I was quite lost, and no words came.

"I'm saying that I've put it off for long enough, but I've got nothing left to prove to myself now, so I'm ready to go." He only paused for a few seconds longer before revealing what any of this meant. "The grand tour of Europe we've been planning – we'll leave in the new year."

My heart sang to hear these words. It had been over eighteen months since he'd promised that we'd go abroad, and I was beginning to worry that he (or I) would get too old for it to happen.

"Do you really mean it?" I'm sure I sounded quite incredulous.

"Of course. First, we'll go to a castle near Florence that belongs to a friend of mine. He's quite mad, but he's been begging me to visit him for some time."

"Florence in Italy?" I thought I should confirm.

"Well obviously not Florence in Staffordshire." He tittered quietly at this. At least he was enjoying himself. "We'll start in Italy, then go on to Spain, France, and maybe Germany. Perhaps I'll feel brave, and we'll venture beyond the Continent. Who knows where the wind will carry us and whether my old knees will take the strain."

I didn't know what to say to any of this, but he didn't seem to notice. In fact, he was nattering away at double speed.

"We'll get Christmas out of the way first, of course. I thought perhaps you'd like to spend it at home with your parents before our big trip, but then I'll book a pair of seats on the Golden Arrow or a flight from Croydon Airport and, before you know it, we'll have crossed the English Channel on our way to foreign climes." He came to a sudden stop and looked at me searchingly through the darkness. "You do still want to go, don't you?"

238

I didn't have to think. I practically shouted the answer. "Yes, of course, I do. The world is our oyster."

The End (For Now...)

Get another

LORD EDGINGTON ADVENTURE

absolutely **free**…

Download your free novella at
www.benedictbrown.net

"LORD EDGINGTON INVESTIGATES..."

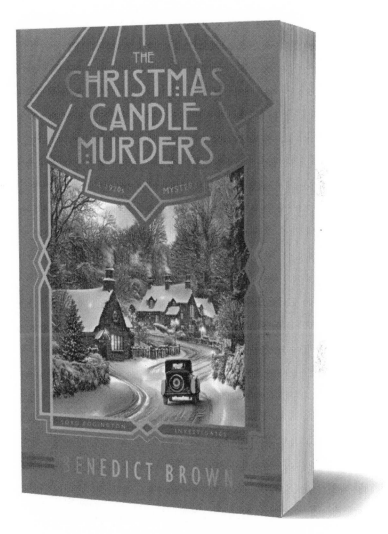

The fifteenth full-length mystery will be available in **November 2024** at amazon.

Sign up on my website to the readers' club to know when it goes on sale.

ABOUT THIS BOOK

I'm aware that at least two other novels in this series have finished in a somewhat similar fashion, but Chrissy and his grandfather really will be heading to Italy in the new year. I must confess it is my fault that Lord Edgington and Co. have taken so long to head off on holiday, but there were so many stories I wanted to tell in Britain that I put off my plan for a year longer than expected. In fact, there are still two books I wanted to write – one about a flying lesson, as suggested back in the first Christmas book, and one exploring Todd's background – but I will try to get around to those at some point later.

As for this book, let's start with the title. Silent Pool is a real place, though I have admittedly changed it somewhat to fit the story. It's located in Surrey, not far from where I grew up, and is most famous for its association with Agatha Christie. In fact, the idea for this book came to me when listening to an excellent episode of the podcast "Shedunnit", which focuses on the Golden Age of Detective Fiction between the two world wars. The episode in question, "The Lady Vanishes", discusses the period when Christie disappeared in December 1926. Her husband had recently revealed that he was having an affair with his secretary (called Nancy, as it happens) and the newly successful detective novelist left her home in Berkshire one evening and drove off into the night. Her car was found the next morning with its lights still on, not far from the edge of Silent Pool, and, for the next eleven days, no one knew where she was.

During that time, at least one senior police officer became convinced that she was dead and quite possibly lying at the bottom of the lake. According to the London Daily Chronicle, Deputy Chief Constable Kenward of the Surrey Police promised, "Every pool and ravine is to be searched, and every yard of ground is to be combed" in an area of forty square miles. Professional divers were brought in to search and then dredge the pool. Obviously, nothing was found, but it did catch the public's imagination, and in several of the articles I've read, they describe the "sinister Silent Pool" and the eerie atmosphere there. I do have to wonder how much of the press and police interest in the place was down to its evocative name!

If you've just read this novel, you'll know that I didn't set out to write an explanation for what happened to Christie during that time. Plenty of authors and screenwriters have already done that and, I think the reality – that Christie went to a hotel in Yorkshire, checked in under the name of her husband's mistress, and wasn't recognised for almost two weeks – is less mysterious than people would like to imagine. The curious part that no one seems to know is how she got from that lake to the hotel in the north of England and whether, as her husband claimed, she really suffered from amnesia and couldn't explain what happened. What interested me was using the beginning of her story as a starting point for a rather unique mystery.

Spoiler alert... skip this if you are one of those people who start at the back of the book! I've never written a story before in which I actually wanted my readers to pick up on every clue. There is a trope in mysteries called the orgy of evidence. This is where the killer has planted so many fake clues that it alerts the detective to their artificiality. I wanted to try a spin on that in which (**here's the spoiler...**) everyone killed someone else. I suppose there is a dash of "Murder on the Orient Express" in this, but I was trying to do it in my own way – which isn't to say that no one has done this before, but it's new to me.

I'm not an author who sets out to include specific tropes in my books – or even writes to a pre-existing structure or template – but I do like playing with ideas that are common in so many mysteries, and I hope I've kept you on your toes this time around. One thing I do include, however, is plenty of references to friends, readers and people from history and popular culture. When I can't think what to call a minor character, I normally search through the names of people I know, and have used most from my extended family by this point. As a result, my cousin Charlotte Elliott was very put out that her brothers had got a mention but she hadn't, so I hope this book addresses that omission. (**Spoiler alert:** I even made her a nice character!)

There's another trope that the book subverts, which I've actively avoided elsewhere. I met someone recently who, when I told her that I was a mystery writer, asked me whether the killer in my books is normally the husband. The most common response I get is the immediate tittering claim "The butler did it!" so this was preferable to that. However, as far as I can remember, I've never had a husband kill his wife and only written a couple of books in which the story begins with a woman being murdered.

I mention this because of the trend of "fridging" which is particularly common in comic books, but also a lot of crime fiction. The term comes from the discovery in a particular Batman comic of a major female character who has been murdered and her body dumped in a fridge. This exemplifies the type of story in which a male protagonist is driven by the need to avenge his lost love. When you realise just how common this plot device is, you'll understand why I've tried to avoid it, and it was certainly fun turning it on its head through the character of Patience Hindmarsh.

Another interesting point about Silent Pool that I didn't get around to mentioning in the book itself is that it has been described as the most haunted lake in Britain. There is a story from the twelfth century that tells of a young maid who was bathing in the water when a well-dressed gentleman rode by and made overtures to her. She spurned his advances, so he rode his horse closer, forcing her into the depths of the lake where she drowned. When her father, a woodcutter, went to look for her, all he found was the nobleman's hat which (shock horror) bore the mark of the wicked Prince John. The first account of this appears, not nine hundred years ago, but in a history book from 1858. Nevertheless, it is said that the ghost of the woodcutter's daughter still appears at Silent Pool at midnight each night. If anyone fancies going to confirm this, please let me know what you find.

Even though I've enlarged the lake, and there is no manor house beside it in real life, I did try to keep some of Silent Pool's unique characteristics. It is believed that it was an ancient chalk quarry that was fed by natural springs, and as a result of the stone, the water takes on a turquoise or greenish hue depending on the light. Although it was recently blighted by an invasive weed, the water is now incredibly clear once more and, since 2014, has been used in the distillation process by the neighbouring Silent Pool Gin Distillery.

As for the house at Silent Pool, or the rather ominous sounding Lodine as no one calls it, the building doesn't feature on the cover for once, so I wanted to create a slightly more modern setting than the houses in most of the novels I've written. In the early part of the twentieth century, architecture was still influenced by the British Arts and Crafts movement. This style was particularly associated with the polymath William Morris, whom I grew up knowing about as his textile factory was close to my childhood home. Morris's own home, the Red House, which was completed back in 1860, was part of the inspiration for the Hindmarshes' property and you can still visit it today.

However, I also looked at more modern buildings, such as Coleton Fishacre, which is not too far from Christie's summer estate at Greenway in Devon. The house was built between 1923 and 1926 for the theatre impresario Rupert D'Oyly Carte, who has appeared in these pages in previous books. The house matched the Arts and Crafts aesthetic by using locally quarried stone, relying on traditional craftsmanship and with its focus on function over style. However, in the interiors, you can see the influence of burgeoning twentieth century trends in the moulded doorways, patterned carpets and use of modern lighting. A few years later, D'Oyly Carte commissioned a refurbishment of his Savoy Hotel, which gave it the Art Deco look it retains to this day.

The Art Deco movement would only have been starting to have an impact in Britain by 1928, and in actual fact, the term was not used until much later. I'm curious how often mystery writers describe Art Deco features in their books set in the twenties, when actually the term wasn't coined until 1966. I had a good look through papers from the period to find out how it was described at the time, and the most common expression seems to be *Style Moderne,* which fits with its roots in France.

I had to do a bit of retconning in this book – that's where writers write something which corrects or changes something that seemed to be an established fact from earlier in a series. If you go back to the first page of the first Edgington novel, you'll see that Chrissy described Delilah as old. On average, golden retrievers live for about twelve years ago. If she was already old back in 1925 and we're on the cusp of 1929, then she wouldn't have much life left in her. As I have no wish to deal with a thousand e-mailed complaints about the tragic bit in a book in which I killed off a beloved dog, I decided to find a fix. Voila! Delilah is now only about five years old and will be with us for a long time.

As I mentioned in my note at the beginning of the book, I wanted this one to be a touch more serious and unsettling, as I know that the following titles are going to stick to the jollier style of mysteries that have been my stock in trade for the last five years. I also wanted to test myself as I'm hoping to have a break from my main genre next year to write a standalone thriller with a bit more edge. I love these books, as you all know, but writing in series can be quite exhausting, and sometimes a change is as good as a rest. I wonder whether I'll be any good at writing books without silly and eccentric characters. You'll just have to stick with me to find out.

If you loved the story and have the time, please write a review at Amazon. Most books get one review per thousand readers so I would be infinitely appreciative if you could help me out.

THE MOST INTERESTING THINGS I DISCOVERED WHEN RESEARCHING THIS BOOK...

Welcome back to the always long and frequently interesting chapter in which I babble on about the things that amazed me when I was researching this story.

Let's start at the beginning with the very first thing I looked up. I needed to know whether ostriches really do bury their heads in the sand, and I was frankly unsurprised to discover that it's largely untrue. It can be said that they will sometimes duck closer to the ground, laying the head and neck flat to stop predators spotting them. However, according to the (of course there is one) American Ostrich Association, the only time they put their heads underground is to check on their eggs, which they bury to keep warm and turn from time to time when needed. This only takes a few seconds and does not fit the metaphor we use of ignoring one's problems.

In fact, ostriches would be unlikely to behave in such a way as they are, to use a technical term, mega badasses. First of all, they are the fastest animals on two legs. They can run at a top speed of 43.5 mph and can keep running at 30 mph for around twenty minutes. I would say they are the roadrunners of the bird kingdom, but that title has already been taken by, well, the roadrunner. Incidentally, roadrunners can only manage a mere twenty miles per hour and, were the cartoon in any way realistic, the coyote is far faster and would be able to gobble up the birdy who causes poor Wile E. so much trouble.

To return to the real king of the birds, the ostrich is also the heaviest and largest avian. It lays the world's biggest eggs and, wait, it can lay claim to an even more impressive superlative. Thanks to its powerful kick, it is the world's most dangerous bird and is responsible for, on average, up to three deaths a year in South Africa – which kind of puts people's fear of pigeons into perspective. All in all, it is a real living dinosaur, and we should admire and fear it in equal measure.

Sticking with fast things, let's talk about Lord Edgington's rarely spotted black Napier limousine. For Edgington car watchers, this is not a new purchase, but an old one he must have had in his massive garage where Todd keeps the cars clean. D. Napier & Son dates back one hundred years from the time when the wily Lord's car was made and started life as a precision engineering company in London. The company would eventually specialise in aeronautical engines, which were included in several famous World War Two aircraft and won many land-speed records, but during the Edwardian era, they built luxury cars owned by royals and politicians. Or, as a Bonham's auction listing put it…

"Napier's list of customers, like the passenger list of the Titanic, recalls all the thundery afternoon sunlight of Edwardian England. Here is ancient, landed wealth: here is the recent profit of industry and finance: here are the rich Radical politicians. Here is a memory of the days when there were forty servants below stairs at Longleat…"[1]

So they made swanky automobiles, but why have I added this otherwise largely forgotten vehicle to Edgington's collection? Well, I read a particularly curious story about them and wanted to repeat it here. Robert Harris, the brilliant British author of "Fatherland" and "Pompeii", has just released a book about the Liberal prime minister, Lord Asquith. Harris's research has thrown light on the period at the start of the First World War during which Asquith led Britain but was at the same time engaged in an affair with a woman thirty-five years younger than he was. I haven't had time to read the book, "Precipice", but it sounds fascinating and describes how Asquith was distracted and even influenced by the affair at a time when he was making such world-changing decisions as taking Britain into a war. But the thing I really liked about the article I read was that Asquith and his lover had steamy rendezvous in the back of his blacked-out 1908 Napier limousine. Scandal!

The car itself is a huge black affair that wouldn't look out of place parked

1   https://cars.bonhams.com/auction/25455/lot/664/the-ex-ivor-read1908-napier-45hp-type-23-six-cylinder-open-drive-limousine-chassis-no-4160/

on the Addams Family's driveway or in a funeral procession. Debate over whether the relationship between Asquith and his daughter's twenty-six-year-old best friend was romantic has raged for some time, though the fact he had his car specially adapted for privacy during their Friday afternoon tête-à-têtes, and that he wrote to her three times a day, should probably have put that question to bed many years ago.

From one man who hid his secrets to another. Harry Houdini doesn't need any introduction, but I did have to find out when he performed in London in Chrissy's lifetime. One of my favourite uses of the British Newspaper Archive is to look for contemporary reviews and listings of newly released books and shows, as it can help to date these events very precisely. Houdini really did perform at the Palladium in May 1920, and was billed as "Houdini (Himself)" to ensure that people knew it really was him. He was apparently paid the modern equivalent of £140,000 a week, which was a record at the time for that venue. That sounds like a lot of money but doesn't compare to the millions a night that Taylor Swift or Oasis are currently making. Still, I wouldn't complain if someone offered me that to get up on stage and read my books.

He did three performances a day for three weeks and was on a bill with singers, acrobats, black-face minstrels and contortionists. Irritatingly and interestingly for me, I searched through the names of the other acts one by one, sometimes quite painstakingly, but there were no magicians or conjurors, so I had to add one. Brian Godfrey really was a magician at the time, but all I could find out about him online was that he invented a particular trick that is still on sale today – featuring oversized cards and a guillotine – was a member of Houdini's Magician's Club, which was launched to rival the Magic Circle, and one newspaper article described Godfrey as "shy". I've no idea whether he was a genuinely good magician, but I have resurrected him here for Chrissy to be amazed by.

Meanwhile, the greatest escapologist in history, or "King of the Handcuffs", as one paper called Houdini, really did have an incredible life, but it's so widely reported that I don't need to go into it here. One final interesting titbit about him, which I didn't know or had forgotten, was that he died on Halloween. I remember when I was five and Halloween really wasn't a big deal in Britain. We were on holiday in a seafront hotel in Portsmouth for some reason, and there was a special episode on TV with the 1980s British equivalent to Houdini, Paul Daniels. He showed a video of Houdini escaping from a straitjacket, and then when the cameras returned to the live audience, Daniels was standing in front of a real iron maiden, which he proceeded to lock himself inside before the spiked door snapped shut. The credits rolled without revealing whether he had survived, and my brothers and I were left terrified. We weren't the only ones. So many people rang into the BBC that after the next programme (a repeat of "Monty Python's Flying Circus") had finished, they had to get Daniels back on to explain that he hadn't been killed. Creepy stuff.

(More spoilers coming now…) Far scarier than that, however, is cancer. Whoa! Sorry for the sudden dip in mood there. That was dark… but true. There is a key plot point in this book which involves lung cancer, and I needed to read up on it a little to check my facts. I have to say that I was amazed by what I discovered, not least because, until the twentieth century, it was an extremely rare disease, and so the sudden epidemic led to doctors searching for an explanation. As Chrissy can attest, by 1928, there were articles in the papers pointing to "meat eating, tarred roads and tea that is swallowed too hot"[2] as the causes.

I was curious to find out when the connection between smoking and lung cancer was made. The most interesting elements are summed up in this brilliant abstract from a paper by Robert N. Proctor, Professor of the History of Science at Stanford University.

"Lung cancer was once a very rare disease, so rare that doctors took special notice when confronted with a case, thinking it a once-in-a-lifetime oddity. Mechanisation and mass marketing towards the end of the 19th century popularised the cigarette habit, however, causing a global lung cancer epidemic. Cigarettes were recognised as the cause of the epidemic in the 1940s and 1950s, with the confluence of studies from epidemiology, animal experiments, cellular pathology and chemical analytics."

Terrifyingly, he goes on to explain the tobacco companies' response

---

2   The Scotsman, Tuesday 09 October 1928

and point out exactly what each life was worth to them. "Cigarette manufacturers disputed this evidence, as part of an orchestrated conspiracy to salvage cigarette sales... As late as 1960, only one-third of all US doctors believed that the case against cigarettes had been established. The cigarette is the deadliest artefact in the history of human civilisation. Cigarettes cause about 1 lung cancer death per 3 or 4 million smoked, which explains why the scale of the epidemic is so large today. Cigarettes cause about 1.5 million deaths from lung cancer per year, a number that will rise to nearly 2 million per year by the 2020s or 2030s, even if consumption rates decline in the interim... Cigarette makers make about a penny in profit for every cigarette sold, which means that the value of a life to a cigarette maker is about US$10,000."[3]

The link to cigarettes was first made in Britain by two researchers with the brilliant names Richard Doll and Bradford Hill. They interviewed 651 lung cancer sufferers in hospitals in 1949 and discovered that all but two of them were smokers. Doll immediately quit his own habit as a result, and the pair later went on to do a similar survey of working doctors. Of the 59,600 they wrote to, 200 of the smokers would be dead in two years compared to very few who abstained. It was this paper in particular which helped to establish the link and may have saved millions of lives over the subsequent years.

I was going to keep talking about poisons now, but despite having to sacrifice a good segue, I'll lighten the mood instead. "The Laughing Song" can trace its history back to a singer called George W. Johnson, who was the first African American star of the recorded era. Released in 1890, it sold more than 50,000 copies in the first four years and became the best-selling phonograph record in the world. What's particularly impressive about this is that there was no way to copy records mechanically, and so Johnson had to record it thousands of times to satisfy demand.

---

3   Proctor RN. The history of the discovery of the cigarette-lung cancer link: evidentiary traditions, corporate denial, global toll. Tob Control. 2012 Mar;21(2):87-91. doi: 10.1136/tobaccocontrol-2011-050338. Erratum in: Tob Control. 2013 Jan;22(1):62. PMID: 22345227.

"The Laughing Policeman" from 1922 owed a debt to, and borrowed the melody from, this original record, but the lyrics were written by a British variety show comedian by the name of Charles Penrose and his wife, Mabel Anderson. Penrose would go on to release various different laughing songs and find a career in radio comedy. He would even make cameos in films in the thirties and forties, often laughing as he did so. It is estimated that his hit record sold over a million copies by the end of the twentieth century. Coincidentally, Penrose was born in Biggleswade, Bedfordshire, a place I've never been to, but after which I quite randomly named a character in the next Marius book.

Staying with music, I tried to find out the cost of a high-end piano in 1928, and I came across an advertisement in the Mirror which gave a long list of prices with names and pictures. Blüthner is one of the classic German piano manufacturers, and their instruments have been used by everyone from Rachmaninoff – he really did make that grand claim which Edgington quotes – to the Beatles. In fact, the Fab Four used a Blüthner to record "Let It Be", their last album in 1970.

There was even such a piano made for the Hindenburg zeppelin. To save weight, parts were made of aluminium, and it became the first piano used in flight as it crossed back and forth over the Atlantic in 1936. Luckily, the piano was removed before the tragic crash a year later; less luckily, it was destroyed when the Blüthner factory was bombed during the war.

The model of the Blüthner I saw in the paper was a "boudoir grand" and so I had to look that up, too. It turns out that this type of piano is slightly larger than a baby grand and known for having a rich, balanced sound. To my surprise, the first image that came up in my search not only belonged to Agatha Christie, but as it happens, I myself played it when we visited her house in Devon earlier this year. What are the chances?

I was tempted to describe the rabbit hole I then went down reading about the Hindenburg disaster, but it is so far removed from the plot of this book that I will only say it is very interesting, and you should give it a read. The events of that fateful night in 1937 seemed to have put paid to airship travel, but a new generation might well be on the horizon. A hybrid electric/helium ship called Airlander 10 has been built in the north of England, and a Spanish airline has already ordered twenty of them, with the first ships arriving in 2026. The plan has been delayed several times, but I can't wait to see them floating past my window (especially as the prototype looks like a giant flying bottom, and I will look at it and laugh and think of Chrissy).

Sticking with... innovation, maybe? The British Empire Exhibition! Such exhibitions were a big deal through the Victorian era and into the twentieth century. It's the kind of thing you'd read about and think, *That sounds nice, why don't they do that anymore?* But the only one that I know of in my lifetime was at the Millenium Dome in London in 2000, and it was widely regarded as terrible, with very little to show for the millions of pounds spent on it.

However, the exhibition of 1924 was (at least conceptually) more successful. It was staged at a time when Britain's power on the international stage was waning, and this was considered a way of reminding people what made the Empire great, even as its exit from India had been confirmed. In preparation, a ten-month tour of the world was organised by one of the managers of the exhibition, and who do you think he invited along with him? That's right (I'll assume you guessed correctly because it seems that almost everything that I research almost magically comes back to her): it was Agatha Christie and her husband, not long before he left her for his secretary...

The planning of the Empire Exhibition was heavily influenced by the then Prince of Wales. He pushed for the exhibition to leave the legacy of a national sports stadium, and so Empire Stadium (or Wembley Stadium as it's now known) was born. It was built on the site of Watkin's folly, an Eiffel Tower-esque structure of which only the first level was ever completed. The iconic stadium remained pretty much the same for the next 76 years before the wonderful Roman and Indian inspired architecture was demolished. Sad as this is, its life could have been a lot shorter, as it was sold for demolition after the exhibition to a financier called James White. Wait, I love this bit. James White was quite a character and has appeared in these pages before. He worked his way up from nothing but wasted his fortune by 1927, partly because he had bought and lost a lot of money on Daly's Theatre in London, where my novel "A Killer in the Wings" is set. You've got to love a coincidence – in fact, I even named a character after him.

The exhibition featured separate pavilions for 56 different nations within the British Empire to showcase their culture and wares – the Australian pavilion had a sixteen-foot ball of wool and, more contentiously, a sculpture made of butter of a famous British cricketer losing to the Aussies. All in all, it sounds like a good day out, with funfairs, international restaurants, a boating lake and even a working model coal mine. However, it was not a financial success and, despite 27 million people visiting over two years, it lost millions of pounds, whereas the twenty-first century expo in the millennium dome cost £789 million, left us without a great legacy, and was visited by just six million people.

More positive are memories of the first ever football match played at Wembley, which became known as the "White Horse" FA Cup Final. It occurred in April 1923 just a few days after the stadium was completed, and the organisers hadn't thought it necessary to introduce ticketing. As a result, anything up to 300,000 people turned up to watch in a space designed for 125,000. There were so many people that the spectators occupied the pitch and there was no room for Bolton Wanderers and West Ham to play. That was until the Metropolitan Police pushed back the huddled fans to clear the way, and a mounted constable by the name of George Scorey and his horse Billy turned up to cut through the crowds. It was an incredible moment, unless you were an Irons fan, as West Ham lost 2-0.

Far away from north London is a place called Russia. How's that for a connection? I have a Russian sister-in-law, so I thought I would be safe to use her name for the fictional countess in my book. Luckily, one of my very first alpha readers speaks Russian and noticed that the surname I had used, Poltorak, was not native. It turns out my wife's brother's wife has Kazakh ancestry, so I had to change the name to Vorontsova, which really was an aristocratic line before the Russian Revolution.

I looked into the history of White Russian émigrés, as they are such a feature of Golden Age detective fiction that I was curious to find out more about them. The term mainly refers to exiles who were against the Bolshevik movement and uprising of 1917. They were not just aristocrats but could be from any class or occupation, from the intelligentsia and nobility to businessmen and the working classes. Between one and two million people emigrated in the three years after the revolution. It's easy to understand why these characters became popular in British literature at the time, as they offered a touch of glamour and the unknown to the largely mono-cultural Britain of the early twentieth century.

Staying with Russia, I had to read up on Victorian criminals and inevitably got sidetracked by Jack the Ripper – bear with me. In 1923, a book was written by author William Le Quex – I'm almost there, I promise! – Le Quex wrote one hundred and fifty novels and, in his somewhat dubious autobiography, he put forward the idea that Jack the Ripper was actually – wait for it – Russian! Segue accomplished!

What's interesting is that Le Quex claimed to have seen a document written by none other than the mad monk himself, Rasputin, which pointed towards a Russian doctor called Alexander Pedachenko, who had carried out his reign of terror in order to undermine the British police – obviously. This claim should be taken with a pinch of salt, however, as Le Quex was something of an eccentric (and a liar).

He was a half-French writer who often wrote invasion literature on the threat posed by the French. He also attempted to mount an expedition to Jerusalem in search of the Ark of the Covenant based on a (presumably unreliable) tip he got from a Swedish civil engineer about a cypher within the original text of the Book of Ezekiel. He was an early radio enthusiast – establishing his own station before many people even had radios – an aeronautics fanatic and something of a self-mythologiser. There is no denying, however, that his brand of sensationalist, fear-mongering, xenophobic fiction had a major impact on readers of the day and led to the "spymania" of the 1910s, which in turn led to the founding of the British Secret Service. From what I can tell, he is the kind of guy who would be fun to have at a dinner party but, just like his Ripper theory, you wouldn't necessarily believe much of what he said.

(Yet more spoilers!) From a famous killer to a famous method of killing. I surely spend more time researching poisons than any other single element in these books. I think I spent four or five hours going back and forth between natural poisons that you would be able to find in an English garden or woodland that would fulfil the conditions I required. I set out to find one that would take an hour for symptoms to show and one that would take three. Monkshood (also known as wolfsbane, leopard's bane, devil's helmet, blue rocket or, more scientifically, aconitum) is a very famous one and fitted the bill perfectly as it affects the victim in the space of an hour and then quickly kills.

A fatal dose can be as little as a gram, and so it could easily be brewed up as a tea. Even handling the plant can lead to sickness, which is why gloves should be worn. Ancient Greek mythology stated that the poison came to Earth when Hercules dragged the three-headed dog Cerberus from Hades and the beast's drool splashed out of its mouth. It has been referenced in literature throughout history, in everything from Shakespeare to Game of Thrones, and accidental poisonings are still common, as the plant can be mistaken for more innocent species.

I believe using parts of the yew tree to kill someone, meanwhile, is less common in fiction, and I was happy to find it as an option. The poison takes longer to have an effect than monkshood, but there is no antidote for either substance, which is what I needed in this story. As Lord Edgington explains, the arils are harmless, but the rest of the plant is poisonous, though some birds have evolved to be able to eat the seeds without any issue. It contains at least ten dangerous alkaloids and even breathing in the sawdust of a cut tree could lead to poisoning. Boudica, the ancient warrior queen of the Celtic Iceni tribe who stood up to the Romans in AD 60 in an uprising that killed around 80,000 people, was eventually defeated and is said to have eaten the leaves of a yew tree to kill herself.

The main thing I have changed to suit my needs is a noticeable lack of gastrointestinal symptoms. In reality, both poisons would induce substantial sickness, but to be honest, vomiting isn't a common element of cosy mysteries, and I decided to cut it out as much as possible. It's also debatable whether the symptoms would come on so suddenly from one moment to the next, but I'll show my poetic licence and move swiftly on.

As mentioned, it was important in this book that neither of the poisons could be reversed too easily, and so I looked once more into the use of activated charcoal. I've spoken of this micro-porous wonder substance before, and it is essential to the treatment of many poisons. In the case of monkshood it could save a life if given in the first hour after poisoning, but in a search of newspapers from the 1920s, there is only one reference to it, so I think it's fair to assume that Edgington and the local doctors wouldn't have known to prescribe it.

If anyone can think of a connection between poisons that grow in British gardens and underwater mammals that live in the waters around America and Africa, please let me know, and I will add it here in future editions of the book. That notwithstanding: manatees! They only got a mention because they rhyme with insanity, but they are one of my favourite animals, and so I had to read about them. I have only actually seen them in Beauval Zoo in France, but they are magical. They form the scientific order *sirenia,* which also includes dugongs and takes its name from the ancient Greek sirens, who in turn lent their name to the Spanish word for mermaid, *sirena.* So I wonder whether sailors in times gone by saw these animals and mistook them for the mythical creatures. N.B., I read bit more and, yes, they did.

Interestingly, manatees' closest relatives are elephants and a small, rodent-like animal called a hyrax that lives in South Africa. One of the things that all these animals have in common is that the male's testicles are concealed within the abdominal cavity, unlike other mammals. Isn't that great that we now know so much that we can link this disparate group? The oldest known manatee in captivity lived to sixty-nine, and these peaceful, herbivorous animals were once used by water treatment plants to keep canals weed-free. And added to all that, they're so cuuuuuute!

I will switch to bullet points for these last few titbits and then finish – as all good things should – with cake.

- I wrote a note for myself which just said "cabbage", which wasn't very helpful. I eventually remembered that I looked into ornamental cabbages – as they are a colourful addition to any autumn garden – and discovered that wild cabbages are rather important. *Brassica oleracea* is a humble plant which grows on cliffs along the English Channel, but it has given us a whole bunch of different foods that are now staples of our diet. Without it, we wouldn't have had cauliflower (though, personally, I doubt that would be a bad thing), broccoli, Brussels sprouts, kale, and collard greens. I like most of these now, but as a child, I would have to stay at the table until I'd finished my then intolerable broccoli. What my mother didn't know was that there was a small shelf under the table where I would hide the detested food while she wasn't looking. I don't remember whether I later returned and put it in the bin when there was no one around. I should probably check that there are no ancient vegetables still festering there.

- Sticking with veg, vegetarianism was already in existence in Britain in the '20s, but the main discussion I could find of it in the papers was its impact on health. It seems that it was largely a wellness fad, rather than an ethical choice. There are thousands of references to the diet throughout the decade, and I even found a joke about it in the sporting pages of one paper. A championship-winning golfer was asked to what he owed his success. He replied, "I've been practically living on greens for the last year," to which the questioner responded, "Oh, I hear the vegetarian diet can work wonders for athletes."

- The Married Women's Property Acts of 1882 came in handy for this book. It stopped husbands from automatically assuming control of their wives' wealth on marriage. Before this, very few married women could be said to own property in any real sense. One example of this was George Eliot, whose copyright for her novels passed to her husband after they wed. It also provides a good motive for a murder in mystery novels as, if a husband legally possessed his wife's belongings, there wouldn't be much point in killing her to inherit them. One of the people who campaigned for this change was Millicent Garrett Fawcett, the suffragette sister of Elizabeth Garrett Anderson, Britain's first qualified female surgeon, over whom I have fawned in these pages before.

- I decided to give Todd a salary of six pounds a week, though this is quite high from what I can tell. I came to this number for a number of reasons. 1) we have been told a few times that Lord Edgington is a generous employer. 2) I had a quick go on the Bank of England's

260

historical inflation calculator to work out what a normal salary would have been. 3) I didn't trust that result and so searched Hansard (the official transcripts of British parliament debates going back two hundred years). What I found was a discussion from 1925 which listed the average salaries certain occupations. Ship building labourers would get the equivalent of a miserly £1.90 a week, able seamen made around £2.50, and engine drivers came out on top with anything up to £4.50! so I figured that Todd deserved even more than them for his dashing nature, cocktail mixing, smooth driving and near-psychic abilities. Interestingly, the data shows that wages had fallen a lot in the previous five years, presumably due to the weak British economy (as Chrissy mentions in this book) and the after effects of the First World War.

- Musical bumps is, like all the best children's games, one that often ends in over-eager kiddies in tears. You have to drop to the floor when the music stops, so a lot like musical chairs, but with less fighting. I found an article from 1923 which claims that children of the day do not consider it a real party if there are no balloons and favours (I agree), and that it is essential to foster a carnival atmosphere in order for the critters to enjoy themselves. Good advice there, parents.

Something else that children enjoy, according to Mrs Beeton, is rolled treacle pudding. It appears to be similar to a treacle sponge pudding and can be boiled or baked. It contains suet and ginger, and she says it is "economical, and a favourite one with children; it is, of course, only suitable for a nursery or a very plain family dinner," not that Chrissy would complain.

Okay, everybody. I hope you feel enlightened and informed. I'm off to write the Christmas book and then I might think about having a day off to tidy the garage. Bye for now!

ACKNOWLEDGEMENTS

This book felt like a bit of a solo effort in the early stages. I wasn't using a real house, so I couldn't rely on the history of it for inspiration, and I wrote it on holiday in Italy with the windows closed because it was so hot and everyone else was having fun without me. So I'm going to thank myself. Wait, no, I'm not that vain. I'll thank Marion and Amelie for keeping our golden-haired cherub Osian busy when I needed to work.

Thank you, too, to my always kind and generous early readers, Bridget Hogg and the Martins. To Lisa Bjornstad, Jayne Kirk and M.P. Smith for arduous close editing. And to my fellow writers who are always there for me, especially Catherine, Suzanne and Lucy.

And, of course, a massive thank you to my ARC team… Rebecca Brooks, Ferne Miller, Melinda Kimlinger, Emma James, Mindy Denkin, Namoi Lamont, Katharine Reibig, Linsey Neale, Terri Roller, Margaret Liddle, Lori Willis, Anja Peerdeman, Marion Davis, Sarah Turner, Sandra Hoff, Mary Nickell, Vanessa Rivington, Helena George, Anne Kavcic, Nancy Roberts, Pat Hathaway, Peggy Craddock, Cathleen Brickhouse, Susan Reddington, Sonya Elizabeth Richards, John Presler, Mary Harmon, Beth Weldon, Karen Quinn, Karen Alexander, Mindy Wygonik, Jacquie Erwin, Janet Rutherford, Ila Patlogan, Randy Hartselle, Carol Vani, June Techtow and Keryn De Maria.

READ MORE LORD EDGINGTON MYSTERIES TODAY_

- **Murder at the Spring Ball**
- **Death From High Places** (free e-novella available exclusively at benedictbrown.net. Paperback and audiobook are available at Amazon)
- **A Body at a Boarding School**
- **Death on a Summer's Day**
- **The Mystery of Mistletoe Hall**
- **The Tangled Treasure Trail**
- **The Curious Case of the Templeton-Swifts**
- **The Crimes of Clearwell Castle**
- **A Novel Way to Kill** (novella available at Amazon)
- **The Snows of Weston Moor**
- **What the Vicar Saw**
- **Blood on the Banister**
- **A Killer in the Wings**
- **The Christmas Bell Mystery**
- **The Puzzle of Parham House**
- **Death at Silent Pool**
- **The Christmas Candle Murders** (November 2024)

Check out the complete Lord Edgington Collection at Amazon

The first twelve Lord Edgington audiobooks, narrated by the actor George Blagden, are available now on all major audiobook platforms. There will be more coming soon.

"THE PUZZLE OF PARHAM HOUSE" COCKTAIL

I completely forgot to put in a cocktail this time around and had to add one in in the second draft. By chance, when looking for something original, I came across the Last Word. I added it, and then realised just how appropriate a name it had. In a way, this drink influenced the plot as (spoiler alert) I then changed certain elements to draw attention to the last words of the victims.

It was first made in Detroit in 1915 and considered a classic prohibition-era drink. In fact, it is said to have been made with bathtub gin, so cocktail purists may want to turn their bathroom into a distillery to get the authentic flavour. Another interesting thing about it is that it almost disappeared. Between a reference in a book in 1951 and hipster millennials rediscovering it in the last twenty years, barely anyone drank it. Here's the recipe…

Equal measures of:

Gin

Green Chartreuse

Maraschino liqueur

Lime juice

Add the four ingredients to a shaker. Shake, then strain the mixture into a chilled glass and add a brandy-soaked cherry to garnish. Yum!

You can get our official cocktail expert François Monti's brilliant book "101 Cocktails to Try Before you Die" at Amazon.

WORDS AND REFERENCES YOU MIGHT NOT KNOW

Odeur de cheval – that would be horse smell in French.

Underwood – another word for undergrowth or scrub.

Bird-high – a high-pitch noise like that which is made by a bird.

Pre-war – In this case, before World War One.

Oracular – like an ancient oracle – wise, able to see the future etc.

Pebble-hearted – a rather pretty term similar to stone-hearted.

Kyphotic – someone with pronounced curvature of the spine – it can be caused by a number of diseases and conditions.

Kellogg-Briand pact – an important plot point in the last Marius book. This was the pact that was signed by many countries, which essentially outlawed war. Its long-lasting effects are debatable (especially in the last couple of years) but it was the legal framework that enabled the Nazis to be prosecuted after the war. Its architect, Monsieur Aristide Briand gets a mention in this book and was a character in "The Castleton Affair".

Doolally tap – unhinged (temporarily or otherwise)! It came from British forces jargon in India and gave us the word doolally.

Super-man – not in the comic book sense (which came a decade later) but the concept of an advanced, amoral human being, as proposed by Nietzsche, whom you could imagine the Hindmarsh men being rather fond of.

Common purpose – this is the idea that someone can be liable for a crime even if they were not instrumental in its execution because of pre-knowledge or a common desire for the same outcome as the culprit. In the true case of Edith Thompson, she was put to death after her lover confronted and murdered her husband, even though she was not involved in the planning of the crime, because she had described a fantasy of murdering him in her love letters. Sad.

Stir my stumps – get moving!

Getting the needle – get angry.

Off my onion – doolally tap!

Brain-sick – Off your onion!

Hidey-hole – a place to hide something.

Muckworms – a very soft insult for a low person. It has also previously meant a miser, a street urchin and now commonly refers to grubs that live in manure.

Knifemanship – no, Chrissy, it's not a word.

Prestidigitator – a conjuror. One of you lovely readers mailed me to suggest I use this word, and I finally found the opportunity to do so.

Tiddlypush – thingamajig. I do always check the usage of the odd words I include in my books, and I found a funny passage in the Daily News from 1925 saying that his friend had bought a motorbike, and he asked for a simple explanation of how it worked, but the young man spoke in a jargon that he couldn't understand… "Oh, it's quite easy," said the youth. "This gadget here fits on to the thingummybob down there, and works a whatyoumaycallit down there by that tiddlypush. Then this howdoyoudo slides in and out that oojah there and causes this umptydoodle to open that plonkidoddle. Now do you understand?"

Unmetaphorically – free from metaphor. I was surprised that this was a real word, but it is!

Innings – No, it's not a typo. In British English, we use the plural form with the singular article. It comes from cricket and if you say someone had a good innings, it will often mean they had a good long life or achieved something.

Victrola orthophonic phonograph – another thing I spent too long reading about. I chose this because it was loud! As opposed to a simple wind-up gramophone, this invention which hit the market in 1925, used electric recordings and even had an automatic disc changer. Its horn was folded into the body of a wooden cabinet which increased its sound capacity. It doesn't appear to have had a volume knob, but you could buy something called a mute ball or silencer to dampen its impressive output, hence Ezekiel saying that he would tell his brother to keep his music down.

Pitcairn Islands – a British territory in the middle of the Pacific Ocean that are just about as remote as you can get. Interestingly, a large part of their tiny population is descended from nine mutinous sailors who stole the famous ship Bounty in 1798. They stripped and burnt the boat and settled on the uninhabited island. I would say they were luckier than other mutineers who were captured and hanged, but the settlement was not a happy one and practically all of them murdered one another before long.

Doyen – the most skilled or experienced person in a particular place.

Nearest and dearest – I was surprised to discover that this expression dates right back to 1598.

Pseudo – the word pseud only exists since 1954, but this was used before that to mean the same thing: someone who is fake and pretentious.

Myrmidon – it can mean a follower in an army or gang, but as an insult it means hanger-on. Another word that means the same that I really love is *cake-fiddler,* but I was pretty sure that no one would have understood what it meant.

"They placed him on his back and tipped his head up to face the ceiling, as most doctors recommend these days in an emergency" – this was the advice before the recovery position was perfected. Please don't do this anymore, as it is more likely for the sufferer to choke.

THE IZZY PALMER MYSTERIES

If you're looking for a modern murder mystery series with just as many off-the-wall characters, try **"The Izzy Palmer Mysteries"** for your next whodunit fix.

Check out the complete Izzy Palmer Collection in ebook, paperback and Kindle Unlimited at Amazon.

THE MARIUS QUIN MYSTERIES

There's a new detective in town. Marius first appeared in the Lord Edgington novel **"A Killer in the Wings"**, and now he has his own series...

 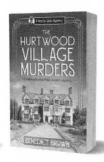  

Check out the complete Marius Quin Collection in ebook, paperback and Kindle Unlimited at Amazon.

ABOUT ME

Writing has always been my passion. It was my favourite half-an-hour a week at primary school, and I started on my first, truly abysmal book as a teenager. So it wasn't a difficult decision to study literature at university which led to a master's in creative writing.

I'm a Welsh-Irish-Englishman originally from **South London** but now living with my French/Spanish wife and our two presumably quite confused young children in **Burgos**, a beautiful mediaeval city in the north of Spain. I write overlooking the Castilian countryside, trying not to be distracted by the vultures, eagles and red kites that fly past my window each day.

When Covid-19 hit in 2020, the language school where I worked as an English teacher closed down, and I became a full-time writer. I have three murder mystery series. My first was **"The Izzy Palmer Mysteries"** which is a more modern, zany take on the genre, and my newest is the 1920s set **"Marius Quin Mysteries"** which features a mystery writer as the main character – I wonder where I got that idea from.

I previously spent years focusing on kids' books and wrote everything from fairy tales to environmental dystopian fantasies, right through to issue-based teen fiction. My book **"The Princess and The Peach"** was long-listed for the Chicken House prize in The Times and an American producer even talked about adapting it into a film.

"Death at Silent Pool" is the fourteenth novel in the "Lord Edgington Investigates…" series. The next book will be out in November 2024 and there's a novella available free if you sign up to my **readers' club**. Should you wish to tell me what you think about Chrissy and his grandfather, my writing or the world at large, I'd love to hear from you, so feel free to get in touch via...

www.benedictbrown.net

CHARACTER LIST

The folk at Silent Pool

Patience Hindmarsh – the matriarch of the family who is missing from the first chapter.

Abraham Hindmarsh – her politician husband. Not the nicest chap.

Elisheba Hindmarsh – the oldest child in the family. She likes flower pressing, is close to Lemuel and is very much Team Mother.

Ezekiel Hindmarsh – the oldest boy, who harbours dreams of following in his father's footsteps. Team Dad.

Hosanna – The middle child, she attempts to remain neutral between the two sides but is critical of her father. Team no one. She also paints.

Lemuel – The middlest brother (still funny). He is athletic and rather easily led. Team Mother.

Josiah – the youngest child. He is his father's biggest admirer. He has a spinal issue called kyphosis and enjoys long walks on sunny beaches and plays the piano (part of that might not be true).

P.C. Rod Argent – he stands by the door. He's not the best officer around.

Blunstone – the rather proud butler.

Countess Marina Vorontsova – a Russian émigré who moves to London and seeks the help of distant family there.

The Duchess of Hartlepool – a wealthy woman in London who has her jewels stolen.

Regulars

Lord Edgington – former Metropolitan Police Superintendent and master sleuth.

Christopher Prentiss – his ever-improving assistant and grandson.

Chief Inspector James Darrington – former colleague and trusted friend of Superintendent Edgington.

Todd – former chauffeur to Lord Edgington, he now does practically everything – though presumably someone else polishes the car these days.

Halfpenny – the Cranley Hall head footman.

Don't worry, all the other regulars will be back in the next book. In fact, Cook gets into an argument with another cook. Fun stuff!

Made in United States
Orlando, FL
09 November 2024

53629520R00164